HOLLY RIVERS

The BOY in the POST

Chicken House

2 Palmer Street, Frome,
Somerset BA11 1DS
www.chickenhousebooks.com

Text © Holly Rivers 2022
Illustration © Caroline Bonne-Müller

First published in Great Britain in 2022
Chicken House
2 Palmer Street
Frome, Somerset BA11 1DS
United Kingdom
www.chickenhousebooks.com

Chicken House/Scholastic Ireland, 89E Lagan Road, Dublin Industrial Estate,
Glasnevin, Dublin D11 HP5F, Republic of Ireland

Cover and interior design by Helen Crawford-White
Cover illustration by Caroline Bonne-Müller
Typeset by Dorchester Typesetting Group Ltd
Printed and bound in Great Britain by CPI Group (UK) Ltd, Croydon CR0 4YY

1 3 5 7 9 10 8 6 4 2

British Library Cataloguing in Publication data available.

PB ISBN 978-1-912626-04-5
eISBN 978-1-913696-54-2

For Fred and Silver,
who I would travel land,
sea and sky to reach.

1

'Surely that can't be it?' said Orinthia, sweeping her dark fringe from her eyes as they came to a standstill at the top of the hill. 'It looks like it's about to fall down!'

She and her younger brothers, Séafra and Taber, were looking down at a ramshackle old windmill which stood in the field below. Its crumbling pink brickwork had been half engulfed by the surrounding woodland, and its sails were frozen like the hands of a stopped clock.

Séafra edged forward, looking equally confused. 'Maybe we followed the wrong path?' he suggested. 'Or made a mistake with the address?'

'Hmmm . . . let me double-check,' said Orinthia. She reached into the front pocket of her duffel bag and pulled out the advertisement which the siblings had taken from the noticeboard on the village green earlier that afternoon. They'd been on their way to Mr Barnabas's sweet shop for coconut ice when they'd come across it – pinned between a poster for SMITH & SONS FUNERAL PARLOUR (BUY ONE COFFIN GET ONE FREE) and a notice from the park warden reminding dog owners that POODLE POO WON'T PICK ITSELF UP.

It had caught their attention immediately. With tomorrow being the first day of the summer holidays, and with Mum far too busy with work as usual, the siblings were going to have to entertain themselves for the *entirety* of the six-week break. Orinthia had been dreading it – the long, tedious days, the endless jigsaw puzzles, the inevitable squabbles with her brothers. The advertisement sounded so much more exciting!

She unfolded the paper and ran a finger from top to bottom. It read:

SCHOOL CHILDREN WANTED FOR PAID SUMMER HOLIDAY WORK

APPLICANTS MUST BE HAPPY WORKING WITH ANIMALS, KNOW HOW TO ADDRESS AN ENVELOPE, AND NOT TAKE UP TOO MUCH SPACE.

FULL TRAINING WILL BE PROVIDED, BUT BASIC KNOWLEDGE OF TEA–MAKING AND EGG–BOILING IS DESIRABLE.

HARD WORKERS ONLY.

MALINGERERS, SHIRKERS, CRYBABIES AND LAZYBONES NEED NOT APPLY.

IF INTERESTED, PLEASE ENQUIRE IN PERSON AT:

TUPENNY MILL,
ST SYLVESTER'S MOUNT,
LITTLE PENHALLOW

'So?' Séafra asked, peering over his sister's shoulder. '*Is* this the right place?'

Orinthia looked around, shielding her eyes from the early summer sun as she tried to get her bearings. 'Well, we're definitely on St Sylvester's Mount,' she replied, scanning their surroundings. 'And that's the only mill *I* can see . . .'

Séafra shuddered. '*Urghhh* . . . But it's so creepy. Who would run a business from a place like that?'

Orinthia surveyed the field below, thinking that perhaps there might be another, less decrepit-looking building nestled somewhere amongst the trees. But there wasn't. Whoever had pinned the job advertisement to the noticeboard worked here in this ancient, tumbledown edifice.

'Rinthi, you said we were going to see some animals!' groaned Taber, shuffling from foot to foot as he looked up at his big sister. He was short for his six years, with a round face and cheeks the colour of peaches. Just like his older siblings, his tresses were jet black, but his were wild and thick, sticking up in unruly tufts. 'Where are the animals? I can't see them!'

'There aren't any, Tabs,' Séafra butted in sharply. 'There's nothing to see here—'

'Oh, come on, Séa,' Orinthia countered, unbuttoning her knitted cardigan and tying it around her waist. 'You don't know that. We should at least go down there and have a look. We've come all this way.'

'Rinthi, are you joking?' Séafra snapped back. 'This looks like the kind of place you'd come across in a ghost story! Who knows what might be lurking inside?'

Orinthia sighed. Why did her brother always have to be so sensible? At eleven years old he was one year her junior, but he behaved like a grumpy old man. 'Séafra Shalloo, you should never judge a book – or a windmill – by its cover. It might be really nice inside.'

'Or it might be even spookier!' snapped Séafra. He snatched the advertisement from his sister and waved it in her face. 'This could be a kidnapper trying to lure us in!'

'Oh, stop catastrophizing, Séa!' said Orinthia with a tut. 'It's probably just an old biddy who wants someone to look after her cats and run her errands.

And besides, it's good to take risks sometimes. Like Ophelia Pearcart always said: *One cannot discover new oceans unless—*'

'—*unless one has the courage to lose sight of the shore*,' interrupted Séafra with a roll of his eyes. 'Yes, yes, we know what boring old Ophelia Pearcart said. You've only told us a squillion times before.'

Orinthia crossed her arms with a huff. Ophelia Pearcart was definitely *not* boring. How could her brother say such a thing about one of the greatest explorers ever to have lived? She'd discovered hidden civilizations deep within the Amazon jungle, and scaled snowy mountains in search of yetis! She'd clambered atop dusty ruins, swum through tropical archipelagos, and sailed across each of the seven seas! Orinthia had read her diaries so many times that she could name every one of her two hundred expeditions off by heart. And when *she* was older, she was going to follow in Ophelia's footsteps and become a famous explorer too!

'I tell you what, Séa,' Orinthia pressed, giving her brother a gentle nudge and softening her voice. 'We'll just take a quick peek inside. We might be pleasantly surprised. And by the end of the day we could have summer jobs!'

'We could be dead, more like,' Séafra muttered under his breath. 'Rinthi, I'm not going in there, and that's the end of it!'

'Fine,' said Orinthia. 'But I am!' She crouched down beside her youngest brother and smiled. 'What do you say, Tabs? Are you coming to see if we can find the animals? Or are you going to stay here with grumpy old Séafra?'

'Find the animals!' Taber replied, jumping up and down excitedly, much to Séafra's annoyance. There was nothing Taber liked more than nature: foraging for conkers and pine cones, or upturning rocks to delight in the swarming masses of creepy-crawlies lurking beneath. 'I want to find the animals!' he continued. 'Animals! Animals!'

'Good,' said Orinthia, looking pointedly at Séafra. 'At least *one* of my little brothers has a sense of adventure.' She took Taber by the hand, and as they strode off down the hill, she called back, 'See you at home, scaredy pants!'

Orinthia grinned mischievously to herself as she headed through the long grasses towards the old mill. She knew it had been childish to name-call, but Séafra was far too much of a worrywart for her liking. He balked at even the slightest hint of danger, and always expected the worst. But what was life without a few surprises? For instance, if all the archaeologists in the world had settled for careers in nice, safe offices, then none of the wonders of the world would have been discovered – the Roman ruins of Pompeii, Easter Island's incredible statues, the beautiful Cave of Altamira! Dr Dawud Charter would never have unearthed those incredible tombs in the Valley of the Kings if he'd thought it wiser just to stay at home with a pot of Darjeeling! Séafra really needed to live life a little more bravely.

'So what animals are we going to see, Rinthi?' asked Taber, skipping through the grasses ahead of his sister as they picked their way towards the mill. 'Will I get to pet a koala bear? Or a tiger?'

'*Awww*, I don't think so, Tabs,' Orinthia replied with a chuckle. 'Probably something a little less . . . exotic.'

Taber cocked his head and thought for a moment. 'Like a zebra?'

'Erm . . . probably not a zebra either.'

'A monkey then? I'd *reeeeally* like to see a monkey!'

Not wanting to completely shatter her little brother's hopes, Orinthia smiled before saying, 'Maybe, Tabs. Let's just wait and see, hmmm?'

Taber nodded, and with the sun warm on their backs, the pair continued down the hill and through the field.

Soon enough they were standing at the foot of the rickety wooden steps which led up to the windmill's front porch. Orinthia craned her neck. The building had looked shabby from afar, but up close it was positively dilapidated. It was like a shrivelling pink gourd which had gone to seed – tiles were missing from the roof, the window frames were rotting and the crumbling bricks were laced together with dark-green weeds.

'Let's go inside! Let's go inside!' said Taber, tugging at Orinthia's arm and obviously still eager to explore.

But just then, Orinthia heard footsteps pounding behind them.

'Hey! Wait up! Wait for me!'

Orinthia turned to find Séafra lolloping towards them through the yellow grasses, his cheeks flushed. When he was a couple of metres away he stopped, resting his hands on his knees and puffing hard.

'You changed your mind, then?' said Orinthia with a wry smile. 'Thought you might.'

'Yes,' Séafra panted, trying to catch his breath, 'but

only because there should be someone *responsible* around to keep an eye out for trouble. I don't want anything happening to Taber.'

Orinthia felt her teeth clench together. She hated the way Séafra had emphasized the word *responsible*, as if she were some reckless hothead who'd happily put their little brother in danger. But she couldn't be bothered to fight with him any more – they had a windmill to explore after all, and as the leader of this expedition she needed to keep her crew motivated. 'So, you're coming in?' she said, trying not to let her eyes betray her annoyance.

'Yes, if I must,' huffed Séafra, wiping sweat from his brow. 'But if we see anything strange – anything at all – we're leaving straight away.'

Taber's eyes lit up and he reached for his big brother's hand. '*Yaaaay!* Rinthi said we're going to see monkeys!' He jumped around like a little chimp. 'I think we might see some penguins, too . . .'

Séafra rolled his eyes in despair, but Orinthia was already leading the way up to the front door. This, she hoped, was going to be the start of a wonderful summer.

2

From the peeling paint it looked as though the front door of Tupenny Mill might once have been bright blue, but it obviously hadn't been touched up in a long time. There were spiderwebs stretching across the windows, and a mouldy-looking doormat lay threadbare at the children's feet.

But none of these things seemed to be deterring Taber. 'Can I knock? Can I knock?' he enthused, pulling himself on to his tiptoes and stretching up to reach the circular brass knocker. He wasn't quite tall enough, so Orinthia lifted him up, and with a gleeful fervour, he curled his chubby fingers around it and rapped down hard repeatedly.

'All right, that's enough, Tabs,' chuckled Orinthia, pulling her little brother away. 'That knocking was loud enough for everyone in the village to hear, let alone the mill!' She put him back down and ruffled his hair. 'Now remember, when we go inside you need to be polite and well mannered. Don't forget your *pleases* and *thank-yous* and no running around.'

As they waited, Orinthia turned her head towards the sun and thought about who might come to the door. *Who pinned the advertisement to the noticeboard?* she wondered. Would they make them do some kind of interview or test? Mummy was always going on about the 'incompetent and underqualified numpties' that wrote to her asking for a job at the car dealership, so Orinthia could only hope that *their* potential employer wasn't going to be quite as much of a taskmaster.

But after a few minutes, no one had come to let them in.

Orinthia cupped her hands around her eyes and peered through one of the adjacent windows, but the glass was so thick with dust, she could barely see a thing.

'Why is nobody answering, Rinthi?' asked Taber, pouting out his lower lip in disappointment. 'I want to go inside!'

'Because there's nobody there, Tabs,' Séafra said smugly. 'Like I said, this has just been a big waste of time.' He grabbed his little brother's hand. 'Come on,

I'm taking you home—'

'CAN I HELP YOU?'

A shadow had fallen over the porch and the children spun around with a yelp. An old man was standing behind them, his face so gnarled that it looked as if it had been carved out of the same wood as the windmill. His tattered three-piece suit had been patched with scraps of mismatched material, and an old flying hat was pulled down over the matted, smoke-coloured hair which hung to his shoulders. His back was slightly hunched, and he edged forward with an unsteady gait.

Orinthia felt Séafra clutch at her arm in fright, but she was more intrigued than scared. From reading Ophelia Pearcart's diaries she knew that the most peculiar-looking people were often the most fascinating, and if that was the case then this man would certainly have an interesting story to tell.

'Can I *help* you?' he repeated. He spoke with a posh, old-fashioned-sounding voice, which seemed at odds with his slightly dishevelled appearance.

Orinthia opened her mouth to answer, but Taber had already begun to speak. 'We want to see the animals,' he said, seeming completely unfazed.

'Is that so?' replied the old man, raising one of his bushy grey eyebrows.

'Yes . . .' said Orinthia. 'I mean . . . we've come about the job vacancy. We found your advertisement on the noticeboard in the village.'

The old man blinked. 'Really?' he said, sounding almost surprised. 'You're interested in the summer work?'

Orinthia went to nod, but Séafra cut in sharply. '*Maybe*,' he said, shooting his sister a stern look. 'We want to know more about what you do first.'

'And very sensible that is too,' said the old man with a nod. He looked the children up and down, then scratched his cheek. 'How about we start with introductions first, hmm? My name is Amos Brock, but most people call me Grandy Brock.'

He held out a large hand for the children to shake, and Orinthia accepted. His palm was rough and calloused, and she suspected that whatever line of business he was in, it required some hard graft.

'My name's Orinthia Shalloo,' she replied. 'And these are my younger brothers, Séafra and Taber.'

'Well, aren't they interesting names,' said Grandy Brock. 'Never heard any quite like that before. Where do they come from?'

Orinthia was just about to elaborate on their names' Irish origins, when all of a sudden she heard the sound of claws scratching against wood behind her. She wheeled around and, to her astonishment, a furry, four-legged creature wearing a little blue hat shot out from behind a potted plant and dashed across the porch. Orinthia saw a flash of bushy tail as it scampered atop the bannister before springing on to Grandy Brock's left shoulder.

'Well, hello there, boy,' said the old man, running a finger down the creature's chest. 'Come to see what's going on, hmmm?'

Orinthia gasped. What *was* this creature? She'd never seen anything like it. Its furry beige frame was slender, and it had a narrow muzzle and small ears. Dark triangles framed its beady orange eyes, and its tail was now curling around Grandy Brock's neck like a black-and-white striped scarf.

'Squirrel!' squealed Taber, pointing excitedly to the creature. 'I want to pet the squirrel! I want to pet the squirrel!'

'*Squirrel?*' said Grandy Brock sharply. 'Goodness gracious me, this isn't a squirrel, dear boy. This is a Madagascan ring-tailed lemur. Or *Lemur catta* to give him his scientific title.' He reached into his pocket and took out a tangerine, which the lemur deftly snatched from his grasp. The animal's hands were small and padded, and as he began to unpeel the piece of fruit, a series of little chirruping sounds escaped his lips, not too dissimilar to those of a bird.

'Wow, he's beautiful,' said Orinthia, fascinated. 'You said he's a boy? Does he have a name?'

'Of course!' said Grandy Brock. 'His name is Fankalazana Solofo Njaka Malagasy. But I like to call him Mr Malagasy for short.'

'Wow, that's quite some name,' said Orinthia, watching as the lemur threw the tangerine peel over his shoulder before beginning to eat.

'A magnificent creature needs a magnificent name,' the old man replied. 'I really can't abide by ridiculous monikers like *Fluffy* or *Rover* or *Tiddles*.' He harrumphed. 'It's just insulting!'

Séafra shot his sister a look as if to say, *Let's go, this man is clearly bonkers*, but Orinthia was completely entranced. She already liked Grandy Brock, and leaving was the last thing on her mind.

'So is Mr Malagasy your pet, Grandy Brock?' asked Taber, looking up at the lemur with wonder.

'Well, I guess he is now,' replied the old man, looking to the lemur. 'I originally acquired him as I thought he'd make rather an able postal worker.' He chuckled. 'And he might have done, if he didn't like eating the stamps so much!' He straightened Mr Malagasy's little blue hat, which Orinthia saw, on closer inspection, was embellished with a silver badge shaped like a postage stamp. 'I let him keep his hat, though, so he still feels like part of the team.'

The Shalloo siblings looked at each other in confusion. Grandy seemed to be talking in riddles.

'Erm . . . I'm sorry?' said Orinthia with uncertainty. '*Postal worker?* You thought a lemur would make a good *postal worker?*'

'Well yes,' the old man replied, as if it were the most humdrum of concepts. 'Perhaps not as good a postal worker as an aardvark or a baboon, but—' The continued look of confusion in the siblings' eyes brought the old man to a sudden halt. 'Oh, forgive me,' he exclaimed, striking a palm to his forehead. 'There's me rattling on about aardvarks and baboons, but of course, you aren't yet familiar with the nature of our work here at Tupenny Mill.'

He looked around suspiciously before bringing his voice down to a secretive whisper. 'I didn't want to reveal any of the specifics in my advertisement because there's lots of nosy parkers around, you see.' His brow darkened as he checked over his shoulder once more. 'In fact, we should probably go inside right away. Someone might be listening in.'

He brushed past the children and made his way to the front door with Mr Malagasy still perched on his shoulder. As Grandy turned the doorknob, Séafra grabbed Orinthia by the elbow and pulled her close.

'Rinthi, we need to leave . . . NOW!' he hissed through gritted teeth. 'This man has clearly got rather a large screw loose. We need to get out of here while we still can.'

But Orinthia didn't give her brother an answer. Even though Grandy Brock was eccentric, there was something about him that intrigued her greatly – a mischievous twinkle in his eyes that hinted at adventure and excitement and fun. She liked how unkempt his clothes were, how knotty he'd let his hair get. And how many people had a ring-tailed lemur living with them? If the summer job involved looking after Mr Malagasy, then she definitely wanted in.

'Right, there we go,' said Grandy Brock, pushing the creaky door open. 'After you.'

Even though she knew Séafra would be livid, Orinthia took Taber's hand. With Ophelia Pearcart's words still ringing in her ears, she stepped inside. *One cannot discover new oceans unless one has the courage to lose sight of the shore.*

3

'In you go, in you go!' said Grandy Brock, ushering the Shalloo siblings into Tupenny Mill before closing the door behind them. 'That's it . . . make yourself at home . . . don't be shy.'

The Shalloo children edged forward, Orinthia and Taber leading the way, with Séafra trailing reluctantly behind. He was mumbling something to himself about *recklessness* and *danger*, but Orinthia was giddy with excitement, her breath coming out in gasps of delight.

They were in a tall, circular space, almost like a gigantic turret. Lit by the oil lamps hanging from the walls and a few small windows, it reminded her of the kind of place a hunter or lumberjack might come back to after a day in the forest. A wood-burning stove stood in a little alcove, its pot belly hungry for the logs stacked alongside it, ready for the colder months.

Antique ephemera covered most of the walls – a rifle rack lined with muskets; antlers; faded maps; an old flag. In one corner a rocking chair sat beneath a taxidermy moose's head, one of its glass eyes hanging from the socket like a loose button. Orinthia squeezed Taber's hand with glee as they looked around. She absolutely loved the place, and judging by the grin on his face, her youngest brother did too.

'Right then,' said Grandy, taking off his flying hat and hanging it on the single peg next to the door. 'You can take off your coats and put them . . . well . . .' He looked around. 'Well, I see you aren't wearing any today, but on the floor is fine in the future. I'll go and get my children, and then we can tell you a little more about what we do here.'

'Children?' asked Orinthia, wondering if Grandy Brock was referring to human offspring, or simply more of the furry kind.

'Oh yes,' said Grandy Brock, crossing the room to the bottom of the rickety wooden staircase which spiralled upwards to the floors above. 'I have five of them!' He put a foot on the bottom step, before putting his thumb and forefinger to his mouth and letting out an ear-piercing whistle. 'CHILDREN!' he bellowed. 'Can you come down please?'

When no answer came, Grandy Brock tutted. 'They *should* be up in their room practising their handwriting,' he said, turning back to the Shalloo siblings. 'But it's very possible that they're actually turning the bathtub into a secret den, or playing hide-and-seek in the airing cupboards. I'll go on up and see if I can find them. Won't be long.'

Orinthia felt herself beaming. She *loved* the sound of these children. Secret dens? Hide-and-seek? She adored both! As Grandy Brock ascended the creaky staircase, she skipped further into the room excitedly, already looking for hiding places.

Séafra, on the other hand, was loitering near the front door with his arms still crossed. His face was like a thundercloud.

'Come on, Séa,' said Orinthia. 'What are you waiting for? You heard what Grandy Brock said. Make yourself at home – take that woolly cardigan off at least.'

'*Pffft*, there's no way I'm taking my cardie off,' Séafra huffed. 'Someone might steal it. Those children sound feral!'

'Don't be so rude, Séa,' Orinthia tutted. 'And besides, who'd want to steal a scratchy old cardigan? Especially one the colour of bogeys!'

Taber giggled as he attempted to wrangle his jumper over his head, before repeating, 'Bogeys! Bogeys! Bogeys!'

'It's *khaki*, actually,' Séafra replied defensively, poking his tongue out at Orinthia. 'And besides, even if no one steals it, it'll get dirty on the floor. This place looks as if it's never seen a dustpan and brush.'

Orinthia rolled her eyes. Séafra was right, of course – the place was definitely not an example of good housekeeping. The floor was dusty, cobwebs stretched from corner to corner, and the windows were filthy. But it felt lived-in, homely, and that's why Orinthia loved it. As soon as they'd stepped through the door, she'd immediately felt a warmth envelope her, and her shoulders had begun to soften. She certainly never felt like this when she walked into their own home. Yes, Mum might have furnished it with chandeliers, and polished marble floors, and antique vases, and furniture upholstered in sumptuous fabrics, but it wasn't cosy like this place. There were no little nooks in which to snuggle up, no knick-knacks on the walls, no roaring fireplace in the winter. In fact, if you were none the wiser, you probably would never have guessed that a family lived there at all.

A sudden rumble of footsteps from above, followed

by a cacophony of voices, made the Shalloo siblings jump. Orinthia looked up to find a throng of dishevelled-looking children jostling down the staircase – all in tattered clothes and muddy wellington boots – with Grandy Brock at their helm. They were a tangle of arms and legs, their hair colours ranging from bright white to brown, from auburn to jet black. There were turned-up noses and sticky-out ears, knobbly knees and dimpled chins.

As they trundled down the stairs, they didn't seem to notice the Shalloos. They were far too busy talking, or in some cases, arguing.

'Kipling, stop it!' shouted a freckly, surly-faced girl, turning to the boy with marmalade-coloured hair behind her. 'You're pushing me!'

'No, I'm not, Peggy,' protested the boy dramatically. '*You're* just grumpy because I beat you to the last sausage at breakfast this morning and—'

'*AHEM!* That's enough of that!' Grandy Brock turned sharply and looked back up the stairs to his brood. 'What have I told you two about bickering, hmm? It's extremely rude.' He gestured to Orinthia and her two brothers, who were looking up at them with wide eyes. '*Especially* when we have guests.'

On hearing the old man's last word, the children

quickly peered over the bannister, and a series of looks were exchanged.

'Ohhhh, Grandy, not *more* children,' groaned a girl with straight black hair. 'It's enough of a squeeze in our room as it is.' Orinthia suspected the girl was probably around her age, but she was much taller, with a frame like a beanpole. 'I don't want to have to share a bed with anyone else, especially if they wriggle around like Peggy does.'

Peggy's face soured and she spun towards her accuser. 'Well at least *I* don't do bottom burps all night like you do, Suki!' she retorted. 'They smell like rotten corned beef! Actually, a rotten corned-beef omelette with—'

'Children, please! Stop this at once,' scolded Grandy Brock once more. He took a deep breath and held up his calloused hands in appeasement. 'Suki, don't worry. They're not coming to live with us. But I am hoping that they'll be coming to work with us.'

He edged downstairs towards the Shalloo siblings and gestured for his offspring to follow. 'Children, I'd like to introduce you to Orinthia, Taber and . . . and . . .' He looked blankly at Séafra, clicking his fingers as if to jog his memory. 'Oh blast, what was your name again?'

23

Séafra scowled, and sensing that her brother wasn't going to help out the old man, Orinthia answered for him. 'His name is Séafra, Grandy Brock.'

'Ah, that's it! Orinthia, Taber and Séafra.'

Séafra rolled his eyes, causing Kipling, the boy with the marmalade-coloured hair, to flash him a warm smile. 'Don't take it personally,' he said. 'When Grandy Brock first adopted us, it took him months to remember all of our names.' He brought his voice down to a whisper. 'And he still calls me Katherine from time to time!'

'Adopted?' Séafra blurted out. 'So you're orphans?'

Orinthia shot him a sharp look – that question was a little blunt, to say the least!

'It's OK,' shrugged a brown-skinned boy with tight black curls. 'We *were* orphans, living at Guttersnipes Home for Boys and Girls. But just after Christmas Grandy Brock turned up looking for children, and our orphanage directress, Madame Fitzwilliam, couldn't get rid of us quick enough.'

'Not that we complained, though,' added Kipling. 'It was like living in a prison up there.' He threw the back of his right hand to his forehead in exaggerated distress. 'Horrible place! Ghastly! Detestable!'

Peggy rolled her eyes. 'As you can see, Kipling can

be a bit of a drama queen sometimes. Wants to be a famous actor when he's older.'

'Not *wants* to be, is *going* to be,' corrected Kipling. He took a low bow before blowing kisses to an imaginary crowd. 'A true thespian cannot veer from the pull of the stage, the smell of the greasepaint . . .'

'See what I mean?' said Peggy. '*Drama queen!*'

'All right, all right, that's enough,' scorned Grandy Brock, shaking his head in dismay. 'Now, why don't we start again? I'd like you all to introduce yourselves properly, please.'

The children nodded sheepishly and one by one they stepped forward and introduced themselves. At thirteen, Suki was the oldest of the brood and was originally from Japan. She loved to play sports, and immediately delighted in showing the Shalloos her collection of gold, silver and bronze medals.

Kipling came next. He was eleven and a half, and for the first years of his life had lived with his two mothers in a townhouse opposite a theatre. This, Orinthia thought, explained a lot!

The boy with tight curls was a ten-year-old named Bramwell who loved stories. He wanted to be an author when he grew up and had already penned six books, two novellas and an autobiography. He was gentle and softly spoken, and seemed shyer than the others. Orinthia found herself drawn to him immediately.

Peggy, they learnt, had just turned seven, and had come from a family of circus contortionists. As such, she had an innate flexibility which, she bragged, made her 'the best tree climber in Little Penhallow'.

Orinthia had wanted to say that *she* was pretty good at climbing too, but decided against it – she still wasn't sure what to make of this prickly little girl and her terrible temper. She seemed to want to argue with everyone.

'And this little fellow,' said Suki, turning around to reveal a bald-headed baby nesting inside a knapsack on her back, 'is Milky.' He had but a single tooth protruding from his top gum and he was dribbling profusely. 'He arrived at the orphanage without any birth certificate, so we decided to name him after his favourite thing! He's not old enough to work yet, so he plays with Mr Malagasy for most of the day. The only problem is that he's starting to speak "lemur" instead of English!'

The baby glanced up, and having taken in the three new faces staring at him, let out a high-pitched *chirrup*.

Orinthia and Taber laughed, and even Séafra couldn't help but crack a little smile.

'And what about you?' Bramwell asked the siblings. 'Do you live round here?'

Orinthia nodded. 'We live with our mum at the bottom of Foxglove Hill.'

Kipling gasped. 'What, in one of those massive houses? The ones with the big gates and gravel drives and hedges trimmed into shapes? Wow, you must be millionaires!'

Orinthia bristled, and as if sensing her discomfort Grandy Brock quickly clapped his hands together. 'There'll be time for chatter later, Kipling. But now that the introductions are done, I think it's time for the guided tour. And after that, we can decide when you'll start work—'

Séafra sprung forward and cut in. 'Hang on – you still haven't told us what work we'd be doing, *if* we were to accept the job.'

Kipling shook his head. 'Seriously, Grandy? *Ufff*, I told you that I should be in charge of auditions!'

'*Interviews*,' Peggy corrected. 'They're not here because they want to be in one of your silly plays.'

Kipling ignored his sister, proceeding to clear his throat as if about to start a Shakespearean monologue.

'Here at Tupenny Mill, we are in the process of creating the first postal service to be staffed entirely by animals or, as we like to call them, *animails*. We're not quite ready to launch yet, but eventually each street, road and cul-de-sac in Little Penhallow will be designated their very own fleet of postal fauna.'

'The slower creatures like the snails and hedgehogs will deliver the second-class post,' Suki explained. 'While the faster ones, like the fruit bats and the monkeys, will be responsible for first class. The most dexterous animals do the sorting, while the ones with long tongues are in charge of licking stamps!'

Orinthia's eyes widened. So Grandy Brock hadn't been joking when he'd talked of animal posties earlier on!

Séafra snorted in disbelief. 'Oh come off it! Fruit bats delivering post? Next you'll be saying that you can train polar bears to mend socks. This is ridiculous!'

Mr Malagasy, as if attuned to Séafra's disbelief, screeched loudly in protest. He leapt from Grandy Brock's shoulder and, within the blink of an eye, he'd reached for a cream-coloured envelope atop the dresser and was scampering towards Séafra with it balanced on top of his head. Orinthia watched in amazement as he dispatched it into Séafra's cardigan pocket as if it were a letter box, before poking out his tongue and blowing a rather loud and extremely wet raspberry.

The other children, including Orinthia and Taber, laughed. Séafra, however, did not.

'Oh dear, I am sorry about that,' said Grandy Brock, obviously trying very hard to repress his own mirth. 'But our animails are very proud creatures, you see. And they do not like people underestimating their abilities.'

Séafra's face flushed, and he looked to his feet in embarrassment. Orinthia gave him a playful nudge and whispered, 'Don't worry, Séa, just try to enjoy yourself and keep an open mind.'

'Exactly!' said Grandy Brock. 'By the time you leave here today, young Séafra, I can guarantee that you'll have had a change of heart.'

Grandy couldn't have heard Séafra muttering *I doubt it*, because he was already lolloping towards the front door with his brood in tow. He reached for his hat and brandished it staunchly in the air. 'To the Mailbox Menagerie!'

4

'Right, well, here we are,' said Grandy Brock, coming to a standstill five minutes later. 'Everyone gather round. I want to go over a few rules before we go inside.'

He and his children had led the Shalloo siblings out of Tupenny Mill and into the dense woodland which engulfed their home. Having pushed their way through brambles and thickets, they'd arrived at the entrance to a gigantic domed glasshouse, which was nestled under a canopy of overhanging trees and completely hidden from the outside world.

Orinthia had to step back and crane her neck to take it all in. It was palatial – constructed from thousands of panes of light-green glass which glimmered, emerald-like, in the afternoon sunshine. Through their verdant lustre she could see that the interior was just as wondrous, with luscious palms jutting from pots, leafy tendrils creeping along walls, and vines dangling from the ceilings like long lime-coloured fingers.

She could hear the animals too. A cacophony of squawks, squeaks, growls and grunts was coming from within, and she inhaled sharply. These were not the sounds of animals you'd find in a pet shop – these were the sounds of exotic creatures and magnificent beasties that came from faraway jungles and deserts and plains!

On hearing the purr of a wildcat, Taber's face immediately lit up. Then, Orinthia thought he might explode with excitement when the chatter of monkeys rang through the air. 'Can you hear that, Rinthi?' he squealed, bouncing from foot to foot. 'I told you there were going to be monkeys! I told you!'

'Yes you did!' said Orinthia, squeezing her brother's hand with a chuckle. And who'd have thought it? Not her, that was for sure!

Grandy Brock edged towards the doorway and adjusted his hat. 'So, are you ready to take a look inside?' he asked with that twinkle in his eye.

Not needing to think twice, Orinthia and Taber nodded enthusiastically.

'Now, a few words of advice before we go in,' continued Grandy Brock. 'All of our animals are extremely friendly, but as with all creatures, you'll need to earn their trust. They have to feel that you are not a threat, and that takes time. I'd recommend not approaching or touching any of them to begin with. Take things slowly and let them come to you, OK?'

Orinthia nodded. She liked the way that Grandy Brock was talking about the animals. The respect he showed them, his understanding of what they needed to feel safe. He obviously really cared about their well-being.

'Oh, and one more thing,' Bramwell added. 'There are no flushing toilets in the animal kingdom, so watch where you're treading! I'm sure your mum won't appreciate it if you traipse hippopotamus poop through the living room later on!'

Orinthia and Taber gasped in unison. Did Bramwell really just say *hippopotamus*? This day was getting more and more remarkable by the second!

'OK, OK, OK,' muttered Grandy Brock, rifling through what must have been at least thirty keys hanging from a brass ring on his belt. When he found the right one he turned it in the lock, before using his shoulder to push the door open.

A rush of warm air burst from within, heavy and humid, and with the same green, vegetative smell that filled your nose when walking into a garden centre.

'Welcome,' said Grandy Brock to the Shalloo children, stretching out an arm in a bow-like gesture, 'please, step inside! Guests first.'

The siblings edged forward tentatively. The Mailbox Menagerie looked exactly as its name suggested: as if a post office had exploded in a zoo. Everywhere Orinthia looked there were animals in little blue hats – reptiles and molluscs, mammals and arachnids, amphibians and crustaceans – all busy undertaking their various postal duties. There were meerkats rifling through mailbags, and alpacas slotting envelopes into wooden sorting cabinets. An aardvark trundled past pushing a postal trolley with its long snout, and all of a sudden a hedgehog appeared from behind a pillar box with a tiny parcel in its mouth.

'Wow,' Orinthia mouthed, her gaze darting from metallic scales to rainbow-coloured feathers, from polka-dotted furs to leathery scutes. Some of the creatures were going about their business on four legs and some on two, while others slithered or slid or even swam! It was like nothing she'd ever seen before, and she almost had to pinch herself as she caught sight of a pink-bottomed baboon sitting on a filing cabinet, franking envelopes with an ink stamp. She even spotted some toucans swooping around in the rafters, transporting postcards in their tangerine-coloured bills.

Grandy Brock, followed by his children, held his arms out wide as he took centre stage in the middle of the menagerie. 'So? What do you think?' he asked. 'Impressive, isn't it?' Mr Malagasy leapt from the old man's shoulder, grabbing on to an overhanging vine and climbing it like a rope.

'It's . . . it's extraordinary!' replied Orinthia, almost speechless. 'Miraculous!' She looked down at Taber, his eyes as wide as saucers and his little body vibrating with excitement as he watched a pair of Sphynx cats busily licking stamps with their long pink tongues. Séafra also seemed mesmerized, his attention being held by the bright-orange octopus in the adjacent tank, who had a beautifully wrapped gift in each of her sucker-covered tentacles.

'Hang on a minute, let me get this straight,' said Orinthia, still trying to get her head around what was going on. 'You're training all of these animals to be postal workers? So you can set up a new kind of postal service?'

'Exactly!' said Grandy Brock, nodding proudly. 'The Mailbox Menagerie is the first of its kind in the entire world! Some of the animails are sorters, some are clerks, some frank envelopes and some do the deliveries. And each of my children oversees a different species.'

'But . . . but why?' asked Séafra, suddenly finding his voice. 'I don't mean to be rude, but don't we have a perfectly good postal service already? The Royal Mail is one of the best in the world.'

'It's because Grandy Brock got fired,' Peggy answered quickly. 'From his job at the—'

'Thank you, Peggy!' Grandy Brock swiftly cut in. 'I don't think we need to go into that right now, *do we?*' A vein twitched at his temple, and he shot his freckle-faced daughter a stern look, silencing her instantly. She had obviously hit a nerve. Grandy Brock had been fired? But from where? And why had that led to him setting up the Mailbox Menagerie?

In an obvious attempt to change the subject, the old man clapped his hands together, before saying, 'Why don't we give you a guided tour, hmmm? Meet some of our animails? The little one seems eager to look around!' He nodded to Taber, now peering into the nearby pen of wombats, who were busy stacking parcels with their short arms.

'Oh, yes please,' Orinthia nodded, the thought of seeing more of these incredible animals quickly distracting her from whatever Peggy had nearly divulged. 'That'd be wonderful.'

Grandy Brock looked to Séafra and raised an eyebrow. 'And what about you, young man? Are you going to join us, or would you prefer to go and wait back in the mill?'

Orinthia turned to her brother, expecting a miserable face, but to her absolute surprise Séafra was grinning. 'Wait in the mill? No way!' he exclaimed, before adding sheepishly, 'And I'm sorry for being a bit grumpy earlier. My brother and sister are much more adventurous than I am. I'm nowhere near as brave.'

'Nonsense,' said Grandy Brock. 'If you ask me, it takes a *very* brave person to admit their fears. A very brave person indeed.' He smiled at Séafra, who instantly stood a little taller, his shoulders inching back with pride. 'Now come along, we have lots to show you. Children, lead the way!'

With Kipling at the front, the Brock siblings set off through the glasshouse, slaloming their way around the various enclosures and terrariums, scratch posts and fish tanks. As they passed a new type of animail, one of them would give the Shalloos a brief explanation of the creature's role in the menagerie. There was a shoal of iridescent fish which Bramwell introduced as the Piscine Posties, and a terrarium of giant, yellow-shelled gastropods which Peggy collectively called the Mail Snails. A family of long-haired guinea pigs (who looked as if they were wearing tiny blonde toupees) were in charge of a sorting cabinet housing parcels – each of them overseeing the maintenance of a different cubbyhole.

As they skirted a pond filled with frogs, a *click-click* drew Orinthia's eyes upwards, and a bat flew overhead grasping a small parcel in its clawed feet. 'That's Titus,' said Bramwell, tracking the path of the brownwinged creature with his index finger. 'He's one of our most capable posties and, as you'd expect, loves doing the night shift!'

Orinthia beamed. Not even Ophelia Pearcart had witnessed such an array of remarkable beasts!

'So, how many creatures do you have exactly, Grandy Brock?' asked Séafra as they meandered into a section of the menagerie devoted to rodents. Orinthia was so glad that he'd started to relax, and he seemed to genuinely be enjoying himself.

'*Hmm*, now there's a question,' replied the old man. He cocked his head to think for a moment, and Orinthia could see him visualizing each individual creature in his mind's eye as he counted. 'Three hundred and fifty-three, I think . . .' he said eventually. 'No, forgive me! Three hundred and fifty-*six*. I forgot that the porcupines have just had a litter.' He pointed to an adjacent enclosure where three tiny prickled creatures were curled up next to their mother.

'*Awwwwww!* Can I touch one? Can I touch one?' exclaimed Taber, running towards them. 'They're sooo cute!'

'Ha! You wouldn't say that if you'd fallen into their enclosure one morning and had to spend the rest of the day pulling quills out of your bottom!' said Bramwell with a chuckle. 'It was so painful, I couldn't sit down properly for days.'

The Shalloo siblings grimaced in unison.

'But they do make wonderful postal workers,' continued the boy, opening the enclosure and stepping inside. 'They're resourceful, quick-witted and' – he reached for a couple of letters from a nearby pigeonhole and slotted them neatly in between the mother porcupine's quills – 'during a delivery, they keep the mail perfectly organized!'

'That's so clever!' said Orinthia, impressed. 'Brilliant!'

'Well, wait until you see what *my* animails can do,' said Peggy, leading them away from the porcupine enclosure. Her pace quickened as she continued to talk, the Shalloo siblings hurrying after her. 'I'm in charge of all the reptiles, you see. Lizards, turtles, tortoises, crocodiles and' – she came to a standstill next to a huge glass-fronted vivarium filled with tropical plants – 'these little beauties!'

To begin with, Orinthia couldn't make out what Peggy was referring to, but as she peered through the glass and scanned the greenery, she found herself inches away from a writhing tangle of jewel-hued snakes. They were svelte and muscular, their forked tongues flickering like blue flames as they twisted and turned.

'*Pythonidae*,' said Peggy with the confident air of an expert. 'More commonly known as the python family!' She opened a hatch on the top of the vivarium and reached in. The reptile she picked up was citrus-green in colour, and it wrapped around her arm like a beautiful bangle (albeit one with yellow eyes and pin-sharp teeth).

'But how can snakes be postal workers?' asked Séafra. 'They haven't got any hands . . . or paws.'

'Watch this,' said Peggy, as if a light were brightening inside her. She tapped gently on the glass, and when she'd got all of the snakes' attention, she took a small whistle from her pocket and blew. 'Thirty-three, Talbot Avenue,' she called out. 'Thirty-three, Talbot Avenue.'

Immediately the snakes began to move, their scaly intertwined bodies unravelling like a loose knot. It was only when Orinthia looked closely that she realized that the snakes had started to manoeuvre themselves into shapes . . . no . . . letters! Their bodies were spelling something out! L . . . P . . . 5 . . . 1 . . . H . . . P.

'Wow! Is that a postcode?' Orinthia gasped.

Peggy nodded proudly. 'Yup. They've learnt the postcodes for every street and road in Little Penhallow. They're going to make brilliant navigators when it comes to deliveries!'

Just then, the snakes began to move once more, and just when Orinthia thought that they were turning themselves into a different postcode, they spelt out the words: CHEESE BREATH.

Peggy grimaced with embarrassment. 'They might have picked up a few rude words along the way too. Sorry about that!'

Orinthia didn't mind. *Cheese Breath*. She'd definitely be adding that to her list of things to call Séafra when he was being annoying.

It took them well over an hour to circumnavigate the entirety of the menagerie, and when they had finished, they all sat down around the baby hippo enclosure to enjoy a cold drink. With Grandy Brock's permission, Taber was the first to pick one of the hippos up, and with the biggest grin, pulled the grey barrel-shaped creature close to his chest. 'Ooooohhhhh, squishy!' he said, squeezing it tight.

'Careful, Tabs!' said Orinthia. 'Be gentle, you don't want to hurt her.'

'Don't worry,' said Kipling. 'Baby hippos are pretty robust little things. I found Milky trying to nibble one's ear one morning and it wasn't fazed in the slightest!'

Orinthia laughed. What a life these children led!

'So, what do you think?' asked Grandy Brock, pouring each of the Shalloo siblings a glass of icy lemonade. 'You fancy being part of our team? You don't need to make up your minds right away, of course. Take your time.'

Orinthia would have been more than happy to accept the job offer straight away, and from the way

Taber was cooing over the little hippo, she thought he would be too. But as always, Séafra was a little more cautious.

'If we *were* to accept your job offer,' he asked, 'what kind of animails would we be looking after? What would our duties be?'

'Aha! Now there's a good question, young man!' Grandy replied. 'And one that I will happily give you the answer to. Follow me. The animails I'd like you three to train are just over here.' He turned on his heel, and the Shalloo siblings followed him to the very back of the menagerie, where something as tall and as wide as a gas stove was hidden under a heavy velvet cloth. 'Now, do you three like birds?' he asked.

'Oh yes!' said Orinthia enthusiastically, her mind swirling with images of hot-pink flamingos and tropical parrots and long-necked swans. She looked to her brothers, who were nodding eagerly in agreement.

'Wonderful,' said Grandy Brock. 'In which case I'd like to introduce you to our newest and perhaps most exciting arrivals!' He whipped away the velvet cloth with the flourish of a magician and stepped back. '*Ta-da!*'

Orinthia's face dropped in amazement. Grandy Brock had revealed an ornate wrought-iron aviary, and inside were two pelicans. One was rather large, with bright-white feathers and a hooked, yolk-coloured beak. The other was much smaller, possibly still a chick, and its plumage was grey and fluffy.

'*Pelecanus erythrorhynchos*,' said Grandy Brock. 'Also known as the American white pelican. The larger one is called Geronimo, and the smaller one is her son, Gungho.'

Grandy Brock opened the door to a frantic flurry of feathers, and with a loud *caw* Geronimo flew from the enclosure and landed on his outstretched arm. 'Gungho hasn't started flying yet, but he will, in time.'

'And you think they're going to make good posties?' asked Orinthia.

'Oh yes, these are no ordinary pelicans,' said Grandy Brock proudly. 'These birds are extremely rare. There's only a few of their kind in the entire world.'

'But what's so special about them?' asked Séafra.

'Well,' said Grandy Brock, stroking Geronimo down her back. 'Have you ever heard of homing pigeons?'

'Yes,' Orinthia nodded. 'I learnt about them in school. During wartime, the military used pigeons to transport messages back to base.'

'Precisely!' said Grandy Brock. 'But Gungho and Geronimo here can go one better! They have an extremely heightened sense of magnetoreception. This means that, thanks to the iron clusters in their upper beaks, they can use the Earth's magnetic field to perceive direction, altitude and location.'

'Like a compass?' asked Séafra.

'Exactly! Like a very powerful and very accurate inner compass!' He ran a finger down Geronimo's white plumage and she let out a raspy honk, somewhere between the *quack* of a duck and the *oink* of a piglet.

'You see,' continued Grandy Brock, 'homing pigeons can only navigate their way back to home territory, but these pelicans can learn to go back and forth between many different locations. With the right training, they'll be able to deliver our post internationally. The people of Little Penhallow will be able to send and receive mail by animail from every corner of the globe.'

'Wow!' said Taber. 'They're very clever birdies! Very, very, very clever!'

And all of a sudden, as if in thanks, Geronimo extended her wings, launching herself from Grandy Brock's arm before coming to land on the six-year-old's head. 'Eeeeeeeeeeek!' he squealed joyfully, reaching up to stroke the bird's tail feathers. 'She's come to say hello!'

'Yes, she definitely seems to like *you*, young man,' said Grandy, ruffling Taber's hair affectionately. 'Either that or you have bird food in that wild barnet of yours.'

'Taber's always adored animals,' said Orinthia, recalling the time when her younger brother had rescued a mouse from a trap in the kitchen, then nursed it back to health with the marrowfat peas left over from dinner. 'But our mum has never let us have one. She works a lot and doesn't really have time for animals.'

'Doesn't have time for animals?' Grandy Brock took a sharp breath, as if it were the most shocking thing he'd ever heard. 'Goodness gracious me, that's a travesty! A life without animals isn't a life worth living, in my book.'

And having spent only an afternoon in the menagerie, Orinthia already completely agreed.

'So, what do you say?' asked Grandy Brock. 'Do you think you'd like to help me train the pelicans? I can't offer you much in the way of payment, but the three of you will get a few coins at the end of each week, and a hot lunch every day.'

The Shalloo siblings didn't even need to discuss the matter. 'YES!' they all said in unison, even Séafra. 'Yes, yes, yes!'

'Wonderful,' said Grandy Brock. 'You'll start tomorrow morning!'

The Shalloo siblings beamed as they walked back through the menagerie, but just as they were making their way out, Orinthia felt something squidgy give way beneath her foot. 'Yuck!' she shrieked. 'Is that a—?' As she looked down, her suspicions were confirmed – a brown animal poo lay squashed beneath her plimsoll.

'I did warn you,' said Bramwell with a wry smile.

Orinthia smiled back. She'd definitely be wearing her wellies tomorrow.

5

The sun was setting, casting a pinkish glow across the fields, as the Shalloo siblings trundled back over St Sylvester's Mount later that afternoon. Séafra was giving a piggyback to Taber who, exhausted from the day's activities, was sound asleep and snoring gently.

'Well *that* was an unexpected afternoon,' Séafra said, looking back at Tupenny Mill. 'I can't believe that there's this amazing place right here in Little Penhallow that we had no idea about!'

'So you're glad you didn't go home?' asked Orinthia pointedly. 'You're glad you listened to your wise big sister?'

'*Yes*,' groaned Séafra reluctantly, hoicking Taber higher on to his back as they crested the hill. 'And I can't believe we start our summer jobs tomorrow. We're going to be training pelicans!'

'It beats a paper round, that's for sure,' said Orinthia with a grin. 'This is going to be the best summer holiday ever!'

Séafra pondered for a moment before they made their descent. 'But . . . do you think we should tell Mum?'

'What's the point?' Orinthia replied with a huff. 'She'd only half listen anyway. The only way to get her full attention is to mention *road tax* or *service plans* or *torque converters*.'

A slight pang of sadness prickled over Orinthia, the way it always did when she thought of how much time their mum actually spent at work. It wasn't that she didn't care about them, it was just that sometimes it seemed that she cared about her business more. When Grandad had died a few years ago, Mum and Uncle Max were left in charge of the family's used-car dealership, Wheely Good Motors. But Uncle Max didn't seem to like working very much, so now Mum spent more time at the dealership than she did at home. She rarely finished before 8 p.m., often worked weekends, and even when she took a day off, most of her time was spent in the study, poring over papers and ledgers and accounts. Orinthia knew that their mother just wanted to honour Grandad's memory and keep the business going, but she wished that she could spend as much time with them as she did with the convertibles and coupes.

'Come on, let's get a move on,' she said, refusing to allow these negative thoughts to spoil what had been an incredible day. She nudged Séafra with her elbow, before picking up the pace and calling back, 'Last one home has to do the laundry all holidays!'

'Hey, that's not fair!' shouted Séafra, trying his best to speed up with the snoozing passenger on his back. 'I've got the equivalent of a baby rhinoceros clinging on to me! I should get a head start!'

But Orinthia was already homeward bound. She sprinted down the hill, ripped across the village green, and turned on to the higgledy-piggledy cobbles of the high street. It was still bustling with people, each of the shop fronts adorned to entice even the most reluctant of passers-by. Mr Barnabas's sweet shop looked especially wonderful, its window display an architectural wonder of treacle toffee, lollipops, bonbons and coconut mushrooms. Orinthia would have usually stopped off to pick up a bag of her favourite chocolate drops, but there was no way she was going to lose this race to Séafra!

When she reached the wrought-iron railings that

surrounded their house she clasped her hands above her head in victory. 'And she's done it!' she cried, mimicking the voice of a news reporter. 'Orinthia Shalloo becomes the first female explorer to single-handedly cross the vast wilderness of Little Penhallow. What an achievement! What an inspiring young woman!'

'Stop showing off, Rinthi,' called Séafra, lolloping behind with Taber still on his back. Their little brother was awake now, and was pretending that he was a jockey and that Séafra was his horse.

'Giddy up, horsey!' he shouted, digging his heels into his brother's thighs as if wearing spurs. 'Giddy up! Giddy up!'

'OK, off you get, cowboy,' groaned Séafra, lowering Taber to the ground. 'Next time, you're giving *me* a piggyback! I don't care that you're half my size!'

The three children laughed and Orinthia pushed open the front gates, giving way to the sprawling gravel drive which led up to their family home. It was a grand red-brick property with a newly tiled roof and decorative leaded windows. As Kipling had pointed out, it *had* cost Mum a lot of money, but it lacked the homeliness of Tupenny Mill. Orinthia couldn't help wishing that they were still there, curled up in front of the fire and learning more about the animails of the Mailbox Menagerie.

Pushing open the front door, the siblings were greeted with the whirring din of the vacuum cleaner coming from one of the upstairs rooms. Their cleaner, Mrs Gastaldini, came once a week to tidy the house, and was obviously hard at work.

'Hello!' Orinthia called up, taking off her (poo-encrusted) shoes before leaving them in the porch. 'It's only us.'

The vacuum cleaner cut out and Mrs Gastaldini appeared at the top of the stairs. She was a squat old woman, dressed in a flowery tabard and a plaid headscarf which was knotted beneath her chin. 'Ah, *ciao bambini!*' she called down in her thick Milanese accent. '*Buonasera! Come stai?*'

'*Bene, grazie!*' chorused the three children, remembering the Italian phrase that the cleaning lady had taught them on her first day at work.

'*Bene, bene,*' said Mrs Gastaldini, unplugging the vacuum cleaner and hauling it downstairs. 'You're so polite! Not like my *nipoti*. They're very mischievous! Never listen to what their grandmother says.'

She put the vacuum cleaner in the cupboard and took her coat from the bannister. 'Well, that's me finished for the day,' she said. 'Are you three going to be OK until your *mamma* gets home?'

'We'll be fine thanks, Mrs Gastaldini,' said Orinthia.

'Well, she works too hard if you ask me,' said the old woman, shaking her head as she made for the front door. 'That lazy brother of hers needs to start helping out a bit more. *Uomo pigro!*' Her hands shot into the air with contempt and even though Orinthia didn't speak Italian, she knew that whatever Mrs Gastaldini had just said about Uncle Max probably wasn't complimentary.

'Here . . .' said Mrs Gastaldini, reaching deep into her coat pocket. She pulled out a handful of toffees wrapped in gold foil and gave one to each sibling. 'Some Italian *caramelle*. But don't eat them until after dinner, OK?'

Orinthia and Séafra nodded, but Taber was already unwrapping his. Mrs Gastaldini laughed, and pinched his cheek affectionately. '*Che carino*. What a little cutie! Anyway, see you soon, *bambini. Ciao, ciao!*'

The Shalloo children waved the old woman off, and once she'd gone they made their way into the kitchen. Like the rest of the house, it was immaculate

– shiny appliances adorned the countertops, alongside vases of perfectly arranged flowers, and a bowl of untouched fruit. A black-and-white photograph of Grandad completing his first used-car sale hung on the far wall, next to a framed certificate bearing the words WHEELY GOOD MOTORS – LITTLE PENHALLOW DEALERSHIP OF THE YEAR.

'OK, who wants a ham sandwich?' asked Orinthia, rifling through the cupboards as her brothers sat down at the dining table.

'Me!' squealed Taber, his mouth still gluey with toffee. 'I want two!'

'Two? That's a lot of food for such a little boy,' said Orinthia, turning towards him. 'Maybe start with *one*, hmmm?'

Taber crossed his arms with a huff. 'They're not both for me, Rinthi. Gungho wants one too, don't you, boy?'

'Gungho?' said Orinthia, turning around. 'What—' She stopped mid-sentence, watching as her little brother reached into his pocket and pulled out the baby pelican that Grandy Brock had shown them earlier that afternoon.

'Tabs!' Orinthia gasped. 'What's he doing here? He shouldn't be out of the menagerie. You can't just take things without asking. Especially not living creatures!'

'I didn't take him,' protested Taber, putting Gungho down on to the table and running a finger along his beak. 'He jumped into my pocket and Grandy Brock said it was OK if I took him home, just for the night! I want to show him to Mummy. I think she'll really like him.'

Orinthia and Séafra exchanged a look. Taber was desperate for their mother's attention, and never stopped believing that someday soon she might have some free time to spend with him. Orinthia and Séafra had been the same when they were younger, but had long since given up hope.

'Tabs, I think you'll be in bed before Mummy gets home tonight,' said Séafra gently, trying to appease his little brother. 'You know how busy she is with work.'

Taber looked up, heartbroken. 'But . . . but Gungho could perch on Mummy's desk and help her with her numbers. Or keep her company when she's on the telephone . . .' His shoulders started to heave and before long, tears were rolling down his cheeks.

'Hey, don't be sad, Tabs,' said Orinthia, coming to

his side and putting an arm around him. 'Maybe we can show Gungho to Mummy another time, hmm? Maybe on a weekend when she's not so busy?'

Taber nodded, sniffing back his tears. 'You promise?'

'I promise,' lied Orinthia, knowing full well that she shouldn't really make such an oath. 'I tell you what, why don't you and Gungho share a tuna sandwich, then we'll take him up to your room? We can make him a nice nest somewhere and you can read him a bedtime story?'

Taber's frown immediately curled upwards. '*Little Red Riding Hood*?'

'Good choice,' said Orinthia. 'Now let's slice some bread. Come on, you can sit up on the counter and help me spread the butter.'

But just as Orinthia was getting up, she heard the front door burst open.

'Children, I'm home!' Mum called from the hall-way. '*Ufff*, it's been such a long day. Sold three saloons this morning, then a lovely red station wagon after lunch. An investor is coming in for a meeting tomorrow too. Could mean very exciting things for the business . . .'

She came into the kitchen and immediately Taber

leapt from his seat. 'Mummy, Mummy, look what I've got!' he shouted, picking up Gungho and bounding across the room. He held up the bird to his mother's face and grinned. 'He wants to say hello to you!'

'That's lovely, darling,' said Mum vacantly, obviously so distracted by thoughts of work that she didn't even question why her youngest son was holding a baby pelican. She was a vision in pastel-coloured clothes – her cardigan matching her shoes, her shoes matching her handbag, and her handbag matching her lipstick. A string of pearls hung around her neck and her hair was set in perfect blonde curls.

'He belongs to Grandy Brock,' Taber continued enthusiastically, despite their mother's lack of interest. 'He has lots of animals up at Tupenny Mill and they're going to send things all over the village. We're going to help him train them—'

'That sounds wonderful, darling,' Mum replied absent-mindedly. She was already walking over to the other side of the kitchen, towards her office. 'Well, it looks like you have everything in hand with dinner, Orinthia. Would you be a sweetheart and put on a pot of coffee for me? I need to go and work out the day's profits – it's going to be another late one . . .'

She didn't wait for a reply from her daughter, and within an instant she was closing the office door behind her.

6

The Shalloo siblings barely slept that night. Too excited to sleep in their own rooms, they all bundled into Orinthia's and chatted into the early hours, enthusing about postage stamps and pelicans, letter-writing and lemurs! They were all keen to get to know Grandy Brock and his brood, and the summer holiday no longer seemed like the long, arduous ordeal that it had only yesterday to Orinthia. In fact, the children were so excited that the sun had barely risen when they got up, sneaked out of the house, and made their way back across St Sylvester's Mount, ready to start their first day at work.

They had all dressed appropriately – teaming their play-clothes with wellington boots and pairs of thick socks. Orinthia had also packed a knapsack inspired by what Ophelia Pearcart used to take on her expeditions: it contained a length of rope, her Swiss army knife, a first aid kit, mosquito spray, a box of matches and sun cream. Séafra had joked that they were only going a few miles from home, not to the Amazon rainforest, but Orinthia knew from Ophelia Pearcart's diaries that it was always better to be prepared.

Walking back into Tupenny Mill made Orinthia's shoulders soften and her heart sing. The Brock children, still in their flannel pyjamas, were sitting around the long kitchen table, chatting and joking as they wolfed down bowls of porridge. The smell of honeyed oats hung in the air, sweet and warm and comforting. Orinthia took in all of their grubby faces, trying to remember their names: Suki . . . Bramwell . . . Peggy . . . and . . . Kipling! Milky the baby was in a wooden high chair, half a banana in hand and his mouth sticky with yellow-brown gloop. Some of the animails had been brought up from the menagerie for a spot of breakfast too, and before she'd even stepped inside, a hedgehog had scuttled across Orinthia's feet with a croissant in its mouth. The place felt homely and welcoming, as if she were being greeted by a dear friend (albeit one that smelt a bit like animal poo and left you covered in fur).

'Here they are!' said Grandy from the kitchen,

gesturing to Orinthia and her brothers to come in. 'My lovely new worker bees!' He was wearing exactly the same outfit as the day before, but today a red fez crowned his head, a long black tassel hanging from its centre. 'How did you get on with Gungho last night, young Taber? Did he behave himself?'

Taber nodded and pulled the little bird from his pocket. 'We read him a bedtime story, then I made him a nest in Orinthia's laundry basket.'

'Well, what a lucky little pelican he is!' said Grandy Brock with a smile. 'Now come and take a seat and I'll get the three of you some brekka.'

The Shalloo siblings sat down, mouths already watering. The breakfast Grandy Brock had laid out looked delicious. There were racks of granary toast accompanied by pats of butter the colour of gorse. There was plum jam and orange marmalade, lemon curd and apricot preserve. Each of the Brock children had their own wooden egg cup, in which nestled a speckled beauty waiting to be cracked open.

Before Orinthia had even reached for her napkin, Séafra and Taber were already filling their plates and tucking in.

'Wowsers trousers, someone's peckish!' said Grandy, as Séafra stuffed a whole round of toast thick with apricot preserve into his mouth. 'Haven't you ever tasted home-made bread before?'

The Brock children laughed and Séafra's cheeks flushed with embarrassment. Orinthia shot him a reassuring smile. If truth be told, he probably *hadn't* tasted home-made bread – not for a long while. Mum didn't have time for that kind of thing any more, so breakfast was usually just a bowl of boring old cornflakes.

'Our mum isn't a very good cook, that's all,' lied Orinthia, coming to her brother's defence. 'She always burns things.'

'Bless you,' said Grandy Brock with a chuckle. 'Well, there's plenty more where that came from. In fact, that reminds me, I must show you where all of our animal feed is kept later on. We try to make our own where possible – gravy bones, chicken nibbles, fish-gut bites, tripe biscuits. And I usually make extra to send to my brother Jobe who lives in New York. He has an animal sanctuary there, you see.'

'That's a great idea!' said Orinthia. 'Although the fish-gut bites don't sound hugely appealing, I must say.'

The children ate with gusto, and when every plate was clean, Grandy got up and began collecting the jars of jams and preserves. 'Right,' he said, 'everyone put your plates in the sink and get into your overalls. Then we'll head down to the menagerie. Kipling, did you say that you wanted to do another test delivery with one of the chinchillas this morning?'

The boy nodded. 'Yes. His sense of navigation was good last time, but he dropped a few letters and got distracted by one of the geckos. I think he can do better today.'

Grandy Brock nodded. 'Excellent. And what about you, Suki?'

The eldest of the Brock children looked up. 'I'm teaching the frogs to hop up garden paths.'

'Wonderful. And you two?' said Grandy Brock, addressing his remaining offspring.

'Bramwell and I are going to see how the snakes are getting on with their door number recognition,' said Peggy. 'And after that we're going to spend some time with Petunia the octopus.'

Grandy Brock clapped his hands together with glee. 'Splendid. In which case, you three' – he turned to face the Shalloo siblings – 'can make a start with Geronimo. Come on, follow me! I hope she remembers you!'

*

The old man needn't have worried about Geronimo remembering the children . . . well, the youngest of them at least! As soon as the aviary had been opened, and just as she'd done yesterday, Geronimo flew out and headed straight for Taber. After a quick squawk and affectionate peck at Gungho, who'd travelled back to the menagerie on Taber's head, she landed at his feet, nuzzling against his calf with the large pouch of her beak. Even though neither she nor Séafra were getting a look-in from the bird, Orinthia couldn't help but beam at the unfolding sight – seeing her youngest brother and the large-beaked bird reminded her of one of those eighteenth-century oil paintings depicting a nobleman and his hound, albeit with a six-year-old boy and his pelican.

'Well, I think we know who's going to be doing the majority of the work with Geronimo,' said Grandy Brock with a chuckle to the two older children. 'It's quite incredible. I've never seen an animail so instantly comfortable with anyone before. I hope you don't feel too left out.'

'It's OK,' said Orinthia, not taking her eye off Taber and his new-found friend. 'I'm happy that Geronimo seems so at ease. She looks really contented.'

Taber seemed equally as smitten. He was now sat cross-legged on the floor, looking up into Geronimo's glassy brown eyes. The bird was standing upright, moving from webbed foot to webbed foot, her plump feathered chest jutting out proudly.

'Well there's no time like the present, young Taber. Why don't you try calling her by name, and get her to come to you from a distance?' suggested Grandy Brock. 'There's a bucket of sprats in the corner. Use them to reward her when she does as you say.'

Taber nodded, and with a few of the fishy treats in hand, he walked over to the other side of the menagerie. In the meantime, Orinthia had scooped up little Gungho, and was cradling the feathery grey puffball in the crook of her arm, ready to watch his mother attempting the challenge ahead.

'OK, I'm ready!' said Taber, crouching down and putting the sprats on the floor beside him. 'Geronimo, *come*!' he called out, gesturing to the pelican with an open hand. 'Come on girl, don't be scared . . .'

The bird and the boy locked eyes, and Orinthia beamed with pride as Geronimo began to cross the floor. She'd always known that her youngest brother loved animals, but she'd had no idea how much they would love him in return.

Grandy Brock seemed equally impressed. 'That's it, that's it!' he enthused as the pelican hopped forward on her yolk-yellow legs. 'Keep calling her name, Taber. She's on her way!'

Taber nodded and leant in. 'Here, Geronimo, come get your fish!'

'Do you think she's enjoying herself?' asked Séafra, watching the bird as she followed the sound of Taber's voice. 'And do you think she'll like being a post pelican?'

'Oh yes!' said Grandy Brock, nodding with confidence. 'It's such good exercise and it'll give her a purpose too, not like those poor old zoo animals that get shut up in cages with nothing to do.'

Orinthia couldn't disagree with that. All of the animals in the menagerie really did seem to be living such happy lives.

'But what happens if the animals *don't* enjoy their postal duties?' asked Séafra. 'Or if they're just not very obedient?'

'Well, I let them retire, of course. Remember I told you about my brother Jobe's animal sanctuary in New York City? Well, if I don't think an animal is thriving here, I'll send them over the Atlantic to live the rest of their lives there. My brother spoils them rotten! We have a couple of raccoons heading over there next week actually – they're really not getting on with the chameleons.'

The thought of an animal retirement home made Orinthia smile. *What might they spend their time doing?* she wondered. *Knitting? Playing golf? Learning to paint watercolours?*

She didn't have the chance to enquire further, however, as just then Grandy Brock leapt to his feet. Geronimo was now only metres away from Taber, and the old man was *whooping* wildly. 'That's it Taber, that's it!' he enthused. 'Now, get ready to give her one of the sprats. You need to show her how well she's done. That's how she'll learn to do as you ask.'

Taber grabbed one of the oily treats by the tail, and as soon as Geronimo was in touching distance, he threw it into the air. The bird caught it deftly in her large bucket beak, swallowing it whole in one greedy gulp.

The rest of the Brock children, who had stopped what they were doing in order to watch, erupted into huge applause.

'I did it!' Taber beamed, his eyes sparkling. 'Geronimo listened to what I said! She followed my instructions!' He threw his arms around her neck, the bird cooing happily at his touch.

And it wasn't long before Geronimo was listening to more of Taber's commands in return for tasty rewards. It was as if they'd known each other all their lives, as if they were speaking a secret avian language. By the end of the morning Geronimo was able to *stay*, *catch* and *turn*, simply by listening to Taber's voice.

'Remarkable,' said Grandy Brock when it was time to go up to the mill for lunch. 'I've never seen anything like it. The boy's a natural!'

And his children were just as dazzled.

'You've done so well!' enthused Bramwell, giving Taber a congratulatory pat on the back.

'I wish Petunia would listen to me like that,' huffed Peggy. 'She's been so naughty this morning. Kept trying to tickle me with her tentacles!'

'Don't worry, Pegs,' said Kipling to his sister. 'All creatures have their off days' – he nudged her in the ribs – 'as *you* know all too well!'

Grandy Brock rolled his eyes. 'Come on, you two, I don't want any squabbling again. Now let's go up to the mill and have some lunch. It's bubble and squeak today!'

As they made to leave, Geronimo let out a loud *honk-honk*.

'Yes, Geronimo,' Grandy Brock called back. 'You can have some too!'

7

For the next couple of weeks, the children visited Tupenny Mill every day. Taber made swift progress with Geronimo's training, and soon enough he was letting the bird out for short flights around the village, in order to test out her homing skills. The connection she had to Tupenny Mill had to be strengthened before she could start making international trips, and as such Taber had been training her to deliver dummy letters all around Little Penhallow before returning to the mill. The practice was known as 'tossing', Grandy Brock had explained, and it was the tactic that pigeon fanciers used when preparing their birds to race.

Taber had started by releasing Geronimo only a mile away from St Sylvester's Mount. Then he'd made a toss at five miles, then at ten, and continued in incremental steps each day. Grandy Brock had driven the boy and his bird the distances in his truck – a rusty old wreck with a clunky gearbox and a horn which sounded like a wheezy chest. Each time they'd set off, Taber had worried that his beloved winged companion might not come back. But he needn't have fretted. Geronimo always returned within hours, swooping back into the menagerie with her beak wide open, hungry for her fishy rewards.

Orinthia and Séafra spent their days helping out with the other animails, as well as looking after Gungho and watching the little pelican grow. His fluffy grey plumage had begun to moult, and in its place the bright-white feathers of a maturing bird had started to appear. He'd still shown no interest in flying, and was at his happiest when snuggled up in the crook of Orinthia's arm or being finger-fed little pieces of mackerel or cod.

Mum seemed to be none the wiser on what her children were up to, and so far hadn't questioned them about how they were spending their holidays. She had been even busier than usual with work, blaming the 'summer spending surge' for the increasing amount of time she was spending at the car dealership.

But just as the children were slipping out of the house one morning, she called down to them from her bedroom. 'Children, is that you? Where are you going?'

The Shalloo siblings froze at the front door and eyeballed each other nervously. Orinthia, silencing her brothers with a finger to her lips, called back, 'Erm . . . we thought we'd go out to the park, Mum. It's meant to be nice and warm today.'

'OK, sweetheart,' Mum replied without further question. 'But could you stop at the post office on your way there? I need you to send something for me – special delivery. It's on my desk in the office.'

Orinthia rolled her eyes. She'd wondered why Mum had suddenly shown an interest in their plans. She had an ulterior motive, *of course*.

Orinthia strode over to her mother's wooden desk, which was strewn with papers and files, documents and ledgers. A well-thumbed copy of *Under the Bonnet: How To Sell Used Cars, Vol III* lay open, with several passages underlined in pencil. Orinthia picked up the large brown envelope, which was addressed to an automobile manufacturer in South Kensington, and put it in her bag.

'Thanks, sweetheart,' said Mum, appearing at the

top of the stairs. She was in her dressing gown, with a towel wrapped around her head in a turban. 'I'd do it myself, of course, but I'm just a bit—'

'Busy,' said Orinthia, finishing her mother's sentence. 'Yeah, we know.'

Mum's face fell a little bit but she quickly forced a smile. 'Thank you, darling, I do appreciate it. And how about we all make biscuits together this weekend, hmm?'

'That sounds nice,' Orinthia replied, but didn't allow herself to get her hopes up. Mum had broken lots of promises like this before.

Mum unravelled her towel turban and gave her wet hair a rub. 'Well, have a nice day then, children. I'll probably be back late again tonight, but there's plenty of things in the fridge to make sandwiches for tea . . .'

Orinthia nodded to her brothers, and without even saying goodbye to their mother they were out of the front door in a flash.

The weather was indeed warm, with not a cloud in the sky. '*Ufff*, I don't want to go to the post office,' Taber groaned as they made their way down to the village. 'I want to go straight to Tupenny Mill to see Geronimo. Can we post Mummy's letter another day, Rinthi?'

'Come on Tabs, don't grumble,' said Orinthia, putting an arm around her brother to spur him on. 'You heard what Mum said – her letter needs to go special delivery today.'

'But I don't like it in the post office. There aren't any animails and Mrs Pauncefoot is scary.'

Séafra shook his head jovially in disbelief. 'Tabs, how can you think such a thing? Mrs Pauncefoot is a lovely postmistress. And she's always so nice to you. Remember the lollipop she gave you last time we went in?'

'She's got scary eyes,' insisted Taber. '*And* a scary mouth. *And* scary ears.'

Orinthia guffawed. 'Tabs, that's absurd! Nobody can have scary *ears*!'

'She has,' Taber replied, crossing his arms.

Orinthia bent down to be eye to eye with her little brother. 'Come on, Tabs, don't be a silly billy. The sooner we post the letter, the sooner we can get to Tuppeny Mill, OK?'

Monday was always the busiest time at Little Penhallow Post Office. When the children arrived there was already a long queue snaking up to the counter, with rope barriers in place to keep people in line.

As they waited to be served, Orinthia looked around, taking in the rows of shelves that were stocked with parcel tape and twine, envelopes and ballpoint pens. In the far corner there was a revolving display stand filled with birthday cards, each one quaintly illustrated with a puppy, or a ballerina, or a boat, and finished with a soppy sentimental message such as '*Birthday Wishes for a Dear Aunty*' or '*Hip Hip Hooray! It's your special day!*'

Above the main counter, a collection of frames displaying various stamps from around the world adorned the wall. There was an oblong-shaped one from Russia decorated with the colourful patterns of St Basil's Cathedral; a square one from China depicting a giant panda munching on a bamboo cane; and a tiny one from Ukraine adorned with botanical folk art. There was even a triangular one from Egypt, made to look like an ancient pyramid. Orinthia marvelled at how such tiny pieces of gummed paper could enable the safe passage of all the mail in the world: birthday cards could be sent from Birmingham to Bolivia, postcards could be shipped from Lisbon to London, packages could arrive in Tenby from Tangiers!

'NEXT!' came Mrs Pauncefoot's voice from behind the glass front of the counter. 'Who's next please?'

'That's us!' gasped Orinthia, shaking herself from her daydream, and pushing her brothers forward. 'Good morning, Mrs Pauncefoot.'

'Good morning, children,' said the postmistress, flashing the siblings a warm smile. She was a meek, elderly lady with a little wrinkled mouth which looked like a raspberry. Orinthia didn't know how Taber could possibly think that she was scary! She was wearing a knitted lilac jumper, embellished with a sparkly brooch, and her greying hair had been pulled into a neat bun. Behind her was a tall wooden sorting cabinet, its shelves filled with envelopes and its drawers housing the books of stamps. 'And what can I do for you today?' she asked gently.

Orinthia took the letter from her knapsack and put it on the counter. 'Our mum has asked us to post this to London. She said it needs to go special delivery.'

Mrs Pauncefoot nodded. 'Pop it on the scales then, ducky, and let's see how much it weighs.'

Orinthia followed the postmistress's orders, watching as the dial on the scales moved round under the weight of Mum's paperwork.

Mrs Pauncefoot eyed the dial as it settled. 'Hand it over and I'll get it on the overnight mail train, OK poppet?'

Orinthia took the envelope from the scales and passed it to the postmistress. With a speed which could have only been honed from working in the post office for many years, Mrs Pauncefoot stuck a stamp in the envelope's top right-hand corner, before throwing it into a large canvas mailbag. 'There you are. All done. Anything else I can help you with today?'

Orinthia shook her head and felt a twinge of guilt in her tummy as she paid. The postmistress had been so nice, so friendly, and little did she know that they were heading off to work for someone who was trying to take business away from her. They were going to be spending the day training birds to do *her* duties.

8

That morning, Grandy Brock declared that it was time for Geronimo to embark on her maiden international voyage. So, after lunch, the old man led a group of very excited children, armed with an even more excited-looking pelican, to the top of St Sylvester's Mount.

It had been decided that Geronimo was to deliver a letter to Jobe's animal sanctuary in New York, the animail's retirement home Grandy had mentioned before – and where Geronimo and Gungho had originally stayed after they'd been rescued. It would be good for Geronimo to be greeted by a familiar face, Grandy had said, and Taber was more than happy to let his prized bird embark on the journey, even though it meant she'd be gone for quite some time.

'OK, this is it, girl,' said Taber, looking down at

Geronimo in his arms as they reached the top of the hill. 'Are you ready to fly? Are you ready to go to America?'

The pelican let out what sounded like a honk of jubilation, and as Taber held her up her wings began to twitch with anticipation.

'Now, you're going to take this to Grandy Brock's brother,' said Taber, taking a postcard from his pocket and slotting it in the pelican's huge beak. The postcard was emblazoned with the words GREETINGS FROM LITTLE PENHALLOW, which arched over a less than inspiring picture of the village hall. It'd obviously been used a few times in training before, as one of its corners had been chewed, and there was a suspicious brown stain across the back.

'Now, go straight to New York and then come straight back, you hear me?' said Taber, adjusting the bird's little blue postie hat. 'No stopping for hot dogs, OK?'

Geronimo started to fuss and peck at Taber's clothes, which was a sign she was ready to be released. Grandy Brock and the rest of the children gathered round, and as Taber lifted the pelican towards the sky, Orinthia felt her heart leap into her mouth. Gungho clearly felt the same, squawking an excited farewell to his mother from the crook of Séafra's arm. The moment was exhilarating, and as Orinthia watched her baby brother bidding his bird goodbye, she felt herself bursting with pride.

'Good luck!' Taber said, releasing his grip from around Geronimo's feathered chest. 'I'm going to miss you! Come back soon!'

He threw his arms into the air and with a noisy shuffle, the pelican spread her wings and was sky bound!

Orinthia and the others craned their necks as she climbed higher and higher. She struck out in an easterly direction, swooping and wheeling before finding her line. There was rapturous applause from the Brock children as she eventually vanished from view, and they all piled around Taber, congratulating him on his achievement.

The small boy beamed as he lapped up the praise, his chubby cheeks aglow. He was barely able to stand still. 'Do you think Mummy will be proud of me too?' he asked his sister.

'Of course,' reassured Orinthia, planting a huge kiss on the top of his head. 'You are a truly, truly amazing little boy.'

She meant every word with heartfelt intensity, and only hoped that someday soon, Mum would have the time to see it too.

9

Each evening for the next few days, Taber kept track of the days since Geronimo's departure by pencilling little pelicans in the empty windows of his calendar. He imagined the places that Geronimo might have flown across that day, and the sights she might have seen. During their lunch breaks at the Mailbox Menagerie, Bramwell and Suki even helped him put his musings on to paper, the three of them writing stories and drawing pictures of Geronimo swooping through the clouds, battling with krakens, and even stealing fish and chips from the hands of beachgoers!

But when there was still no word of Geronimo's arrival after a week, Orinthia and Séafra began to fear the worst. Grandy Brock had spoken to his brother Jobe every day since the pelican's departure, but she'd still not arrived in New York. Had Geronimo got lost en route to America?

Not wanting to upset Taber, they found themselves making excuses every time he asked where his beloved pelican was:

'Geronimo has probably just made some new birdie friends and is spending some time with them.'

'The weather's been bad so she's probably sheltering somewhere.'

'Pelicans never fly on Wednesdays.'

'Pelicans never fly on Saturdays.'

'She probably fancied taking the scenic route home.'

But Taber wasn't stupid, and when Grandy Brock called everyone for a meeting in the kitchen a couple of days later, it didn't take the six-year-old long to realize that something was horribly wrong.

Grandy Brock stood nervously at the head of the table in a grey homburg hat. His hands were trembling and his eyes were glossy. 'Children, I've brought us all together because I want to talk to you about one of our animals. Unfortunately, it's not good news.'

There was a knowing look amongst the older Brock children, and Orinthia felt a lump rising in her throat.

'As much as it pains me to say it,' Grandy continued, 'and believe me, this is not a conversation I want to be having with you all today, but . . .' He trailed off for a moment, his face grave, then continued. 'I spoke to my brother in New York again this morning, and unfortunately Geronimo still hasn't arrived at the sanctuary.'

A melancholic murmur passed around the table, as the children let the information sink in, but nobody looked as crestfallen as Taber. 'But . . . but where's she gone?' he said, looking to Grandy Brock for reassurance. 'Is she lost? Do you think she went the wrong way?'

'Maybe,' said Grandy Brock gently. 'But sadly, Taber, I think we also have to prepare ourselves for the possibility that Geronimo might be . . .' His breathed hitched. 'Well, that she might be gone for good.'

Orinthia's heart sank. Deep down she'd known that this day was going to come, but it didn't make it any easier. She looked to Taber with huge guilt, watching as he tried to process the enormity of the news he'd just heard.

'But . . . but I want Geronimo!' Taber cried. 'I want her back! She's going to come back!' He was sobbing now, barely able to talk.

'There's plenty of other animails in the menagerie that would love for you to look after them,' said Suki softly. She pointed to Mr Malagasy, who was picking fleas from his fur and putting them into his mouth. 'I tell you what, why don't you help me pack up the crate of animal feed that we're sending to Uncle Jobe's sanctuary tomorrow? You can choose what treats we put in—'

'No!' shouted Taber. 'I just want Geronimo . . .' Taber's words trailed off and Orinthia buried her face in her hands. What could she possibly say that would make her baby brother feel better?

'I think maybe we should take him home, Grandy,' said Séafra, pushing his chair back from the table.

'Oh my goodness, I'm . . . I'm so sorry,' said Grandy Brock, his brow creasing. 'I didn't mean to upset him. I just thought it was better to be honest, that's all.'

'It's OK, Grandy,' said Orinthia, as they made their way to the door. 'We know you meant well. And Taber will be OK. Just give him a few days and he'll be right as rain.'

10

The Shalloo siblings walked home in silence, their chins on their chests, their faces forlorn. Orinthia had never seen Taber so sad – not when he'd lost his favourite toy car, not when he'd had to spend Christmas in bed with the flu, not even when Mum had missed his fifth birthday party because she was finalizing a deal on a vintage Rolls-Royce. He kicked the dust as he walked, his eyes puffy and red with tears.

'Hey, how about we play a game when we get home, Tabs?' Orinthia suggested, in a desperate attempt to lift his spirits. 'Snakes and ladders? Or pick-up-sticks? You like that one.'

Taber didn't reply. His arms hung slack at his sides as he looked to the ground with an empty stare.

'And didn't Mummy mention that she was going

to do some baking with us this weekend?' Séafra persevered. 'That'll be nice, won't it?'

Still no answer.

And the day only continued to get worse.

When the siblings arrived home they found their mother in the driveway, loading luggage into the boot of her car. She was wearing a rigid pencil skirt in baby blue, with a matching pussy-bow blouse, and the pointy shoes she always put on when she was going somewhere important.

Séafra and Orinthia turned to each other, sharing a knowing look. This could mean one of two things – either they were going on holiday or their mother was going away on business. And knowing Mum, the latter was no doubt the most likely.

'Wait here with Taber,' Orinthia mouthed to Séafra before their little brother could see what was going on. She didn't want him getting even more upset.

Séafra nodded, and Orinthia crunched up the gravel driveway, feeling her fists clench in her pockets. Of all the days for Mum to be swanning off to the city, this was possibly the worst.

'Ah, Orinthia, you're back!' called Mum, looking up as she clocked her eldest child coming towards her.

'I was just going to leave the three of you a note.' She shoved the last of her suitcases into the boot before slamming it shut with a *thump*. 'I've been called to London, you see. A very important buyer is in town and he wants a meeting. Interested in buying up a few of our sports cars. Isn't that exciting?'

'But who's going to look after us?' Orinthia asked.

'Mrs Gastaldini has agreed to look after you for the weekend. That's nice of her, isn't it? I'm sure you'll have lots of fun.' She nodded up to the house, where the cleaning lady was standing in the front doorway in a pair of fluffy slippers.

'*Ciao bambina!*' she called down to Orinthia with a wave. 'Nice to see you!'

Orinthia returned the wave meekly before turning back to her mother. 'But Mum, you promised we'd do some baking this weekend,' she began. 'You said we could all make biscuits and—'

'I'm sorry, sweetie, I really am,' her mother interrupted before Orinthia could protest any further. 'But be a grown-up girl and don't make a fuss, hmm? I can't turn down this opportunity. It's good news for all of us.' She picked up her handbag and swung it over her shoulder. 'You want the business to do well, don't you? Make Grandad proud?'

Orinthia sighed heavily. She hated questions like that. *Of course* she wanted the family business to succeed; *of course* she wanted Grandad's legacy to be honoured. But at the same time she also wanted a mum who spent time at home, doing all of the things that mums were supposed to do – cooking roast dinners on a Sunday, playing games in the garden, reading stories, giving cuddles on the sofa.

'Mum, please,' Orinthia persisted, following her mother as she made her way to the driver's seat. 'Can't Uncle Max go to the meeting just this once . . . ?'

Mum adjusted the front mirror and pulled on her seat belt. 'It would be really great if you could set a good example to your brothers and not make this difficult, darling.' She looked over to where Séafra was trying to distract Taber by pointing out birds in the hedgerow. 'Can you do that for me?'

Orinthia looked to her feet, crestfallen. This was a battle she was never going to win. 'Yes, Mum.'

Mum smiled. 'That's my girl. And I tell you what, why don't you and Séafra take Taber to the shops and buy all the ingredients you'll need for making those biscuits?' She reached into her handbag and pulled out a crisp banknote, which she handed to her daughter. 'There you go. I'm sure Mrs Gastaldini will be more than happy to help you in the kitchen.'

Orinthia nodded and took the money, not saying a word. Mrs Gastaldini had come to stand by her side, and she felt her hand squeezing her shoulder.

'Have a good trip, Mrs Shalloo,' she called to her employer. '*Buon viaggio!* And don't worry about us, we'll be absolutely fine!'

'Thank you, Serafina!' Mum replied. She slammed the car door and put the keys in the ignition. The engine roared as it turned over, and within the blink of an eye the shiny red motor was trundling up the driveway and screeching on to the high road.

On seeing their mother zoom past, Taber ran over to his sister. 'Rinthi, where's Mummy going?' he asked, panic flicking across his face.

'Mummy had to go to London, Tabs,' Orinthia replied. 'She'll only be gone for a couple of days, though, so Mrs Gastaldini's going to look after us.' She flashed the banknote she'd just been given. 'And look! Mummy left us some money to buy the things we need to make our biscuits. We can get chocolate chips and raisins and syrup. It's going to be great!'

But Orinthia's forced enthusiasm for the bake-off proved useless. On top of everything that had happened with Geronimo, it seemed as though their mum's departure was just too much for Taber. His face crumpled, and all of a sudden he burst into tears once more.

'Awwww, *piccolo carino*,' said Mrs Gastaldini, bending down to be at his side. 'There's no need to be upset. Mrs Gastaldini is here to look after you. Although you're such a big boy now, that you probably don't really need much looking after.' She smiled, a twinkle in her eye. 'In fact, *you* might have to keep an eye on *me*!'

The corners of Taber's mouth turned upwards slightly and he wiped his eyes.

'There, that's better,' said Mrs Gastaldini, pinching his cheek with affection. 'Now come on, let's all go inside, hmmm? I've prepared something nice for lunch . . .' Her hands launched into the air in a flourish of culinary passion. '*Spaghetti alla bolognese.* My great-great-great-grandmother's recipe!'

11

Orinthia awoke before sunrise with a strange feeling in her tummy. It was not so much a malaise or a pain, but more of an anxious fluttering, as if she were anticipating that something bad was about to happen.

Suspecting that maybe she'd just awoken from a bad dream, she sat up and began to plump up her pillows. If she could get herself nice and comfy, then no doubt she'd be back asleep in no time. She took a sip of water from the glass on her bedside table, before snuggling back down.

But ten minutes later she was even more awake, and still had the fluttering feeling in her tummy. She reached for her dressing gown hanging on the bedpost before pulling on her slippers and creeping down the hall to Séafra's room. Taber had asked if he could sleep in Séa's spare bunk last night and, sensing his little brother needed the company, Séafra had agreed.

Orinthia gently opened the door and looked in. At first glance all seemed to be well. It was only when she edged towards the bunk beds that she worked out what was amiss – she could only hear one set of snores! She could hear Séafra's soft sighs, but Taber's sleepy wheezes were completely inaudible.

Strange, she thought. Her baby brother was usually such a noisy little sleeper. One night, when her brothers still shared a room, Séafra had had to put him in a sleeping bag in the bath in order to get any rest!

Orinthia crossed the room in the hazy half-light and peered into the lower bunk. 'Tabs?' she whispered. 'Tabs, are you OK?'

There was no answer.

'Tabs?' she tried once more.

Silence.

Feeling the fluttering increasing in her tummy, she whipped back the sheets. But her little brother wasn't there.

'Rinthi, what is it?' groaned Séafra from above. 'It's not time to get up yet, is it?'

'It's Taber,' Orinthia replied, stepping back. 'He's not here. He's not in his bed.'

Séafra huffed and rubbed his eyes. 'Well, he's probably just gone to the toilet, or back to his own room . . . or sneaked downstairs to have another one of Mrs Gastaldini's special Italian pastries.' Séafra pulled his duvet over his head and turned towards the wall. 'He'll be back in a bit. Go back to sleep.'

But Orinthia didn't return to her bed. She couldn't explain why, but she knew something wasn't right. She crossed the landing and opened the door to Taber's room – she could see straight away the little bed hadn't been slept in.

'Taber?' she whispered, edging towards the bathroom at the end of the landing. 'Taber, are you in there?' She peered inside and reached for the light. There was a minty white mess in the sink from where they'd indulged in a toothpaste-spitting contest the previous night, and three flannels hanging over the bath. But no Taber.

Orinthia's heart was pounding fast now. Clutching on to the glimmer of hope that Séafra was right, that their little brother *had* just sneaked into the pantry for another of Mrs Gastaldini's *cannoli*, she pelted down the stairs and into the kitchen.

'Tabs?' she whispered. 'Tabs, are you—?'

She froze in her tracks.

A sliver of early morning light was streaming in through the window on to the dining table, and in its path was a note. It had been folded up and propped up against the vase of hydrangeas, her and Séafra's names written across the front in bright-red crayon.

Orinthia ran towards it, her heart like a drum in her chest. She knew that handwriting, and with trembling fingers she unfolded the paper and read.

To Rinthi and Séafra,
I haf gone to lwk for Geronimo in New York. I know she isn't lost and she is probly sad and lonely bai herself. I didn't know how to get to the airpot or the train stayshun so I'm going in the post.
I haf taken a ham sanwich, lots of biscits, the fish paste and some milk.
I will come bak home when I haf fawned Geronimo.
from Taber X

The note fell to the floor as Orinthia's hands shot to her mouth. She must have let out a scream because within seconds, as she slumped into a chair, Séafra was barrelling down the stairs. 'What is it, Rinthi?' he said, bursting into the kitchen. His eyes were sleep-sodden, his hair a sweaty mass. 'What's the matter?'

Orinthia looked over to him, and without saying a word, nodded to the note on the floor, not even able to bring herself to pick it up.

With furrowed brow, Séafra reached for the note and read. All the while, his face looked more and more confused.

When he had finished, he looked over at his sister and laughed nervously. 'It . . . it has to be a joke,' he said. 'Taber's just playing a trick on us, surely. He's having us on . . .'

But from the panicked look in her brother's eyes, it was clear to Orinthia that he knew this wasn't a game. 'But . . . what does it mean?' he said, looking at the note once more. 'He says "I'm going in the post"?'

Orinthia thought for a moment, then suddenly, with adrenalin surging through her, she leapt to her feet. 'Remember yesterday when Suki mentioned the big crate of animal feed that was set to go to Jobe's animal sanctuary in New York this morning? I bet that's how Taber's planning to get there.'

Séafra balked. 'What? You think he's stowed away with those dog biscuits?'

Orinthia nodded. She knew it in her heart, she felt it. Taber might only be six, but he was fearless, adventure-seeking, determined. She had encouraged him to be all of these things. Why was he so much like her?

Séafra began to pace, his face fear-stricken and the colour of ash. 'Rinthi, what are we going to do? Taber could be in danger!'

Orinthia looked up to the kitchen clock. 'We need to go to Tupenny Mill immediately,' she said determinedly. 'It's still early – the courier might not have picked up the crate yet.'

'You're right!' said Séafra, trying to breathe deeply. 'We might be worrying over nothing. Taber might not even have left the village yet!'

Not stopping to even get dressed, the siblings pulled on coats over their pyjamas and shoved their feet into their boots. But just as they were making their way to the front door, Mrs Gastaldini appeared at the top of the stairs.

'Children?' she called out with confusion. 'Where are you going?'

'Erm . . . we're just going out for . . . erm . . . an early morning walk,' lied Orinthia, having to think quickly. 'We like to listen to the birds, you see. Hear the dawn chorus.'

'And the little one?'

'He's . . . erm . . . still sleeping,' Séafra improvised. 'And he likes a lie-in during the school holidays, so he'll probably stay in bed for another few hours.'

Orinthia coughed. 'You should do the same, Mrs Gastaldini. Go back to bed for a bit? It's still very early. We can bring you up a cup of tea when we get back from our walk.'

Mrs Gastaldini smiled. '*Miei cari figli!* Such thoughtful children. Maybe I will do that. The bed in the guest room *is* very comfy. But it's coffee for me, not tea, *per favore*. I'll see you in a few hours.'

The morning sky was burnt orange as Orinthia and Séafra ran pell-mell towards Tupenny Mill. Orinthia was desperately clinging on to the hope that Taber would still be in Little Penhallow, trying her best to quell the growing cloud of dark thoughts that was commandeering her brain. Surely the crate wouldn't have been picked up yet? It was barely even breakfast time; no one started work this early, did they?

When they crested St Sylvester's Mount, the siblings stopped momentarily to catch their breath. 'So, what's the plan?' panted Séafra. 'Should we tell Grandy Brock what's happened?'

'No,' said Orinthia between deep breaths, her mind spinning as she thought everything through. 'We're simply going to go inside and find out if the crate has gone or not. With any luck, Taber won't have gone anywhere. There's no point in us worrying Grandy Brock and the others unnecessarily.'

Séafra nodded. 'And knowing Taber, he probably got restless waiting in the crate, and went in to join the Brocks for some breakfast anyway.'

Hoping with all of her being that Séafra was right, Orinthia sprinted off down the hill towards Tupenny Mill. Its front door had already been unlatched, and without stopping to knock, she burst inside, with Séafra following closely behind. Taber was nowhere to be seen, and Orinthia's stomach twisted.

'The crate with the animal feed!' she blurted out without as much as a hello to the Brock children sitting at the table. 'Where is it?'

Grandy Brock, who was wearing a tartan tam-o'-shanter, turned from the ancient-looking gas stove and harrumphed. 'And a very good morning to you too, young lady,' he said, raising an eyebrow. 'Someone forgotten their manners this morning, eh?'

Orinthia felt her cheeks redden. 'I'm sorry, Grandy,' she said brusquely. 'But we just need to know if the crate has gone. Has it been picked up yet?' Her voice had risen, and every pair of eyes in the mill was looking at her with confusion. All of a sudden the sweet, yeasty smell of fresh bread that hung in the air made Orinthia feel queasy.

'Is everything OK, Rinthi?' asked Suki from the breakfast table. 'Why are you shouting?'

'I'm not shouting!' yelled Orinthia. 'I just want someone to answer my question!'

'All right, all right, no need to get in a tizz,' said Grandy Brock, obviously taken aback. 'And in answer to your question, yes, the courier came to pick the crate up about an hour ago.'

Orinthia felt the colour draining from her face and she gazed at Séafra, the horror she was feeling mirrored in his eyes. If the crate was on its way to New York, then so was Taber! 'No!' she gasped, her breath quickening and her hands beginning to tremble. 'No, no, no . . .'

'Orinthia, are you sure you're all right?' asked Bramwell, coming to her side. 'You really don't seem yourself this morning.'

Orinthia ran a hand through her hair, trying to curb her panic. 'It's . . . it's nothing,' she said, blinking back the tears that were already stinging her eyes. 'I'm fine.'

Grandy Brock's brow furrowed – he was clearly unconvinced. He pulled back two chairs and gestured for her and Séafra to sit. 'Come on, why don't you both join us for a nice bit of brekkie before we start work today, eh? I've got some eggs boiling too. Can do you a nice runny yolk?'

'No!' snapped Orinthia. She instantly regretted her tone. She looked to Séafra for backup. She couldn't hold it together and it was showing.

'I'm sorry, Grandy,' said Séafra. 'But what Orinthia meant was that . . . well . . . we can't stay today. We need to be heading home.'

'Oh?' Grandy Brock replied, reaching for a bread knife. 'Everything OK? In fact, where's Taber today? Is he feeling better?'

Orinthia and Séafra shared a nervous look.

'Taber's fine, everything's fine,' said Orinthia. 'We just have to go visit our granny today, that's all.'

Grandy Brock nodded. 'Ah, I see! Well, no bother. Have a nice time with your grandmother. The three of you'll be back tomorrow, though, yes? I know the animails will miss you today.'

Orinthia looked to her feet. She wanted to tell Grandy Brock that no, they wouldn't be returning to the mill tomorrow, if ever. She wanted to tell him that Taber had posted himself to New York in one of *his* crates, in order to search for one of *his* pelicans. But she was too scared of involving him. As much as she adored Grandy, he was a grown-up, and grown-ups *always* liked to involve other grown-ups when things went wrong. He'd call Mrs Gastaldini, who would call Mum, and she and Séafra would be in so much trouble. So instead, Orinthia nodded and said, 'Yes, of course we'll be back tomorrow. See you then.'

With forced smiles emblazoned across their faces, the Shalloo siblings left the mill to a chorus of *good-byes* and *have a good days* and *see you soons*. But outside, once they were far enough away, Orinthia broke down. 'Oh Séa, this is terrible,' she cried, burying her face in her hands as she slunk down against a tree trunk. 'How could we have let this happen?'

'Rinthi, this isn't our fault,' said Séafra, putting an arm around her shoulder. 'We didn't know Taber was going to do this.' It was strange for him to be comforting her. Taber was the one who usually gave her cuddles when she was feeling sad, or when she needed a pick-me-up. She already missed his milky, cotton-like smell, and his little hands tight around her neck.

'Séafra, we have to post ourselves to New York too,' she blurted out suddenly. 'We have to go after Taber. We must!'

Séafra's face dropped. 'Rinthi, you're not serious, are you?' he spluttered. 'We can't do that—'

'Why not?' snapped Orinthia, letting her idea spiral. 'If Taber was brave enough to go after Geronimo, then we need to be brave enough to go after him. We'll find another freight crate from somewhere and put ourselves through the post too. If we do it today then we won't be far behind Taber.'

'But Rinthi, we're living, breathing human beings – not dog food to be packed up and transported. It's dangerous. Who knows what might have happened to Taber already—'

'NO! DON'T SAY IT!' snapped Orinthia, not wanting Séafra to vocalize the same dark thoughts that she was already contemplating. She shook her head, trying desperately to clear her mind of the image of their baby brother trapped in a crate without much food, much water, much air . . .

'Look, Rinthi, I'm sorry,' said Séafra with a sigh. 'But I think we should just phone Mum.' He reached a hand out to his sister but Orinthia quickly pulled away, not wanting him to see the tears that were about to roll down her cheeks.

'What's she going to do about it? You know she won't listen – she never does!' Orinthia said. 'Besides, this is our problem. *We* should've been looking out for Taber. Now *we* have to fix it. Ophelia Pearcart always said that the leaders of an expedition should take responsibility for the rest of their crew—'

'But Rinthi, we're not the leaders of an expedition, we're children!' snapped Séafra. He paused before running his hands through his thick dark hair. 'I know we need to get Taber back, but I don't think putting ourselves at risk is the answer. Sorry, I'm not doing it. I'm not going to post myself to America.'

The effect of her brother's words was instant-aneous. Orinthia felt disappointment and anger and hurt bubbling up inside her, making her limbs tingle. 'Fine,' she hissed, sprinting off towards home. 'But *I* am!'

12

As soon as they got home, Séafra ran upstairs, leaving Orinthia alone in the hallway. She couldn't believe that her brother was refusing to go with her to America. Being too scared to join her on adventures around Little Penhallow was one thing, but this was an emergency! How could he be so cowardly?

But she couldn't dwell on that now. She had a mission ahead of her, an expedition to organize, a postal journey to plan! As she hung up her coat, she began to make a mental list of all the things she would need in order to post herself to New York. She was going to have to find a big box or crate of some kind, large enough to accommodate her, her duffel bag and a substantial amount of provisions. She'd need to address it to New York and attach a stamp, then somehow stow away inside before the postman picked it up. Despite the knot of worry in her chest about Taber, a delicious shiver of excitement shot through her like electricity. No wonder Ophelia Pearcart went on so many expeditions if this was how they made you feel!

Mrs Gastaldini was in the kitchen, the rich smell of coffee wafting from the stove. As Orinthia went upstairs, the cleaner called out, 'Did you enjoy your walk, bambinos?', but Orinthia merely shouted back a cheery 'hello' before fleeing to her room. Once inside, she slammed the door shut behind her. She had to hurry! Thankfully Séafra didn't disturb her – Orinthia could hear him moving around in the attic above, no doubt hiding away like the coward he was – so she was free to get on with her planning in peace.

First, she took Ophelia Pearcart's diary from her bookshelf. She couldn't think of a better source of guidance. If anyone was going to be able to help her travel to the other side of the world, it was her hero.

Sitting down at her desk, Orinthia began to read. She had looked through the book so many times that the corners were worn and the binding was coming loose in parts. She flicked through the pages, allowing the yellow light of her desk lamp to pick out the beautiful illustrations of deserts and oceans, mountains and rivers. Normally, if she was down in the dumps, she'd try to distract herself with thoughts of the incredible places she'd journey to when *she* was a famous explorer – the Atlas Mountains of North Africa, Peru's Inca temples, Turkey's Byzantine cities, the lofty plateaus of Tibet!

But today, there was only one place on her mind.

New York City.

Eager to find out what route a parcel might need to take to get there, she turned to the centrefold, where a world map was spread over the first two pages. The meridians and latitudinal lines had been picked out in gold and an ornate compass rose sat in the top-right corner. Orinthia placed her index finger on the little island of Great Britain, before moving it west across the page, tracing the journey over the North Atlantic Ocean to America. New York State was on the east coast of the country, sandwiched between Pennsylvania, Vermont, Massachusetts and Connecticut. It was going to be a long and arduous journey, especially by post. She would probably be taken to a port by mail train, then put on one of the packet ships headed for New York City.

As she continued to read, Orinthia's thoughts

turned to Taber once more. Maybe, if she found him relatively quickly, they might be able to explore the city together! She closed her eyes and began to conjure up the fun they'd have climbing to the top of the Statue of Liberty, or heading to Coney Island for a ride on the famous Ferris wheel. They could wander around Grand Central Station, gaze up at the magnitude of the Chrysler Building, and at the end of the day treat themselves to a pastrami-and-pickle sandwich at one of the famous delicatessens! Séafra would wish that he'd been brave enough to make the journey then, that was for sure.

After a long afternoon of studying, Orinthia meandered downstairs to make herself a snack. Eager not to bump into Mrs Gastaldini, she tiptoed as quietly as she could, but just as she was reaching the bottom of the staircase, the doorbell rang.

Orinthia froze.

Through the frosted glass of the front door she could see several people moving around outside, and she could hear a throng of voices. She immediately started to panic. Was it the police? Had something happened to Taber?

The doorbell continued to ring. It came in short, sharp bursts, as if the ringer was growing impatient, and just then a shout came through the letter box. 'Orinthia? Are you there? It's me, Bramwell. And I've got all of the gang with me!'

Orinthia exhaled, relieved it wasn't the police – but this was almost as bad. What on earth was she going to say? Maybe she should just tiptoe away . . .

'Orinthia, open up!' came a different voice. It belonged to Suki, and she sounded rather stern. 'We know you're in there. The lights are on. And I can see your shoes in the hallway. Let us in. We're not going anywhere until you do.'

Orinthia huffed. She supposed she'd have to answer the door. If she didn't, she'd run the risk of the Brock children telling Grandy that something was amiss. She didn't want to arouse suspicion.

Quickly checking that Mrs Gastaldini wasn't around, she opened the door.

'Ah, there you are!' said Bramwell, stepping back. 'We've been ringing the bell for ages! Didn't you hear us?'

'Sorry, I was . . . erm . . . in the shower,' Orinthia lied, trying to sound as blasé as possible. 'Anyway, is everything all right? What are you doing here?'

'We were worried about you, Rinthi,' said Peggy. 'You and Séafra were acting really weirdly when you came up to the mill this morning. All that talk of the dog-food crate. And then you just ran off without saying a proper goodbye!'

Orinthia bristled. 'I'm fine. Like I said, we had to go and see our grandmother this afternoon. We were in a bit of a rush, that's all.' But as the untruthful words left Orinthia's mouth, she could already feel her bottom lip beginning to tremble. All of a sudden, tears began to fall down her cheeks.

'Hey, Rinthi, what is it?' said Bramwell. 'What's wrong?'

'Oh, I'm in so much trouble,' she said, between sobs. 'Something terrible has happened.'

'What?' asked Kipling.

Orinthia sighed. She hadn't planned on telling her friends about what was going on, but she couldn't hold it in any longer. Closing the door behind her, she slipped outside. 'It's Taber,' she whispered, not wanting to alert Mrs Gastaldini. 'He's gone to find Geronimo. He's posted himself to New York!'

'What?' said Suki. 'What do you mean *posted* himself?'

Orinthia took Taber's note from her pocket and unfolded it. 'He must have got in the crate that Grandy was sending to his brother's animal sanctuary.

Look – his plan's all in there.'

Furtively, Suki took the note and read. With every line her eyes widened, her breath hitching as she came to the end of each sentence. 'Oh my goodness, Rinthi, this is awful!' she exclaimed. 'No wonder you were so upset this morning when Grandy Brock said the crate had been taken.'

The note was passed around the rest of the Brock children, their jaws slackening and their eyebrows rising as they took in Taber's waxy red words.

Suki reached for Orinthia's arm. 'Well, I think you and Séafra should come back to Tupenny Mill with us. You have to tell Grandy Brock what's happened. He'll know what to do, he always does—'

'No!' snapped Orinthia. 'I don't want any adults getting involved. And besides, I've made up my mind. I know what I'm going to do to get him back. Come up to my room, I'll tell you all about it.'

13

'I'm going to go after Taber myself,' Orinthia announced, once they were all settled in her bedroom. 'I'm going to post myself to New York, just like he's done. If I do it first thing tomorrow then I won't be too far behind him.' For a moment no one said a word. As Orinthia had anticipated, her idea garnered a few stunned faces, and even more raised eyebrows. 'Well?' she said impatiently. 'Don't just sit there like lemons. What do you think?'

'Well,' began Kipling, 'it's a bold move, that's for sure . . .' His brow was furrowed and Orinthia assumed that she was going to be hit with a tirade of disapproval. 'But . . . I think it's a brilliant idea. Bonkers, but absolutely brilliant. You've always wanted to be an explorer, and this can be your first overseas expedition!'

The other children agreed, their heads nodding fervently as they showered Orinthia with words of encouragement and support.

'If anyone can pull this off, it's you,' said Suki.

Orinthia smiled, touched by the faith her new friends had in her. 'Thanks. I just wish that Séafra would get on board too. He thinks it's a terrible idea. He hasn't spoken to me all afternoon. He's holed himself up in the attic.'

'Don't worry, Rinthi, he'll come round,' said Bramwell. 'But posting yourself to the other side of the world isn't going to be easy. How are you going to do it? You're not exactly letter shape . . . or size! It's not like you're going to be able to walk into the post office and ask them to put a stamp on your head.'

'Oooh! I know!' said Peggy excitedly. 'How about we invent a special size-changing machine that could shrink you down to the size of a baked bean? Then, you'd be small enough to fit inside an envelope!'

The children burst out laughing.

'Nice thinking, Peg,' said Orinthia. 'But I'm not sure if any of us have the scientific capabilities to pull that one off.'

'Hang on a minute,' Bramwell exclaimed suddenly, his eyes twinkling. 'I think I might have thought of something!'

Orinthia's ears pricked up. 'Go on!'

'Well,' said Bramwell, edging forward in his seat, 'there's a little antiques shop off the high street, opposite the orphanage where we used to live.'

'Yes, I remember,' said Suki. 'Honest Heirlooms.'

Bramwell nodded. 'I always used to see the shop owner, Mrs Oglesby, leaving huge freight crates full of antiques outside, ready for the postman to collect. She had buyers from all over the country and they'd pay to have their purchases sent to them.' He broke off for a moment and cleared his throat. 'Maybe you could go to the shop, and then, when no one is looking, readdress one of the crates so that it's bound for New York and stow away inside!'

Orinthia clasped her hands to her chest, and for a moment she was completely silent.

'You think it's a stupid idea, don't you?' said Bramwell. He shrugged, his smile fading. 'You're probably right—'

'No!' Orinthia blurted out. 'I think it's a fantastic idea! Do you think the crates will be big enough?'

'If they're big enough for marble statues and Victorian tables, then they're big enough for you.'

'Brilliant,' said Orinthia, her brain already going

into overdrive. 'But if this is going to work, I'm going to need to plan everything down to the very last detail. There can be no room for error. Will you all help me?'

'Of course!' said Kipling, without hesitation. 'Just tell us what you need us to do.'

'OK,' said Orinthia, standing up. All of a sudden she was a tangle of nerves and excitement, but mainly determination. 'Let's meet at the antiques shop at eight thirty tomorrow morning. In the meantime, I have some jobs for you all. Bramwell, let's start with you. You have the neatest handwriting by far, so I'd like you to write out a new postage label to stick on the crate. It needs to be addressed to the Brock Family Animal Sanctuary in New York. You can find the address, right?'

'Of course,' said Bramwell, his eyes brightening at the prospect. 'And I'll use my favourite ink pen to write it. Any particular font?'

'It doesn't matter,' said Orinthia. 'As long as it's clear and legible. I don't want to end up in Outer Mongolia!'

Bramwell nodded, his inky fingers already wiggling at the prospect of the challenge.

'And what about me, Rinthi?' asked Suki. 'What can I do to help?'

Orinthia turned to her. 'Well, I'm going to need some provisions for my journey. I daren't take anything from here in case Mrs Gastaldini catches me. Do you think you could find some food back at the mill? Choose things that are long-lasting and nutritious' – she smiled mischievously – 'but make sure that they're tasty too, of course.'

Suki smiled. 'So basically you want me to find a month's worth of biscuits?'

'Pretty much,' said Orinthia. 'And maybe a few cold sausages if Grandy has some in the fridge.'

Suki nodded. 'Roger that.'

'Next,' said Orinthia, stroking her chin in thought, 'we're going to have to figure out a way to break into one of Mrs Oglesby's crates. They're bound to be padlocked if they contain expensive antiques.'

Peggy leapt up. 'I could help with that. We had an escapologist in the circus for a while. The "Great Zamora", he called himself. Used to escape from a sealed casket by picking the lock with a hairpin he had hidden up his nose! He showed me how to do it once. It was a long time ago but I think I can remember the steps.'

'Brilliant!' said Orinthia, giving her friend a thumbs up and smiling as she pictured the escapologist's secret nasal hiding place. 'That sounds like a great solution.'

Peggy smiled proudly. 'Then we can just lock you back inside with one of your own padlocks, which you have the key for.'

Orinthia pondered this momentarily. 'But how will I get out if I need to use the toilet or stretch my legs? It's a long journey to America.'

'I know!' Kipling exclaimed. 'We can cut a hole in the crate just big enough for your hand to go through. Grandy Brock has plenty of tools up at the mill we could use. Then you'll be able to just reach out and turn the key in the lock when you know nobody's looking. And it will allow some fresh air to come in too. If you aren't able to bathe it's going to get rather pongy in there pretty quickly!'

'Perfect!' Orinthia sat back, pondering what she needed to figure out next.

As if reading her thoughts, Kipling leant in. 'You're going to need an international stamp to put on the freight crate, Orinthia. Royal Mail won't take it to New York if Mrs Oglesby has only paid for it to go to Scotland, or France or Sweden.'

'Good point,' said Orinthia. 'But where am I going to get one?' She looked up at the kitchen clock. 'The post office will be closing soon, and I really don't want to have to wait another day. Taber will be long gone, and I'll have no chance of catching up with him.'

The Brock siblings looked at each other, and Orinthia could see mischief light up in their eyes.

'Are you thinking what I'm thinking?' Peggy asked her siblings.

They all nodded.

'What?' asked Orinthia.

Peggy grinned deviously. 'Well . . . you could always break into the post office?'

Orinthia was shocked at the suggestion. She was all for taking risks and breaking rules, but stealing? That definitely wasn't something she approved of.

'I don't think that's such a good idea, Peg,' she said sheepishly. 'I'm really grateful that you'd do something as risky as that for me, but Mrs Pauncefoot would be so upset. I don't like the idea of stealing from her. It's just not right!'

'Not right? Ha!' said Kipling dismissively. 'What Royal Mail did to Grandy Brock *wasn't right*!'

'Kipling, *shhhh*!' chided Suki. 'We're not supposed to tell—'

'Tell me what?' asked Orinthia, suddenly feeling completely in the dark. 'What did Royal Mail do to

116

Grandy Brock?' She glared intently at her friends until they had no choice but to open up.

Suki sighed, and began to fiddle with her fingers. 'Orinthia, can you remember that day in the Mailbox Menagerie when Peggy blurted out that Grandy Brock had been fired?'

'Yes,' said Orinthia, thinking back to their first visit to the mill. 'I thought it was a bit strange at the time, and I was going to ask you about it, but I completely forgot.'

'Well,' Kipling continued, 'he was fired from his job at Royal Mail. He used to be a postman, you see. Had been in service for over twenty years.'

'But why was he fired?' asked Orinthia. 'What did he do?'

'Nothing!' said Suki. 'Grandy was framed! He found out that Mrs Pauncefoot was running a fraudulent business from the back of the post office. She was pilfering books of stamps and selling them cheaply on the black market! And she's still doing it. Grandy Brock thinks she's made a fortune over the years.'

'What?' Orinthia exclaimed in disbelief. 'Mrs Pauncefoot? But . . . but she's such a sweet old lady.'

'A lying and cheating old witch more like!' said Kipling in his usual dramatic fashion.

'Anyway,' said Bramwell, continuing with the story, 'Grandy confronted Mrs Pauncefoot about what she was doing, and threatened to go to the authorities if she didn't stop. But the next morning when he turned up for his shift, Grandy wasn't allowed in. His desk had been cleared, his uniform had been taken. Mrs Pauncefoot had gone to the postmaster general and said that *he* was the one who'd been stealing stamps!'

It took a moment for Orinthia to process everything she'd just heard. Mrs Pauncefoot was a crook who had framed Grandy Brock and got him fired! The Mailbox Menagerie made perfect sense. No wonder Grandy Brock wanted to launch a rival postal service.

'What a horrible, horrible woman,' said Orinthia, shaking her head. 'After everything she's done, Mrs Pauncefoot deserves a taste of her own medicine.' She got up and stomped a foot to the ground with resoluteness. 'In fact, I've changed my mind. I *will* break into the post office tonight.'

The Brock children looked at each other and beamed.

'But surely you're going to need a wingman to help you?' said Kipling with a cheeky grin.

'You volunteering?' Orinthia replied wryly.

'Try and stop me!'

14

'OK, we're nearly there,' whispered Orinthia to Kipling, as the two of them ducked behind the red postbox that stood on the corner of the high street. It was dark, and they were dressed in disguises from Taber's dressing-up box – Kipling sporting a cowboy hat and fake nose attached to a pair of glasses, and Orinthia dressed in a long, hooded silk robe that she'd once worn for a school nativity. The post office was in sight and only a few metres away, safely shut down and locked up for the night.

Kipling was confident that they could break in without being caught. He knew from what Grandy Brock had once said that Mrs Pauncefoot always left a spare set of keys beneath the doormat outside, just in case one of the postmen needed to get in.

The problem was that there were still quite a few

people milling around on the high street – revellers trickling in and out of the Drunken Duck, shop-keepers pulling down their shutters for the night, street cleaners sweeping debris from the pavements. There were even a couple of policemen on the beat, patrolling the streets with handcuffs jangling at their belts. Orinthia recognized the taller of the two immediately. His name was Inspector Snodgrass and he'd given a rather boring talk called 'The History of Truncheons' at her school the previous year. She pulled herself and Kipling further back into the shadows, knowing that seeing two children out after dark would immediately give the policeman cause for concern.

Orinthia and Kipling had to crouch in their hiding place for quite a while before the high street started to empty, and when it was as quiet as it was ever going to be, they seized their chance.

The pair sped at a crouch towards the post office, and having looked over his shoulder for prying eyes, Kipling swiped the spare key from beneath the front mat and opened the door.

They were in!

As Kipling closed the door behind them, Orinthia flicked on her torch, allowing its soft yellow beam to pick out the path ahead. It was strange being in the post office after dark. There were no parcels being weighed and no stamps being licked; no old ladies talking about the price of cauliflowers as they waited in line for their pensions; no savings being deposited; no mailbags being emptied.

'OK, let's find what we need and get out of here,' said Kipling, ducking under the rope barriers and heading towards the front counter. Orinthia pictured Mrs Pauncefoot sitting at her desk behind it, greeting customers with her trademark smile, all the while running a black-market stamp racket! What a rotter!

'She keeps the stamps in those drawers,' whispered Orinthia, pointing through the glass to the sorting cabinet.

But the door leading to the back room wouldn't open.

'Oh blast!' said Kipling, rattling the handle to no avail. 'It's locked. And I don't know where the key for this one is.'

Orinthia felt her heart sink. Now she would have to wait another day before she could post herself. *And* she'd have to come to the post office again and force herself to make polite chit-chat with Mrs Pauncefoot.

Hoping that it might illuminate another way for

them to get into the back room, Orinthia angled her torchlight through the glass and leant in. But she wasn't in luck – the only thing piquing her interest was a framed photograph on the back wall showing a younger Mrs Pauncefoot with her arm around a familiar-looking young man. Was it the late Mr Pauncefoot, perhaps?

It was only as she craned her neck and ran her hands through her hair that Orinthia thought of something; it was all she could do not to shout out *Eureka!* Mrs Pauncefoot's collection of framed stamps was displayed above the counter! Surely there'd be one suitable for her international journey?

Orinthia lifted her torch and angled it at the rows of frames, letting its wide yellow beam illuminate their beautiful designs. She was looking for one marked 'Worldwide Service' and it wasn't long before she spotted it.

'Hold this,' she said to Kipling, handing him her torch. 'And keep it pointing at those frames.'

Kipling did as she asked, quickly catching on to her plan. Orinthia pulled herself up on to the counter and stretched up. She lifted the frame she needed from the wall, and looked down at it in the torchlight. The stamp behind the glass was like a miniature work of art – a majestic yellow flower in full bloom, with a single leaf growing from its thorny stem, against a deep-purple background. Orinthia felt a prickle of excitement tighten her skin. This little piece of gummed paper was her ticket to America – and to finding her little brother!

Slipping the frame inside her coat, she crouched down, and as quickly and as quietly as she had ascended, lowered herself back to the ground. 'OK,' she whispered to Kipling, her voice spiked with adrenalin. 'Let's get out of here!'

15

After such an eventful day, Orinthia thought that she'd fall into a deep slumber that night, but she couldn't settle. Every time she was on the verge of dropping off she'd panic about oversleeping, worrying herself about not waking up in time to get to the antique shop, find herself a crate and catch the morning post. Séafra had already been fast asleep by the time she'd returned from the post office, and she hadn't dared to wake him to tell him about the plan she and the Brocks had cooked up – that would only have put him in even more of a bad mood.

As she lay awake, her mind whirled with thoughts of Taber. Where was her little brother now? Was he still in the crate? Had he been caught by the post-master or the police? Was he OK? The prospect of waking up and turning on the radio to bad news plagued her thoughts. It was like being trapped in the most unimaginably awful nightmare. How could she have let this happen?

She was out of bed before the sun had even risen, and as she listened to the birds tweeting their dawn chorus, she went through her knapsack once more, making sure she had everything she'd need for the perilous journey ahead.

Water? Check!

Clean socks? Check!

First aid kit? Check!

Padlock and key? Check!

Pen knife? Check!

Bottle of glue? Check!

Mum's biscuit money? Check!

She'd also considered packing a few of her favourite books to read in case she got bored, but on remembering Ophelia Pearcart's words, she'd decided against the idea. *She who would travel happily*, her hero had once said, *must travel light.*

As the grandfather clock in the hallway struck eight, Orinthia got up and put on her wristwatch. It was the 'Aqua Aeon 100' – a diver's timepiece which she'd saved up for over a year to buy – perfect for adventures! As she made for the stairs, she peered into

Séafra's room, where he was still snoring in the top bunk. She wondered whether to wake him to say a proper goodbye, but she was still hurt by the things he'd said and the fact that he was refusing to join her on the postal journey. Instead, she climbed the ladder and planted a small kiss on the top of his head, before tiptoeing downstairs.

She was out of the house in a flash and on her way towards the village. The night before, she and the Brock children had decided that once they'd reached the antique shop, one of them was going to need to distract Mrs Oglesby while Orinthia stowed away. Kipling had naturally volunteered for the job, and was going to pretend to be one of the posh boys from Stricton Academy who was interested in buying an antique brooch for his mother's birthday. 'It will be my greatest performance to date!' he'd declared. 'And one of the greatest deceptions of our era!'

Orinthia crossed the village green, and once she'd reached the high street, she pulled up the hood of her duffel coat. The shops' shutters had already been pulled up, and shopkeepers were busy sweeping their doorways and putting out their A-frames. It was imperative that she wasn't seen. Little Penhallow was a tiny place, and gossip travelled fast.

However, she couldn't help but take a sideways glance at Mr Barnabas's sweet shop as she swept past. Outside, a red-headed girl wearing a green deerstalker hat was looking through the window, ogling the jars of strawberry bonbons, humbugs and chocolate limes which lined the back wall. A pale-skinned boy with bright-white hair was standing next to her, pointing to abox of sugar mice. They looked so happy, so contented, and Orinthia imagined them skipping home with their bags of sweets, their parents waiting for them with open arms . . .

'*Pssst!*' came a loud whisper from not too far off. 'Rinthi, over here! Come on!'

Orinthia whipped round to find Kipling, Bramwell, Peggy and Suki peering out from a small side street not far ahead, their heads stacked one on top of the other like four parts of a totem pole. Orinthia quickly ran to their side.

'Morning,' she said. 'How did you all get on? Did you manage to do all your jobs?'

The Brock children nodded proudly in unison.

'I got you these,' said Suki, handing Orinthia a canvas bag full of provisions. 'They should keep you going for a few days at least!'

Orinthia looked inside. There were two crusty

bread loaves, along with a large chunk of cheddar wrapped in brown paper and a wedge of potato pie. A couple of cold sausages and a bag of oranges were also part of the loot, as well as a jar of jam, several scones, a pat of butter, some biscuits and a pot of pickled gherkins.

'And the pièce de résistance!' said Suki, pulling a striped paper bag from behind her back. 'Gobstoppers from Mr Barnabas's shop! He let us sneak in early to buy some.'

'Of course, we *had* to try a couple first,' said Kipling, his eyes twinkling mischievously. 'To check that they weren't poisonous.'

Orinthia smiled as she put the bag of sweets in her coat pocket. What lovely friends she had.

'Do you want to see the label I've done?' Bramwell said proudly. 'I found the address of the animal sanctuary.' He held up the label for all to see.

'It's perfect,' said Orinthia. 'Well done, Bram.'

He puffed out his chest with pride. 'And before I forget, I've got something else to give you.' He reached into his pocket and pulled out a beautiful silver pen. 'It was my pa's, but I want you to take it for good luck. Maybe you could keep a diary of your travels, just like Ophelia Pearcart used to?'

Orinthia took the pen with a trembling hand, and looked down at the words which had been engraved on to its side: *Happily Ever After*. She was almost speechless. 'Are you sure?' she said, running a finger along the length of the pen. 'It's beautiful.'

'I want you to have it,' said Bramwell, determinedly. 'You know how much I love a story, and yours is going to be one of the greatest of all time!'

'Thank you, Bram. I'm honoured to have it. And who knows, maybe my handwriting will have improved by the time I get back!'

The children laughed.

'How are you feeling anyway, Rinthi?' asked Suki. 'Did you sleep OK?'

'Pretty well,' Orinthia replied, trying to sound self-assured. She'd learnt from Ophelia Pearcart that even if you were scared, even if you were terrified, it was good not to show your nerves to your crew. A confident leader made for a confident crew, and she didn't want her friends to notice how petrified she actually was. 'Now come on, let's put this plan into action. We haven't got much time before the postman starts doing his pick-ups!'

The children made their way to the end of the street and, when they were only a few doors away from Honest Heirlooms, they ducked behind a nearby motor car, watching the shop as if they were part of a police stake-out. As Bramwell had predicted, a large wooden crate had been left outside the shop for the postman to collect. It was about two metres square, its corners reinforced with metal brackets, and its lid fastened with a padlock. Upward-pointing arrows had been stamped on to each of its sides, accompanied by the words 'THIS WAY UP'. Orinthia wondered what was inside it. An Edwardian armchair? An antique chest? A gargantuan Venetian mirror? Whatever it was, it was soon to be replaced with a twelve-year-old girl!

'So, what are you going to call it?' asked Kipling.

Orinthia scrunched up her nose in confusion. 'Eh?'

'The crate! Every vessel needs to have a good strong name. My mum's old motor was called Pandora!'

'Hmmm,' said Orinthia, thinking hard. 'Good question.'

'I know! How about the *Penny Black*?' suggested Bramwell. 'It was the name of the world's first adhesive postage stamp. Grandy Brock was telling us all about it the other day.'

'That's perfect,' said Orinthia. 'I love it! A pioneering

name for a pioneering journey!'

A sudden tinkling of bells sounded from the antiques shop and the children looked up.

'OK, there's Mrs Oglesby!' whispered Bramwell, pointing to the woman coming out of the shop. She had frizzy hair the colour of honey, and was swathed in heavy, jangling jewellery. A green feather boa had been tossed around her neck. 'Kipling, are you all set? Ready to perform?'

'*Kipling?*' Kipling replied in his best upper-class accent. 'I think you mean *Maximilian Walter Boniface*. But yes, *one* is most definitely ready.'

Orinthia couldn't help but laugh. Kipling was such a good mimic, and really sounded as if he were speaking with a plum in his mouth – just like the boarders at Stricton Academy!

He tipped his straw boater as he sauntered off towards the antiques shop, and the children watched intently as he approached Mrs Oglesby and began his performance. They couldn't really hear what they were saying, but after a minute of chit-chat the shopkeeper was leading him into the back area of the shop with a pleased smile on her face. As Kipling went inside, he deftly turned the sign on the door to read 'CLOSED', before giving them all a big thumbs up.

'OK, let's go,' said Orinthia, jumping to her feet and scampering down the street with her friends in tow. As planned, Suki stood guard at the end of the road, while Orinthia and the others went to the crate.

'Did you manage to work out how to pick the lock?' Orinthia asked.

Peggy nodded, and with a mischievous grin, she put a finger up her right nostril and pulled out a silver hairpin. 'Ta-da! Just like the Great Zamora!' She slotted it into the lock, and with a quick twist, it was prised open in no time. They opened the lid and peered inside – poking out from a nest of shredded newspaper was a marble statue of what looked like a Roman god. He was crowned with a laurel wreath and draped sparingly in swathes of carved cloth.

'*Urchh*, who'd want *that* in their house?' asked Peggy, her face twisting. 'He hasn't got any clothes on! Gross!'

'Someone with more money than sense, that's for sure,' said Orinthia, looking at the price tag, which had more zeros than she could count.

'Now quickly, let's get him moved before Mrs Oglesby comes back out!' said Bramwell. 'Kipling's got a big mouth, but he'll only be able to keep her chatting for so long.' He took hold of one of the statue's arms, before gesturing for the girls to do the same. 'One . . . two . . . three . . . lift!'

The three children heaved the statue out of the crate and began to shuffle as fast as they could towards a nearby hedge. 'That's it,' said Bramwell, giving out directions as they manoeuvred. 'Left a bit . . . now right . . . Orinthia, watch out for that pothole in the road . . . Peggy, look where you're going!' The antique was even heavier than it looked, and they puffed and panted, desperately trying not to drop it. An expensive relic smashing into a million pieces across the pavement was *not* going to be conducive to a successful clandestine operation.

Before long (but with a lot of huffing and puffing) their mission was complete, and the hideous statue was tucked away in the hedgerows and completely out of sight.

'Well, I guess it's time to say good luck and good-bye,' whispered Bramwell, as Orinthia clambered inside the *Penny Black* and sat herself down. 'Are you sure you're going to be all right in there?'

'I'll be fine.' Orinthia placed her knapsack and food bag to one side and looked around the space that was to be her carriage for the foreseeable future. It was hardly first class – the leg space was cramped and the floor was hard, but at least she could sit upright. It was sturdy too, with no cracks in the wooden sides. Its musty smell wasn't exactly comforting, but she was sure she'd get used to it soon enough.

'OK, Peggy, did you bring one of Grandy Brock's tools to cut the hole for my hand to go through?' Orinthia asked.

The red-headed girl nodded eagerly, pulling a gimlet and a small handsaw from her coat pocket. 'Grandy Brock showed me how to use them last night,' she said, quickly getting to work. 'I told him I was interested in taking up carpentry over the summer holidays.'

Peggy worked deftly, and once the hole had been made in the Penny Black, Orinthia did a test run to make sure she could reach through it and put the key in the new padlock with ease. It worked like a dream!

'Well, let's get you to America then,' said Bramwell. He reached into his pocket and took out the new label. He stuck it down over the existing address, before licking the stolen stamp and pressing it down alongside it. He paused for a moment before saying, 'I'm really going to miss you, Rinthi.'

'Me too,' Peggy agreed. 'We all are.'

Orinthia was just about to say that she was going to

miss them too, terribly, when the sound of approaching footsteps made her heart freeze. She pulled herself up slowly, and there, walking towards them, was Séafra. He had a duffel bag on one shoulder and a wide-brimmed sun hat pulled down over his black curls.

'Is there room for one more in there?' he said, nodding to the crate with a smile. 'I'm coming too!'

16

Orinthia's heart began to race as her brother approached. 'Séa? You've . . . you've changed your mind?'

Séafra nodded. 'I still think that your idea is one of the craziest things I've ever heard in my life, but it's worth a shot. If we're going to get Taber back, then we're going to get him back together.' He edged forwards. 'If you still want me to come with you, that is.'

'Of course I do,' said Orinthia, throwing her arms around her brother's neck. 'As long as you promise to at least *try* and not be so grumpy. We're going to be spending a lot of time together over the next couple of weeks, in very close proximity, and we're going to need to keep positive.'

'I'll do my best,' said Séafra, before adding with a

wry smile, 'As long as you don't do anything to *make* me grumpy!'

'But how did you know I was going to be here?' asked Orinthia. 'How did you know where to find me?'

Séafra smoothed down the front of his shirt with a grin. 'Suki and the others came to find me in the attic when you and Kipling were breaking into the post office last night. They told me all about your plan, just in case I changed my mind!' He clambered into the crate and sat down next to his sister, swinging his bag from over his shoulder. Orinthia shot Suki a grateful glance. The older girl was still keeping lookout, but flashed a smile over her shoulder at the reunited siblings before returning her attention to the street.

'And what have you got in there?' asked Orinthia, as Séafra put his bag down between them. 'You haven't brought too many home comforts, have you? It's pretty cramped in here as it is.'

Séafra's eyes glistened. 'Well, I picked up some extra food, some more blankets and . . .' He opened up the bag just the tiniest bit. There was a flurry of movement from within. A flash of beak and wing. A squawk. 'Ta-da!'

Orinthia peered in to find a pair of glossy, brown-black eyes staring back at her. 'No?' she exclaimed. 'Is that Gungho?'

Séafra nodded. 'I decided to stop by the menagerie and bring him along too. I thought he might help get Geronimo back . . . if she's still out there.' He turned to Peggy and Bramwell. 'You won't tell Grandy Brock I've taken him though, will you?'

Peggy and Bramwell looked at each other mischievously, and in unison, as if butter wouldn't melt, replied, 'Tell Grandy Brock *what*?'

Séafra smiled. 'Thanks. I'll take good care of him, I promise.'

Just then, Suki came running towards them, her arms waving above her head in warning. 'Orinthia, Séafra, quick!' she hissed, looking back over her shoulder with urgency. 'The mail van is just around the corner! You need to get in the crate now!'

With no time to lose, Orinthia and Séafra hunkered down, and within the blink of an eye, Bramwell had jumped into action and was lowering the lid of the crate.

'Good luck,' Peggy whispered, peeking in. 'And don't forget to bring us back some of those famous New York hot dogs, will you?'

'We'll see what we can do!' Orinthia replied. And as the honk of the postman's van sounded from the end of the street, Bramwell closed the lid, plunging the siblings into near darkness. He locked the padlock before posting the key back through the hole.

'This is it, Séa!' Orinthia whispered. Her body was shot with a tingling combination of nerves and excitement. 'There's no going back now. We're going to New York City!'

Eager to hear what was going on outside, the two siblings pressed their ears against one side of the crate and listened. Orinthia heard her friends scampering away, and it wasn't long before she heard the rattling of the mail van pulling up alongside them, followed by the slamming of its door and the pitter-patter of the postman's approaching footsteps.

'Right, what have we got here then?' came his voice from above. '*Ooh!* Something going to America! Very fancy!' He slammed a hand down on top of the crate, making Orinthia's ears ring. 'Right, let's get you in the van.'

Orinthia could hear the postman grappling to find purchase on such a big crate, and anticipating being hoisted into the air, she reached for Séafra's hand. But no sooner had the postman lifted the crate a few centimetres from the ground, than he quickly dropped it to the pavement once more.

'Hell's bells!' he exclaimed. 'What on earth has Mrs Oglesby got in there? Bricks? I'm gonna need some help to move this one!' He stormed off, muttering something about *sciatica* and being *too old for this job*.

Orinthia felt her heart quicken. Where was he going? Was he going into the shop to ask Mrs Oglesby for a helping hand? What if she came out to discover that her crate had suddenly doubled in weight? They'd be caught before they'd even left the country! Before they'd even left Little Penhallow!

For a few tense minutes all the siblings could do was wait, their panic only easing when they heard the postman returning alone. He'd obviously gone to his van to fetch some kind of trolley cart, because within seconds he'd scooped the *Penny Black* from the ground, and Orinthia and Séafra felt themselves being tipped backwards as if in a dentist's chair.

It was a bone-shaking ride across the road to the van – the cobbles felt like mountains beneath them and Orinthia could feel every crack in the road, every pothole. She held on to her brother tight, trying her best not to make a sound, as they were tossed this way and that.

Just when she feared she might be sick, the postman came to a stop. He opened the van door, and with no regard for the words 'THIS WAY UP', tilted the trolley forwards, sending the crate tumbling into the van. Orinthia felt her stomach turn, and the next thing she knew, she and Séafra were lying on their fronts, their faces flat against the crate's side.

But Orinthia couldn't help but grin. Even though they were going to be trapped in this crate for the foreseeable future, it was the freest she'd ever felt.

17

'Rinthi, Rinthi, wake up! Quick!'

Orinthia hadn't even realized that she'd been sleeping until the sound of Séafra whispering her name pulled her from her slumber. Disorientated, she opened her eyes slowly. She felt very confused. Why wasn't she looking up at the ceiling rose in her bedroom? Why hadn't her alarm clock gone off? And why wasn't she wearing pyjamas?

Then Séafra's voice came again, his hands on her shoulders. 'Rinthi! Come on,' he whispered urgently. 'Get up! Get up!'

'*Ufff*, what is it, Séa?' Orinthia groaned, still half asleep. Somewhere in the distance she could hear the sound of someone shouting, and a whistle being blown. 'And why is Mum shouting so loudly? Why is she blowing a whistle?'

'*Mum?*' Séafra replied through the darkness. 'Rinthi, have you forgotten where you are? That's not Mum. It's a station controller. I think we've been put on a mail train! And it's about to depart!'

The words *mail* and *train* brought Orinthia to her senses like a bucket of ice-cold water to the face. Of course! They were in the *Penny Black*. They were on their way to New York. She must have been in such a deep slumber!

'Why didn't you wake me up before?' she grumbled, coaxing her feet from beneath her. As she pulled herself on to her knees her legs began to tingle, fizzing with an agonizing bout of pins and needles. 'Why did you let me sleep for so long?'

'I only just woke up myself,' said Séafra. 'We must have nodded off in the postman's van. I only opened my eyes because Gungho was pecking at my nose. I think he knew that we wouldn't want to miss the experience of a train ride.'

Orinthia felt around for the little pelican, letting her fingers run across his downy back. 'And you were right about that, boy!' she said, suddenly buzzing with energy. 'I can't remember when we last took a train journey. This is going to be great!'

She put an ear to one side of the crate and listened.

She could hear the buzz of the station echoing all around – the rumbling of wheels clacking over tracks, the hissing of brakes, the billowing of steam through funnels, and then, an announcement being made:

'*ALL ABOARD! ALL ABOARD!*' a crackled voice came over the tannoy. '*THE ELEVEN FORTY-FIVE MAIL TRAIN IS READY TO DEPART! STAND CLEAR!*'

Orinthia's heart quickened at the words. This was it! They were about to embark on the next part of their adventure! There was an ear-piercing whistle, and with a jolt and a jerk, the train was on the move. A wave of exhilaration rippled through Orinthia as the locomotive began to pick up pace. She could feel the vibrations of the wheels trundling along the track, and the gentle sway as the train took its first bend. It was so exciting. But where was the train heading? She turned to her brother. 'Did you hear anyone say what our destination was?'

'No,' Séafra replied. 'A couple of train guards came into our carriage shortly after Gungho had woken me up, but all they were talking about was which flavour crisps they thought was the best. I had to stop myself from shouting out loud when one of them said *cheese and onion*! Yuck!'

Orinthia pondered for a moment. She knew that a train could only take them so far – a locomotive couldn't cross the Atlantic after all – so she imagined that they were probably en route to a port where they would be transferred to a packet ship.

'Do you think it's safe for us to get out for a bit?' Séafra asked. 'I don't think I can sit in this position for much longer. It feels like my legs are going to drop off.'

Orinthia considered this. Surely they could get out just for a little while? It wasn't like they were on a passenger train. No one would be coming around to check their tickets or to offer them refreshments. 'OK,' she whispered. 'But let me check that the coast is clear first. Don't move until I say so, and keep a tight hold of Gungho. The last thing we need is another pelican going AWOL.'

Séafra nodded, picking up the little bird and clasping both hands around his feathered body.

Orinthia reached into her sock and pulled out the little key for the new padlock – which, after a little fumbling in the dark, clicked open.

She took a deep breath and slowly pushed up the lid of the crate. The thinnest ray of sunlight shone in, but having been cooped up in the dark for so long, it felt dazzling. She blinked her eyes into focus, and peering through the crack, studied the sliver of carriage beyond.

There was no doubt that they were indeed in a mail train. Their crate was surrounded by dozens of bulging hessian sacks, the words 'ROYAL MAIL – UNITED KINGDOM' stamped across each one in bold red letters. There were parcels of all shapes and sizes too, as well as wooden freight crates not dissimilar to the one they were in. On the wall opposite was a sign bearing the words 'THE PARCEL TAPE EXPRESS – COACH B'.

Orinthia clambered out, before extending a hand to her brother, who had Gungho nestled under one arm. 'That's better,' he said, stretching out as he stepped into the freedom of the carriage. 'I didn't think it was possible for pins and needles to have their own pins and needles, but I do now.'

Orinthia giggled as she rolled back her shoulders. 'I know. My neck is so stiff. I feel like a jack-in-the-box who hasn't been let out in centuries.'

The siblings shared a grin, and began to take in their surroundings. Since Gungho couldn't fly yet, they decided it was safe to let him run around and stretch his legs. The carriage smelt strongly of paper, a musty aroma like that of an old library, but not entirely unpleasant. It was stuffy, though, so Orinthia pulled down one of the windows to let in some fresh air.

By the time she'd turned round, Gungho was hopping from post sack to post sack and Séafra was rifling through the food bag. 'I thought we could have something to eat,' he said, bringing out some of the brown paper parcels and licking his lips. 'I'm absolutely starving, and it is nearly lunchtime after all.'

'Yeah, good idea,' Orinthia replied, suddenly feeling pretty peckish herself. 'But we need to ration the supplies. We've got a long journey ahead of us and we don't want to find ourselves short.'

Séafra nodded, and within minutes, the delicious provisions Suki had taken from Tupenny Mill had been laid out like a little picnic. The siblings dived in, munching their way through hunks of bread, lumps of cheese and cold sausages. Orinthia picked up one of the scones and pulled it in two, before slathering each half with butter and raspberry jam. The scone was a little stale but the toppings more than made up for it – the sweet fruity layer oozing deliciously into the creamy yellow one.

Séafra, meanwhile, had a wedge of pie in one hand and a biscuit in the other, and was chomping intermittently into both. 'Mmmm, this is so good,' he said. 'I didn't realize how hungry I was!' He picked up a sausage before saying, 'Hey, Rinthi, can you remember that picnic that Mum and Grandad took us on when we were little?'

Orinthia nodded wistfully. Yes, she could remember – it was pretty much the only fond memory she had of their mother. They'd driven out to the countryside with a big wicker basket and a flask of tea, and had sat in the shade, eating and drinking and talking until the sun went down. It had been magical.

Once they'd finished their rations, and with their bellies full, the two siblings flopped back on to a couple of mail sacks, enjoying the temporary luxury of being able to stretch out their stiff limbs. Gungho settled down on Séafra's stomach, munching on some of the bird feed he'd brought along. Through the window they could see the countryside rumbling past: fields and paddocks and rivers and meadows.

Orinthia's attention, however, was quickly drawn to an envelope which had fallen out of the mail sack by her side. It was gold, and the address on the front was written in beautiful flowing script. The frank mark showed that it had been posted in Aberdeen, so it had travelled quite a long distance already. Who might have sent it, she wondered. Was it a birthday card? An important manuscript? Or an invitation to a party? 'Hey, Séa, look at this,' she said, showing it to her brother. 'Want to take a look inside?'

'Rinthi, no!' Séafra replied, snatching the letter from her hand. 'It's not polite to look at other people's mail. We can't do that!'

'Oh, come on, Séa, you know you want to,' Orinthia persisted, sitting up straight. 'We can just have a little peek and then close the envelope back up again. I have a bottle of glue in my bag.'

Séafra sighed. 'OK. But just a quick peek, and then we're putting it straight back.'

Orinthia clapped her hands together and swiped back the envelope. Then, as carefully as possible, she prised open the triangular flap and pulled out the letter inside.

Dear Romilly,

My heart is breaking without you by my side. I miss you more with every minute we spend apart and I long to have you in my arms once more.

But soon we will be together again, and until that day I shall treasure your sweet smile in my heart.

Yours, forever,

Otis XXX

'That's so gross,' said Séafra. 'I'd be sick if anyone ever wrote me a letter like that. It's so soppy.'

'Does that mean . . . that we should open another one?' asked Orinthia mischievously as she glued the first one back together. 'To see if we can find something a little less sentimental?'

Séafra raised an eyebrow, then, ignoring all of the concerns he'd had only a minute ago, reached for another envelope and carefully prised open the flap. The letter inside had been written on a typewriter, and he coughed before reading aloud:

Dear Mrs Scantlebury,

You visited us two weeks ago with a complaint of severe flatulence and were prescribed Milk of Magnesia to be taken two times daily.

I am writing to inform you that we have booked your follow-up appointment on 15 November at 2 p.m.

Your medical well-being is important to us, so if you cannot attend this appointment, please let us know at your earliest convenience.

Yours sincerely,

Dr M. Lawrence and team

The siblings burst out laughing. 'Oh dear!'

exclaimed Orinthia, her mouth twisting. 'Severe bottom burps! I wonder if Mrs Scantlebury is related to Mr Malagasy? It certainly sounds like it.'

Séafra laughed. '*Smells* like it, you mean!'

'Come on, let's open another one. My turn!' Orinthia dove into the mail sack once more, and for the next couple of hours the siblings took it in turns to read aloud. They came across letters to pen pals, invites to lavish weddings, and messages of good luck. There was even a court summons written to a woman charged with stealing a garden gnome from someone else's front lawn!

It was only when they'd decided that it was probably time to put the envelopes back in the sacks that something extraordinary happened.

Now perched upon Séafra's shoulder, Gungho began to flap his wings. His motions were tentative at first – a twitch of his feathers, a jerk of his chest. But soon he was gaining confidence, and within a few minutes he had launched himself from his perch and shot into the air. He was like an athlete in a race, flying lap upon lap of the carriage, determined and focused.

Elated, Orinthia craned her neck to follow the bird's path. 'Oh my goodness, Taber's going to be so happy when he sees this. Gungho's finally learnt to fly!'

'I . . . I can't believe it!' said Séafra, equally as mesmerized. 'He probably just needed a change of scenery!'

But the siblings' jubilation was short-lived.

They'd completely forgotten about the window that Orinthia had opened, and with a loud *squawk*, the little pelican swooped towards it, flying through the gap and into the afternoon skies.

'Gungho, no!' shouted Séafra, leaping to the window. He leant out as far as he could, swiping a hand through the air. 'Gungho, come back! What are you doing? You're going to get lost!'

But the bird did not turn around. His wings were feathery white paddles pushing him forward, his tail feather guiding him through the sky like the flight of a dart.

And before long he was already in the distance, climbing higher and higher until he was no more than a moving speck on the horizon.

18

'NO!' wailed Séafra once more. 'Gungho, come back! Please, come back!' He was frantic now, leaning out of the window as far as he could, swiping through the air with the hope that the pelican might still be in his grasp.

Orinthia dashed towards him, all at once feeling his pain, but at the same time worrying that his shouts might alert the crew. 'Séafra, you need to stop shouting,' she said, trying her best to calm him. 'Someone's going to hear you. And it's not safe to lean out like that. Come back in.'

Séafra turned sharply to his sister, his eyes wide and his breath fast. 'Don't tell me to be quiet!' he snapped. 'This is all your fault! *You* opened that window. Gungho would still be here if we'd kept it shut.'

Orinthia let out an incredulous gasp. 'My fault? You're the one that decided to bring Gungho with us in the first place – and we *both* decided he needed to stretch his legs!' She took a breath, trying to centre herself. 'Look, Séa, what just happened is awful, but neither of us realized that Gungho had learnt to fly—'

'No, but . . . but . . . *uffff!*' Séafra's anger fizzled out and he let out a loud groan. He slumped down against the carriage wall, burying his face in his hands. 'We'd already lost one of Grandy Brock's birds, and now we've let another one escape! I promised Peggy and Suki that I'd look after Gungho.'

'It's OK, Séa,' whispered Orinthia, coming to kneel by his side. She tried to comfort him with a stroke of his hair, but he shrugged her away, refusing to meet her gaze. 'Séafra, look at me, please,' she persisted. 'This is nobody's fault. Not yours, not mine, it's . . . it's just nature. And a little bit of bad luck.'

Séafra looked up, still sniffing. His eyes were red and he struggled to take a deep breath. 'What do you mean, "it's nature"?'

Orinthia sighed. 'I mean that birds are meant to exist out in the open. Keeping Gungho in such a small space probably wasn't the best thing for him. Back in the menagerie, he had lots of space and things to do –

but here he was just cooped up in a box. That must've been tough.'

Séafra wiped his eyes. 'But . . . but I thought he liked being with us.'

'Of course he did, Séa.' Orinthia put an arm around her brother's shoulder. 'But now he has the opportunity to feel the wind through his feathers. And you never know, he might even be trying to get home to Little Penhallow.'

Séafra looked up and gazed out of the window, his eyes glassy. 'Taber's going to be so upset when he finds out.'

'Yes,' said Orinthia. 'He probably will be. But he'll have *you* by his side to comfort him. His big brother.'

Séafra sniffed, and on spotting a rogue white pelican feather in the middle of the carriage, he reached forward and picked it up. 'I'm really going to miss him,' he said, twirling it between his thumb and forefinger.

'I know,' said Orinthia. 'And I will too.' She paused. 'Apart from those nasty white splatters and his fishy breath, of course!'

Séafra's mouth began to turn upwards, but the sudden sound of approaching footsteps snatched the smile from his face. The Shalloo siblings froze.

'I'm tellin' ya, Bert, I heard somethin',' came a male voice as the strides drew closer. 'It was comin' from Coach B. Really high-pitched, like a kid screechin' or somethin'.'

'A kid screeching?' was the mirthful reply. 'Nah, it's just these old trains, Bob. They're falling apart! Probably one of the axles needs oiling, that's all.'

'Well, I'm gonna check anyway,' said Bob, now dangerously close. 'We had some stowaways on board last month and I'm not taking any chances. I'm already in trouble with the gaffer for not pressing my work trousers well enough . . .'

The siblings looked at each other, and without needing to say a word they leapt to their feet, frantic- ally picking up all of the letters and envelopes which they'd left strewn across the floor. They stuffed them in a sack, and were back inside the *Penny Black* in a flash, pulling the lid down just as the carriage door burst open.

Orinthia listened as Bob and Bert strode inside.

'See, it's just one of the windows that's fallen open, Bob,' said Bert. 'You must have heard the wind whistling, that's all.' He pushed his way through the bags of mail, before pulling the window closed with a clatter. 'I told you it wasn't anything to worry about.

You need to relax a bit, old boy. Come on, let's go and have a nice cuppa. Got some cheese and onion crisps that we can have too!'

Bob let out a disgruntled huff, and as the two guards left, Orinthia and Séafra breathed out a shared sigh of relief.

'Oh my goodness, that was close,' whispered Orinthia.

'*Too* close,' Séafra agreed.

'I think we should stay in here from now on, until we reach the port, at least.'

19

When Orinthia opened her eyes the next morning, she knew they were no longer on board the *Parcel Tape Express*. The rumbling of the wheels along the tracks had ceased, and there was no chuffing of smoke bellowing through the chimney. She felt cold, and in an attempt to warm up she blew on her fingertips before pushing her hands deep into her coat pockets.

Where are we? she wondered for the second time in as many days. Was this now going to be her daily routine until they reached New York – rousing from slumber completely oblivious to where she and Séafra were? It was a frightening feeling, but at least with every sunrise, she knew that they were a step closer to Taber.

She put her ear to the side of the crate, and listened

carefully. Somewhere in the distance she heard the faint sound of a foghorn. There were low, guttural voices, the sound of heavy footsteps, and the rumbling noise of things being dragged across wooden walkways. And then she heard it – the clue she had been waiting for – the crashing of water and the squawk of a seagull. She knew where they were now. A dock!

With excitement coursing through her, Orinthia pulled herself on to her knees and pushed up the lid of the *Penny Black* the tiniest bit. It was just enough to see a line of boats bobbing at anchor, their masts reaching into the skies. She let her gaze trail across their colourful hulls, reading the names that had been painted in fancy scripts across their prows: *PRINZ EUGENE . . . THE MAGDALENA . . . TEMERAIRE III . . . THE ATHENIAN . . .* and finally . . . RMS *MOLLUSCA*.

Orinthia's eyes lit up. She knew what RMS stood for! *Royal Mail Steamship.* This was the boat that would be taking them across the Atlantic! Buzzing with anticipation and eager to see more, she pushed up the lid of the crate even further, and gazed upwards. The *Mollusca* was a huge vessel, immaculately kept and painted a fresh, bright white. It had three stout funnels, and a tall mast crowned with a flowing red flag. Orinthia's body fizzed with delight, and she couldn't help but let out a little yelp of elation. She was going to be crossing the Atlantic in a boat, just like Ophelia Pearcart had once done!

Too exhilarated to enjoy the moment alone, she gave Séafra a nudge with her foot.

'*Urghhh*, Rinthi,' he said, letting out an irritable groan as he forced his eyes open. 'What's happening? Why are the lights on?'

'It's the sun, silly!' she said, turning to her brother without letting the lid drop. 'We're at the dock. We're going on a steamship!'

Séafra rolled his shoulders and shook out his mop of hair, before joining his sister at the lookout.

'That's the one I think we're going to be sailing on,' enthused Orinthia, nodding her head in the direction of the *Mollusca*. 'Isn't she a beauty?'

'Erm . . . yeah . . .' said Séafra with nonchalance. 'If you can call a big floating box beautiful.' He slunk back into his corner and closed his eyes once more.

Orinthia tutted, letting the lid of the crate fall closed as she slumped back down to sitting. 'I thought we'd agreed that you were going to be a bit more positive from now on? A bit less . . . moody? If you don't want to be here, then you can just—'

'OK, OK, I'm sorry,' said Séafra defensively. 'It's a lovely boat, really it is. I just still feel so guilty about Gungho, that's all. I was up half the night thinking about him. And my legs ache. And I'm hungry. And I really need a wee.'

Orinthia smiled, unable to stay angry with her brother for long. And besides, she'd be lying if she said that she wasn't hungry and achey and in need of the toilet too. 'Don't worry,' she reassured her brother. 'As soon as we're on board you can sneak out of the crate and . . . well . . . spend a penny.' She smirked, and gave Séafra a playful elbow. 'Or should that be . . . a penny black!'

Séafra shook his head with a low moan, but Orinthia knew he liked her joke really. 'And it's OK to feel sad about Gungho, you know,' she added. 'But we mustn't let it get us down. We need to keep focused and positive if we're going to get to Taber.'

Séafra looked to the floor. 'I know. But I was thinking, after we've found Taber and we're back in Little Penhallow, maybe we could use the money in our piggy banks to buy Grandy Brock a couple more pelicans?'

'I think that sounds like a brilliant idea—' began Orinthia, eager to try and cheer up her brother.

But her words of encouragement were cut short.

Out of the blue she felt something crashing into the *Penny Black* from behind, and she winced. A violent kick had sent the crate jerking forwards, and the Shalloo siblings clutched on to each other, barely daring to breathe.

'Drake, what are you playing at?' came a salty female voice from above. 'You know we're not meant to kick the cargo! The captain would go berserk if he caught you.'

'Sorry, Duffel,' replied a husky-voiced man. 'It just looked really heavy, that's all. I couldn't be bothered to pick it up.' He slammed a hand down on to the roof of the crate, making both children jump. 'Anyway, are we putting all these crates in the hold now?'

'What time is it?' asked Duffel.

There was a pause before Drake answered. 'Eleven o'clock. Just gone.'

'Nah, we'll do it later. The *Mollusca* ain't sailing until three, so let's go and get some grub. The Whiskered Kipper is just over the road and it does the best pies and ale in town. As long as we're back here for two-ish, we'll have plenty of time to get the heavy stuff in the hold.'

'Good idea,' said Drake. 'A meat pie and a nice

pint of ale. Can't argue with that!'

Their voices trailed off and as soon as their footsteps were far enough away, Séafra let out a loud whimper of complaint. 'Ow! Rinthi, I can't wait in here until they come back and put us on board. My bladder is going to explode!' He crossed his legs in pain, his face contorting like that of a particularly gruesome gargoyle. 'Can I get out, just for a bit? I'll be really quick.'

Orinthia thought for a moment. It *would* be risky to leave the crate before they'd made it on board the packet ship, but she probably couldn't hold on to her wee for that long either. And besides, they'd already eaten most of the food they'd taken from home, and at the rate Séafra was guzzling down biscuits, this might be a good opportunity to stock up on supplies before they left dry land. She'd brought the money that Mum had left them after all.

'Rinthi, please, I need to get out. I can't hold it much longer!'

'OK, OK, calm down,' Orinthia replied. She lifted the lid of the *Penny Black* a fraction once more. 'Now here's the plan. We sneak out of here, quickly use the toilet and then we go and buy some more supplies to take on board. But we need to make sure that we get back here before Drake and Duffel return from the pub.'

Séafra nodded, and when Orinthia was sure the coast was clear enough, the siblings scampered from their hiding place.

20

They began to weave their way through the dock, zigzagging through the salt-encrusted maze of crates and creels, barrels and buoys, dugouts and dinghies. At the harbour wall they crouched behind an abandoned rowing boat, which Orinthia thought would serve as a good makeshift toilet, and once they were finished they began to climb the rickety stone steps up to street level. Orinthia loved the sensation of the breeze whipping against her face as they ascended, and she was now more fired-up than ever to be heading out on RMS *Mollusca*. In her diary, Ophelia Pearcart had written extensively about her nautical voyage from England to America, in search of the Puebloan sandstone ruins of Colorado. Now, in a few hours' time, *she* would be sailing the Atlantic – following in the same path!

'Woah, look at that, Rinthi,' said Séafra, stopping to take in the view as they reached the top of the steps. 'What a sight!'

It was indeed. A huge city was stretching out before their eyes like an image from a postcard. A domed cathedral dominated the skyline framed by huge bridges which, in turn, were flanked by stout grey chimneys belching smoke. It was so different to Little Penhallow – here, the buildings were tall and narrow, and the sky overhead was as thick as pea soup. Somewhere in the distance a clock chimed the hour, making Orinthia gasp. Hang on a minute – she knew that sound! It was Big Ben!

She leapt from the harbour wall on to the pavement below. 'Séafra, we're in London!' she exclaimed with delight. 'We're in the capital city! Come on, let's go!'

'OK, but stay close,' said Séafra, following in her path with excitement. 'London is a very busy place and I don't want to lose a sister as well as a brother.'

They set off at pace, heading away from the dock and into the murky grey metropolis that stretched out before them. After a near miss with a speeding tram, they jinked left through the grounds of a colossal red-bricked museum, before darting beneath a bridge. They found themselves at the beginning of a wide cobbled street, with buildings rising up on either side of it.

Orinthia took a deep breath. To say that it was bustling would have been an understatement, and her eyes darted frantically this way and that, trying to take it all in. They were standing in some kind of open market. Everywhere she looked there were hawker carts and grocery stalls, buyers and sellers, loiterers and workers.

On one corner people were queuing outside a butcher's shop, where a man in a striped apron was hanging strings of sausages in his window. A few metres down, a woman in a straw hat was selling flowers from a wooden cart. And across the street, a man with a twirly moustache was standing on a soap box trying to flog bottles of his 'Miracure Medicinal Ointment' to a quickly growing crowd. 'Roll up! Roll up!' he crowed. 'One hundred per cent success rate. No boil too big, no headache too painful, no stool too loose.'

The siblings made their way into the crowd, but as they meandered through, Orinthia couldn't help but notice a few people looking at them. An old woman selling bunches of lavender did a double take as they passed by, and a man in a tall hat scanned them from head to toe as they approached his bric-a-brac stall. Maybe they looked different to city children? Or maybe it was unusual for youngsters to be out alone in London? It was much busier than Little Penhallow after all.

Not thinking any more of it, she and Séafra weaved in amongst stalls and carts, and pressed their noses up against shop windows. It was hard to not get swept away by the delicious-looking delicacies on offer, and Orinthia felt her tongue falling further and further from her mouth with every step they took. There were gypsy tarts and jars of pickles, freshly baked loaves and bundles of herbs. A fruiterer in a starched overcoat was selling his wares from a covered pitch. There were pyramids of shiny red apples, deep purple plums, greengages and the largest pears that Orinthia had ever seen. 'Come on, me lovelies!' he bawled. 'Get your sweet nectarines, ripe for the plucking!'

It was the fishmonger that got Séafra's attention, however. 'Rinthi, look at that!' he said, pointing to the icy display in the open shopfront. It was packed with all manner of deep-sea denizens – an iridescent arrangement of pink, red and silver scales. Behind the counter, a buxom woman in a white coat was scaling a gigantic turbot, while her young apprentice was busy preparing jellied eels. Orinthia and Séafra wandered over to the apprentice. 'Wanna try?' the young man asked, scooping up a spoonful of the wobbly grey gloop and offering it to Séafra. He was wearing a flat cap at an angle, his face long and gaunt. 'The best in the East End, these are!'

'*Yuck!* No way!' Séafra replied, pulling away. 'They look like fishy bogeys! Gross!'

'Séafra, don't be so rude!' Orinthia scorned through gritted teeth, before apologizing to the young fishmonger. 'I'm sorry. My brother's not very adventurous with his food.'

'Oh, don't worry about it,' replied the boy with a chuckle. 'Jellied eels ain't for everyone, that's for sure. Nice bit of rock salmon instead maybe? I can do you a good price.'

Orinthia declined politely and was just about to ask if there was a bakery nearby, when a strange look passed over the boy's face. It was as if something had suddenly dawned on him, like a flash of realization, an epiphany. His gaze darted to Séafra then back again and a knot of anxiety started to form in

Orinthia's tummy. She didn't know if she was being paranoid or not, but she could have sworn that the young fishmonger knew who she was . . .

Before he could say another word she edged back, pulling at her brother's coat. 'We . . . we have to go now,' she blurted out in panic. 'Our parents will be wondering where we are.' She tugged at Séafra's arm, before turning and dragging him away in her wake.

'*Ouch*, Rinthi, you're hurting me!' yelped Séafra, trying to yank his arm free, seemingly oblivious to what had just gone on. 'Why the rush? I hadn't finished looking.'

'Nothing,' lied Orinthia, not wanting to burden Séafra with her (hopefully unnecessary) concerns. 'We just haven't got time to loiter, that's all. Come on, let's go and find some bread.'

They headed further into the market in search of a bakery and Orinthia started to relax. Maybe she'd been mistaken; maybe the fishmonger's apprentice hadn't recognized them at all. She had just spotted a bakery at last, the fresh yeasty smell of bread filling the street, when she stopped suddenly with a gasp, spotting something very troubling on a lamp post.

A wanted poster printed in bold, black letters.

POLICE NOTICE

WANTED

The following siblings have absconded
from Little Penhallow:

Orinthia Shalloo

Twelve years old. She is about five feet two inches and is
of slim build. She has bobbed black hair, green eyes and a
small nose. She has a small scar across her left eyebrow
and a deep dimple in her chin.

Séafra Shalloo

Eleven years old. The boy is approximately five and
a half feet tall and is of extremely slim build.
Séafra has curly black hair. His upper front
teeth have a gap between them.

The siblings were last seen on Little Penhallow High
Street on 20 August, and it is believed that they are
trying to make their way to America.

If you see either of the children, do not hesitate to
contact Inspector Jeremy Snodgrass,
Little Penhallow Constabulary.

A sizeable cash reward is on offer to anyone who
provides information leading to their arrest.

Orinthia quickly snatched the poster from the lamp post and looked down at it with horror. Beneath their descriptions, there was a black-and-white photograph of her and Séafra, sitting atop a grassy bank in the sunshine. Her breath hitched. She knew exactly where and when this picture had been taken – Grandy Brock had bought a new lens for his camera a couple of weeks ago, and had taken them and his children to the top of St Sylvester's Mount to try it out.

Orinthia's insides hardened to stone as she realized what this meant. Inspector Snodgrass must have gone looking for them at Tupenny Mill, and the Brock children must have come clean about them stowing away in the *Penny Black*. They'd broken their promise; they'd divulged the secret they'd sworn to keep. And now the police had branded them criminals just for trying to get to America! There was a warrant out for their arrest!

'Oh my goodness, Rinthi, how could they have told on us?' Séafra gasped, obviously thinking exactly the same thing. 'They were meant to be our friends!'

'I know,' said Orinthia with increasing trepidation. 'They've betrayed us.'

Séafra's lower lip began to tremble. 'D-d-do you think we should hand ourselves in? Should we go to the police? Wanted . . . capture . . . This poster makes us sound like criminals, not runaways.'

'No!' said Orinthia sharply. 'We can't do that!' She ripped the poster into shreds and threw the pieces on to the ground. 'We need to find Taber. As soon as we're on board the *Mollusca* and it sets sail, we'll be safe—'

'Is that so, little girl?'

A sharp voice from behind made Orinthia gasp, and she spun around to find the tip of a walking cane centimetres from her face. It was being brandished by an old man with a scowling expression and a twisted parsnip of a nose. He edged forward slowly with a crooked gait, not letting his cane drop for a moment. 'Aha! My suspicions were correct,' he yelped, looking the children up and down. 'I thought I recognized you both outside the fishmonger's earlier on. You're the children the police are looking for, aren't you? The criminals!'

'N-N-No!' spluttered Orinthia, throwing herself in front of Séafra as the man drew nearer. 'K-keep away from us! Or . . . or I'll shout for help. I'll say you're trying to kidnap us!'

The man snorted. 'Shout all you like. I'm sure the police will be very eager to "come to your assistance".'

He smiled cruelly, spittle gathering in the corners of his mouth. 'In fact, let's call them over here now, shall we?' He turned to the street corner, where a gangly policeman in a dark-blue helmet was standing with his hands resting at his duty belt. 'Officer! Officer, over here!'

'No!' pleaded Orinthia. 'Please don't! We're not causing any trouble. We're not the criminals they're making us out to be—'

But it was too late.

The police officer on the corner looked up from beneath the peak of his hat and as his eyes met Orinthia's, his posture spiked. As he ran towards the children, he reached to his belt and pulled out a two-way radio. 'This is PC Williams requesting backup to Pigget Square,' he said into the mouthpiece. 'I repeat, backup required in regards to Operation Narcissus. Over.'

21

Panic flooded Orinthia's belly. She stole a look at Séafra, who was trembling helplessly, and she slipped her hand into his. There was only one thing for it: they couldn't let the police catch them.

'RUN!'

Orinthia's shout momentarily startled the policeman, who skidded on the cobblestones barely a few feet away. Dragging her brother with her, she muscled past the old man with the cane and hurtled back down the busy street towards the dock. Sirens sounded somewhere nearby.

'Oi!' shouted PC Williams. 'Come back here! Come back here now!'

Orinthia could hear his footsteps thundering behind them, his boots heavy with determination. He blew his whistle and, chancing a look backwards,

Orinthia saw that another police officer was already running to his aid. This one was boxy in stature, with barely any neck and a horseshoe-shaped moustache framing his mouth.

The siblings picked up their pace, their feet slapping hard against the cobbles as they threaded through the labyrinth of hawkers, barrows and carts. They dodged everyone they met, weaving from stall to stall and ducking under the swathes of overhanging awning, heading back the way they'd come. Orinthia hadn't realized how far into the market they'd wandered and bitterly wished they had stayed closer to the docks – and the *Penny Black*. As she ran, she tried to think of all the instances when Ophelia Pearcart had escaped from an enemy – the yeti attack in the Himalayas, the rogue crew member on board her private Zeppelin to Nairobi, the buccaneers over the Mediterranean Sea! And with visions of her hero spurring her, she battled on, her heart hammering in her chest. All they needed to do was keep going and get themselves back to the *Penny Black*.

But it wasn't long before the people of Pigget Square began to notice what was going on. Instead of meandering from stall to stall, many had stopped to watch the unfolding chaos, and they'd started to point and stare.

'Hey! Isn't that the missing children?' shouted a floral-scarfed woman outside the bakery.

'Goodness, yes it is!' said the woman next to her. 'The ones the police are after!'

A tornado of heckles followed suit:

'Don't let them get away, officers!'

'They're dangerous!'

'Stop them at once!'

Orinthia felt sweat beading on her forehead, and from her side, Séafra yelped, 'Rinthi, what should we do? Everyone's watching us! We're going to get caught!'

Orinthia stole another backwards look, and to her horror saw that the two policemen were gaining on them fast, and were now dangerously close. She could see the resoluteness in their eyes, and any moment now she was going to feel a heavy hand on the scruff of her neck, and cuffs would be snapped around her wrists . . .

But skirting around a dropped banana peel, an idea flashed across her mind. It wasn't foolproof but it was worth a try, anything to momentarily widen the gap between them and their pursuers. Without stopping, she reached into her coat pocket and pulled out the bag of Mr Barnabas's gobstoppers that Suki had given to them.

'Rinthi, what are you doing?' shouted Séafra from her side. 'This is no time to eat sweets! Put them away!'

'I'm buying us some time!' she replied, and without a second to lose, she upended the bag of sweets, causing the sugary white balls to tumble across the cobbles like marbles. She didn't hang around to witness the chaos that she hoped would ensue, but the subsequent *ARGGGGGGHs*, followed by the *DMFFFF* of two bodies hitting the ground, told her that her plan had worked. The police officers had tripped and crashed to the ground. Bingo!

'Nice one!' exclaimed Séafra, as they continued through the crowds. 'But what now? They're not going to stay down for long.'

Orinthia swallowed. She hadn't really thought about that. 'Just keep running,' she panted, streaking on up the street. She could see the dock in the distance, the white of the boats, the blue of the Thames. 'Just keep heading towards the— *AGGGGGHHHH!*'

Orinthia skidded to a sudden halt, her words evaporating into thin air. Up ahead, the butcher she'd seen earlier had appeared from his shop and was striding purposefully towards them. His apron was stained with congealed blood, and he had knives hanging from his belt, sticky with remnants of raw meat. Orinthia tried to dodge around him, but he swooped in to block her path.

'Gotcha, you little chitterlings!' he grunted. 'Game's over!'

Orinthia felt her chest tighten, and she pulled her brother in close. Adrenalin was shooting through her veins, making her muscles twitch. She looked around for a friendly face, but nobody was coming to their aid. Shop owners and shoppers alike were slinking towards them like predators. There was a price on their heads after all.

The butcher pulled a cleaver from his belt and its blade caught the morning sun. 'Come on children, you've had your fun. Just hand yourself in, eh? Then things won't have to get nasty.' He looked over Orinthia and Séafra's heads and called out to the policemen, 'Don't worry, officers, I've got them. They ain't going anywhere.'

Orinthia turned to find the two policemen limping down the road towards them. They were hot-cheeked and panting, PC William's helmet knocked sideways and his colleague's trousers scuffed after their fall. 'Thank you, sir,' gasped PC Williams. 'We'll take it from here.'

Orinthia's heart sank.

This was it.

They'd been caught before they'd even got to New York.

They'd been caught before they'd even left the country!

What a disastrous first expedition. What a terrible explorer she was.

But just then, something odd happened – a dollop of something grey and slimy landed at Orinthia's foot, making her flinch. It was a jellied eel! Being careful not to alert the police, she glanced slowly to where it had been thrown from, and there, next to the entrance to the fishmonger's, a narrow door was slightly ajar. A thin sliver of light was coming from within, and as Orinthia squinted, she saw a face peeking out. It was the young fishmonger's apprentice from earlier on.

'In here,' he mouthed, beckoning to her frantically. 'Quick!'

Orinthia didn't know what to do. Was he trying to help them? Or was this some kind of trap?

'Come on,' he mouthed once more.

Orinthia swallowed. What would Ophelia Pearcart have done? Gone with the police (no way!), trusted a stranger she'd only spoken to once, or tried to escape another way? The boy had seemed pleasant enough earlier, but looks could be deceiving . . .

There really wasn't time to ponder any more – the two policemen were reaching for their handcuffs. Orinthia *had* to make a decision, and throwing caution to the wind she grabbed Séafra by the arm and bolted in the direction of the fishmonger's.

'OI!' shouted PC Williams, swiftly leaping into action. 'Come back here now!' He pounced in their direction, but wasn't quick enough. The Shalloo siblings had already dashed through the narrow doorway, and once inside, the fishmonger's apprentice slammed it closed behind them. Orinthia watched as, with trembling hands, he turned the key in the lock before bolting and double-bolting the latches. At closer glance, he was probably not much older than she was, although his tired, sunken eyes suggested otherwise.

'Thanks!' panted Orinthia, trying to catch her breath. Fists pounded at the door as they followed the fishmonger's apprentice down the corridor beyond. They were surrounded by icy crates laden with fish and seafood. The pong was overwhelming, but being in close proximity to a few smelly sardines was definitely preferable to being caught by the angry mob outside.

The Shalloo siblings scampered along behind their rescuer, unable to believe their luck. 'You saved our lives back there,' Orinthia called out. 'What's your name?'

'It's Noah,' the boy said over his shoulder. 'But we really haven't got time for pleasantries. Those locks aren't gonna hold for long!' He nodded back to the door which, by the sound of it, was now being struck from the other side with something large and heavy, causing the chains to rattle and the hinges to shudder.

At the far end of the corridor, Noah stopped. 'OK, down here,' he said urgently, shifting a wheeled shelving unit full of dried fish in sealed tubs and unlocking a small door beyond. He opened it up to reveal the inky black mouth of a tunnel. A gust of ocean-cold air whooshed forth from its depths, bringing with it a fetid, briny stench that made Orinthia's stomach turn.

'W-w-what's down there?' Séafra stuttered, peering into the gloom. His words echoed through the darkness, bouncing around the cavernous walls.

'It's a smuggler's tunnel,' Noah replied. 'A secret one, leading down to the docks.' He reached for a lantern hanging on a hook above the lintel before taking a box of matches from his pocket. He struck one and held it to the lantern's wick, the resulting flame illuminating the low, curving ceilings overhead. 'Pirates used to use it to sneak contraband from their ships into the city. Now we only use it occasionally to transport our fish up from the boats.'

'Wow . . . thank you,' said Orinthia again, not really knowing what to say as she ducked into the darkness after Séafra. Everything had happened so quickly. One minute this boy was offering them jellied eels, and the next he was helping them escape down a creepy smugglers' tunnel!

'You're not going to send the police down after us though, are you?' probed Séafra.

'Pah! Of course not!' Noah replied. 'I'd run away too if I had somewhere else to go and a few pennies in my pocket. I'm fed up of stinkin' like a sea bass!'

CRASH!

Someone landed a violent kick to the front door, making the children jump.

'OK, you *really* need to go now!' urged Noah, handing Orinthia the lantern.

'But what about you?' said Orinthia. 'Aren't we going to get you into trouble?'

'Probably,' said Noah. 'But I'm used to it!' And with that, he pushed the Shalloo siblings into the smugglers' tunnel and locked the door behind them.

Orinthia heard the storage unit being dragged back into place.

She shuddered. Being down here was like being inside the belly of a whale – the stench of rotting molluscs hung thick in the air, and the ground squelched beneath her boots as she led the way further down. She dreaded to think what she was treading in – seaweed? Mackerel guts? She was almost glad that the light that Noah's lamp afforded them was so dim.

'Rinthi, we're in so much trouble, aren't we?' said Séafra as they headed off into the gloom. 'The police are saying we're criminals. What's going to happen to us?'

'We'll be OK,' said Orinthia, linking her arm through her brother's. 'As soon as the *Mollusca* leaves the dock we'll be on our way. Once we're in New York they'll never catch us. It's one of the busiest cities in the world.'

Orinthia couldn't be certain of this, of course, but she had to say something to calm her brother. After losing Gungho, he wasn't in the best state of mind, and it wouldn't take much for him to start giving up hope. Even though she'd once thought of herself as a brave, intrepid explorer, secretly she knew she couldn't do this without him.

The tunnel twisted and turned like a dark, mulchy river. A droplet of something plopped down on to Orinthia's head. She looked up – the curved stone ceiling was covered in slime, and dripping oozy, green globules. Just as she was thinking that her surroundings couldn't get more disgusting, something scuttled across her feet and she bristled, imagining the rats and mice and goodness knows what else that might be lurking in the shadows.

But as Orinthia's thoughts started to spiral, she heard something.

It was a loud blast, coming from not too far away.

She turned to Séafra, whose ears had also pricked up. 'Séa, was that a . . . ?'

'A foghorn?' her brother replied. 'Yes! I heard it too! It means that we must be close to the dock, right?'

Orinthia nodded, and the pair immediately picked up their pace. They tore through the tunnel, the cold water splashing up their legs, their footfalls echoing around them. With every step they took, the passage seemed to be widening, the air beginning to freshen. They turned a sharp corner and Orinthia felt relief flooding through her. Their passageway had opened up into a stone railway arch, framing the dock beyond as if it were a picture.

'We made it!' said Séafra, jumping up and down for joy. 'We made it! We made it!'

Not usually one to dampen anyone's spirits, but wary that they shouldn't speak too soon, Orinthia hung Noah's lamp on a hook next to the entrance to the tunnel and put a hand on her brother's shoulder. 'Let's not get too excited just yet, Séa. We need to go and check that the *Penny Black* is where we left it. And remember, the police are going to be looking for us everywhere, so keep your head down.'

Séafra nodded and they scampered over the damp earth, weaving through abandoned kegs and barrels and fishing nets. Once outside, they headed along the bank of the Thames, the sun now nowhere to be seen, and the sky a gloomy watercolour grey.

When they reached the dock, some of the boats they'd seen earlier on had now gone, and for a horrible moment Orinthia thought that the *Mollusca* might have set sail already too.

But she hadn't.

Smoke was billowing from her three funnels, and her red flag was flying high in the breeze like a beacon. The *Penny Black* was still on the gangway too, and as the Shalloo siblings pelted towards it, and clambered to safety, Orinthia had never felt so relieved.

22

At last, the children were on board RMS *Mollusca*, and as four blasts of the horn sounded somewhere above deck, Orinthia knew they had left the shore. From inside the *Penny Black* she bid London farewell and felt her body relax for what felt like the first time in hours.

It had been a bit of a rough journey from the dock into the hold. The *Penny Black* had been shoved, spun, dragged and flung from pillar to post, with Orinthia and Séafra being thrown around like laundry in a washing machine. At one point their world had gone completely topsy-turvy, and they'd had to claw on to the sides of the crate for dear life. To top it off, they'd been dropped into the cargo hold from a fair height, and had crashed to the ground with bone-shaking force. If any of the other passengers were expecting their possessions to be intact at the end of the voyage, they were going to be sorely disappointed. But the Shalloo siblings were finally on their way to New York, and the prospect of seeing Taber within a few days was worth the bumps to the head and bruised limbs and sore bottoms.

For their first night on board, the children didn't dare move from the safety of the *Penny Black*. They had been badly spooked by their encounter with the police and were terrified of being seen. What if the officers were on board? What if they were poised to search the hold? It was hard being cooped up again in such a cramped space – especially with the swaying and rolling of the vessel – but they couldn't take any more risks. But by the next evening, and with the last of their food now gone, Orinthia's hunger had begun to outweigh her fear. 'Come on, Séa,' she said, reaching for the padlock. 'It's been long enough; let's go and stretch our legs – we need to eat.'

'Really?' said Séafra, his face dropping. 'Is that wise, Rinthi? We're wanted criminals after all!'

'I know that, but we can't survive on thin air. According to Ophelia Pearhart's book, the voyage from London to New York takes about three and a half days by ship. That means we still have two days left. Can you go without food and water for another forty-eight hours?'

Séafra's grumbling stomach answered the question, and Orinthia couldn't help but think of Taber. *Is he rationing his supplies?* she wondered with a tightening chest. *Is he hungry?* She really hoped that the biscuits and fish paste and ham sandwiches were enough to keep his strength up.

Orinthia looked down at her wristwatch. It was quarter past nine. 'Come on, the kitchens will probably be closed for the evening, and hopefully there might be some leftovers hanging around.'

'OK,' said Séafra, warily. 'But I think we should just go there and then come straight back. I don't fancy another chase, thank you very much.'

Orinthia agreed, and having checked to see that the coast was clear, she hopped out of the *Penny Black*. The cargo hold was damp and fetid – a faintly lit cavern reeking of salt and algae and engine oil. Orinthia looked around. It was strange to think that they were actually below sea level. There were probably shoals of fish swimming only a few metres away from them; octopuses maybe, or even sharks! This didn't scare Orinthia though – it was the people on board the *Mollusca* that were their biggest threat at the moment.

Not taking any chances, she quickly hunkered down in the shadow of a large freight crate marked with the words 'THE DRIP-DROP LIQUOR CO. – HANDLE WITH CARE'. It seemed to be just one of many strange things that the *Mollusca* was transporting to America in its cargo hold. There were mailbags, of course, but also rolls of linoleum, a gramophone, pallets of soap and candles, bales of leather, and even a grand piano.

'OK, let's go,' said Orinthia, looking around for a way to the upper decks. 'But if it's busy we should keep at a distance from each other. Some of the passengers and crew might have seen our photographs on the wanted posters and they'll be keeping their eyes peeled for *two* children. If anyone does stop you, say that you're on board the ship with your parents. You have a cabin in first class, but you're exploring the ship while your mother and father finish their after-dinner coffees.'

Séafra nodded, and with the hoods of their duffel coats pulled up, they set off to clamber over the surrounding cargo. A rickety wooden ladder led up to the hatch in the ceiling, and they scampered up the rungs as deftly as possible, trying not to pay too much attention to the sensation of the steps giving way as the ship rose and fell.

Once they'd reached the top of the ladder, Orinthia pushed up the wooden hatch above, just the tiniest bit.

She listened carefully.

There was the whir of machinery, the sloshing of water through pipes, the humming of a generator, but she heard no evidence of people. 'I think this might be the engine room,' she whispered to Séafra. 'Let's go.' She pushed open the hatch to a blast of heat and the stench of fuel, and as she'd predicted, they found themselves in a vast engine room. It was a metallic maze of tanks, pumps and machinery, with copper pipes cross-hatching the ceiling, and levers and dials at every turn. Orinthia could feel the vibrations of the machines pulsing rhythmically through her body, the hum of white noise filling the air like static.

'Wow, this is incredible!' she whispered in awe, spinning around to take it all in. 'It's just like the engine room of the *Salty Maelstrom*, the ship that Ophelia Pearcart captained on her amazing voyage across the Indian Ocean!'

'Erm . . . didn't her ship capsize during that voyage?' asked Séafra.

'Well . . . yes. But Ophelia survived. And she only lost *one* finger to the great white!'

Séafra rolled his eyes. 'How encouraging.'

Orinthia was just about to offer her brother some more incredible facts about her hero's unfortunate encounter with the hungry shark, when a sudden *miaow*, followed by the sound of heavy footsteps on a nearby stairwell, stopped her in her tracks.

'Hey come back, you mangey mog!' came an angry voice. 'Animals ain't allowed in the engine room!'

There was a flash of ginger fur as a scruffy-looking cat sped past, and without needing to say a word, the Shalloo siblings quickly bolted behind a nearby boiler. They pulled themselves flush against its metal shell, holding their breaths and listening as the footsteps reached ground level.

'Come back now!' chided the cat's pursuer once more. 'You can't hide from me!'

Orinthia recognized the voice now. It belonged to Drake, one of the two crew members that had gone off to the Whiskered Kipper pub earlier on. He stopped not too far away from where the siblings were hiding and Orinthia felt her heart racing. She could see him now. His weathered face looked as if it had been carved from barnacles, and his hairy biceps were mapped with faded nautical tattoos – there were anchors, compasses, mermaids and a giant squid wrapping its tentacles around a human skull. 'Love' had been inked across the knuckles of his right fingers, the word 'Hake' across those of his left.

'Hey, Drake, have you found her?' came a second booming voice. This one was female but equally as hoarse: it was Duffel.

Drake was silent for a moment, obviously surveying his surroundings for the miaowing runaway. 'Nah, I can't see her. Probably fallen into the water tank. Oh well, if she drowns, she drowns. It ain't my responsibility to look after 'er.' His words echoed loudly around the engine room, bouncing from pipe to pipe and making Orinthia's breath hitch. What a horrible thing to say. That poor, poor cat.

'Oh, and by the way, I forgot to tell you,' shouted Duffel, 'the boss said that we should keep an eye out for them missing children everyone's talking about. They was spotted in London apparently, and the police think they might have somehow sneaked on board a ship to America.'

'What, you mean them urchins on the posters?' asked Drake.

'Yeah, that's them. Little scallywags. I dunno what they've done though. The police are keeping it all very hush-hush.'

'Well, you can tell the boss that they're not gonna to be sneaking down here,' said Drake. 'Not on my watch, that's for sure.'

Duffel laughed. 'You sure about that? You've just been outfoxed by a geriatric cat!'

Drake snarled. '*Ufff*, whatever. Come on, let's go up on deck.'

The pair retreated back up the metal stairwell, and as a door slammed behind them, Orinthia and Séafra sank to the floor.

'That was close,' said Orinthia, passing a hand over her forehead, which was now dripping with sweat.

'Too close,' Séafra replied. 'Do you think we should still go and look for food?'

Orinthia puffed out her cheeks, before letting out a long breath. 'Well, I guess we're going to have to do it at some point. But we'll have to be *extra* careful now. Straight to the kitchen, and then straight back again.'

She got up and brushed herself down, just as the ginger cat appeared from behind one of the engines. Duffel hadn't been wrong when she'd described it as geriatric! She was extremely scrawny, with matted fur which was balding in places, and from the state of her gnarled left ear, Orinthia suspected that she had definitely been in a few scraps in her time.

'Here, puss-puss,' Orinthia said softly, bending down and holding out a welcoming hand. 'Come on, don't be scared.' The cat came to her immediately, nuzzling up against her calf.

'Poor thing,' said Séafra, crouching down beside his sister. 'She must be the ship's cat. Looks as though she hasn't had a good meal in ages though.'

Orinthia ran a hand along the creature's back and she started to purr contentedly. 'Probably hasn't. Not if Drake and Duffel have anything to do with it. I tell you what, if we manage to find some food in the kitchens, maybe we could share some with her?'

'That's a good idea. A few sardines and a saucer of milk and she'll be much happier.' He extended a hand to the cat and she sniffed his fingers. 'What do you think, puss? You stay here and we'll try and bring you some food. Would you like that?'

The cat licked her lips and let out a loud miaow.

'Well, that's settled then,' said Orinthia. She nodded to a door on their right. 'Let's try through there.'

23

Stepping out from the engine room and into the main body of the ship was like going from night into day. The area they'd arrived in was like a floating palace, with lavish interiors and all sorts of beautiful embellishments.

But with so many passengers wandering around, Orinthia and Séafra needed to be careful. They pulled up their hoods once more, and set off in search of the kitchens with their heads down. They made their way through the ship's many corridors, skirting past elegant reception rooms, comfy lounges, smoking areas, cabins and even a Turkish bath!

The vessel was like nothing Orinthia had ever seen before, and she wished more than anything that they could wander around freely like the carefree children that crossed their paths. So when they found themselves in a grand hallway, she couldn't help but stop for a moment. It was incredible – its walls adorned with mahogany panels and its floor carpeted in opulent red. It was furnished with wicker chairs and soft leather settees, with potted palms adding a tropical touch with their lush green leaves.

'Wow,' said Orinthia, arching her neck and turning round to take it all in. 'This is so beautiful. Look at those stairs!' She pointed to the sweeping staircase which was rising up from the centre of the hallway, its balustrades crowned with ornamental cherubs. A large, ornate clock graced the landing, and above it all, the evening sunlight spilt in through a great glass dome. 'Imagine sliding down those bannisters! It would be like taking a ride on a helter-skelter!'

She was so swept up in the moment that she'd almost forgotten that they weren't meant to be loitering, and Séafra looked uneasy. 'Come on, Rinthi,' he said, pulling at her sleeve. 'I don't think we'll find the kitchen anywhere around here. It's much too posh.'

'You're right,' said Orinthia, shaking herself from her trance. 'I think we must have stumbled into first class.' She was just about to turn back the way they'd come when all of a sudden the scruffy ginger cat they'd met in the engine room shot past them. She bounded up the staircase and stopped at a door on the landing, before starting to viciously claw it, as if she wanted to be let in.

Orinthia looked closer. Instead of having a number on it like the other cabins they'd passed, this door had been embellished with a crown-shaped golden plaque. *Who sleeps in there?* Orinthia wondered. *Someone important, that's for sure.* Could it be a famous actress? Or the prime minister? Maybe the cat belonged to them and had been locked out!

Remembering Drake and Duffel's disdain for the poor creature, and fearing what might happen if the wretched pair got hold of her before she'd been reunited with her owner, Orinthia bounded up the plush carpeted steps.

'Rinthi, what are you playing at?' hissed Séafra from the bottom. 'Come back down, you're going to get us caught!'

Orinthia turned and whispered back. 'I think the cat is locked out of her cabin. I'm just going to see if her owners are inside—'

'Rinthi, for goodness' sake,' said Séafra, bounding up the stairs and putting a hand on his sister's shoulder. 'You can't be thinking of a cat right now. Someone's going to—'

He didn't get any further.

Orinthia had already knocked on the door, and when no reply came, she closed her hand around the gold doorknob and turned.

For a moment she could do nothing but gawp. The cabin was palatial – a sprawling, luxurious space screaming of riches. Cut-glass chandeliers hung overhead and a decorative frieze adorned panelled walls. A velvet chaise longue sat beneath an oversized porthole offering incredible views of the sea, and a dressing table was lined with all sorts of perfumes and potions.

The cat had already shot inside, dashing beneath the gargantuan four-poster bed at the far end of the room. It was swathed in heavy drapes, and dressed with silk sheets and a plethora of tasselled cushions.

'Wow, look at the size of that!' said Orinthia, as she laid eyes on it. 'Come on, Séa, let's try it out!'

'Rinthi, no!' Séafra piped up. 'What happens if someone comes in? The police are looking for us, remember?'

But Orinthia had already skipped across the room. She flopped back on to the bed and instantly let out a groan of delight. It couldn't be further from the hard floor of the wooden crate that they'd been travelling in. The pillows were feathery soft and the mattress so supportive that it felt almost as if she were floating. 'Séa, you *have* to try this,' she said, looking over to her brother. 'It's so comfy!'

'No!' he snapped sharply. 'We need to get out of here.'

'Just for a minute, and then we'll leave, I promise.'

Séafra looked over his shoulder nervously before caving. 'OK,' he said, shutting the door behind him and tiptoeing towards the bed. 'But just for a minute. And then we're going straight back to the *Penny Black*. I'm not even hungry any more.'

Orinthia moved up, and as Séafra lay back, his previous trepidations seemed to melt away.

'Nice, eh?' asked Orinthia knowingly.

'It's like lying on a cloud or something,' Séafra replied dreamily, stretching out his long legs.

'When I'm older I'm going to have a bed this size all for myself,' said Orinthia dreamily. 'So I can splay out like a starfish every night.'

'But where will your husband sleep?' asked Séafra.

'Husband?' said Orinthia with disdain, turning to face her brother. 'Famous explorers don't need husbands.' She thought for a moment. 'No, the only companions I want are a compass and map.'

Séafra rolled his eyes. 'So this journey hasn't put you off adventures then?'

'Are you joking? I'm just getting started.' She smiled. 'And what about you? What do you want to be when you're older?'

Séafra shrugged. 'I don't know. I've been thinking that maybe I might take over Grandad's business like Mum did.'

Orinthia raised an eyebrow in disapproval. 'Really, Séafra? You want to be a car salesman? You want to spend every minute of every day talking about tyres? You could be anything you want. An astronaut, an Olympic swimmer, an opera singer! You could even join me on some more of my expeditions if you wanted.'

'We'll see,' said Séafra, pulling himself up. 'Let's complete *this* adventure first, eh? And anyway, I think selling cars might be interesting. Remember how happy it used to make Grandad? It only seems like an awful job because it takes up so much of Mum's time and makes her so stressed.'

Orinthia nodded. He was right, she supposed. Grandad had been as passionate about engines and gearboxes as she was about exploring the world. And he definitely would have loved one of his grandchildren to follow in his footsteps.

'Anyway, I think we should probably get out of here now, Rinthi,' said Séafra, sitting up. 'If we get caught we might never make it to New York at all.'

'OK,' Orinthia replied. 'But before we leave . . .' She reached over to a box on the bedside table which had caught her eye. It was intricately embossed, and inside she found four rows of beautifully decorated sweets, each one sitting in a frilly paper case. 'Just one each. I'm sure whoever's room this is won't miss a couple.'

Not even Séafra could refuse, and as his gaze moved from one row to the next, his mouth began to water. He eagerly reached for a chocolate decorated with a pale-green swirl, and popped it in his mouth. 'Mmmm . . . peppermint,' he said with delight. 'Yum!'

Orinthia was just trying to decide between the hazelnut praline and the marzipan strawberry when the cabin door swung open.

'OI! WHAT ARE YOU TWO DOING IN HERE?'

The siblings leapt to their feet with a gasp.

A freckle-faced boy, probably not much older than Orinthia, was standing in the doorway with a scowl on his face. He was obviously a member of the ship's crew and judging by the bucket and mop he had in hand, he was on his way to scrub the decks. A blue handkerchief was knotted around his neck, and a flat cap was pulled down over wild auburn hair.

Orinthia and Séafra looked at each other, united in utter panic. How on earth were they going to explain themselves out of this?

24

'Well, I'm waiting,' said the boy sternly, striding into the room. His boots squelched with seawater as he walked, and he brought with him the smell of someone who hadn't had a bath in a while. 'You shouldn't be in here, you know. What's going on?'

'We were just . . . erm . . .' Orinthia began, her tongue in knots. 'We were just looking for the way up to the deck. Our mummy and daddy said we could explore, but we got lost.'

The boy raised an eyebrow. 'And you thought that having a snoop around in the royal suite would help you get your bearings, hmm?' He strode forwards and snatched the chocolate box from Orinthia's hands before putting it back in its place. 'A likely story!' The boy crossed his arms and glared at the siblings. 'So, why are you *really* in here?'

'We already told you,' said Séafra, sticking to their story. 'We took a wrong turn and got lost, that's all.' He made to move, pulling Orinthia with him. 'Come on, let's go, Mummy and Daddy will be waiting for us—'

The boy blocked their path.

'I don't believe you,' he said, looking them up and down. He studied each part of them intently, making Orinthia's skin prickle with goosebumps. Suddenly, a look of realization flashed in the boy's eyes and he sucked in a shocked breath.

'Hang on a minute!' he yelped. 'I thought you two looked familiar. You're them two runaways that the police are looking for, ain'tcha? I saw your mugs on the posters they put up at the dock. You're wanted criminals!'

Orinthia bristled. 'I-I don't know what you're talking about,' she said, trying to feign ignorance. But she knew as soon as the words left her lips that the boy wasn't going to buy them.

'Oh I think you do,' he said, rubbing his hands together with glee. 'They've been talking about you on the radio, too. That Inspector Snodgrass fella was being interviewed and he said he ain't going to stop searching until you're found.' He smirked. 'You wait until I tell

Captain Binnacle about this. I'll be promoted from cabin boy to first mate before we've even got to shore.'

'No, please don't!' Orinthia broke in, stepping forward. 'We're just trying to reach our little brother. It's a long story, but he's on his way to America by himself and we need to find him. He's only six.'

'I see,' said the boy, obviously intrigued.

'We're not causing any trouble,' said Séafra. 'And we can stay down in cargo from now on. You won't see us up here again.'

The boy considered this, chewing on the inside of his cheek as he thought. 'And what's it worth for me to keep quiet, hmm?'

Orinthia felt her teeth clench. 'You're blackmailing us?'

'Well, not the term I'd have used,' said the boy, cockily. 'More like . . . seeking a little sweetener.'

'But we don't have anything to give you,' snapped Orinthia, feeling herself getting angry. 'All we have is the clothes on our backs and the shoes on our feet. If you want my smelly socks you can have them by all means, but that's all I can offer.'

The boy sighed. 'Well, that's a shame. I wanted to help you out, but I guess I'll be telling the captain instead . . .'

He turned on his heel, but once more Orinthia stopped him in his tracks as she remembered she *did* have something else. 'WAIT! Wait a minute!' She reached into her coat pocket and brought out the silver pen that Bramwell had given her before they left. She didn't really want it any more anyway, not after he and the other Brock children had betrayed their trust so badly. 'What about this? Would this buy your silence?'

The boy took the pen, and even though he said nothing, Orinthia knew from the way his eyebrows were moving upwards that she'd piqued his interest. He held the pen up in front of him, and it glimmered in the moonlight streaming in through the porthole, reflecting the greens and blues of the sea.

'It's a very nice piece,' said Orinthia, pretending to know more about the pen's provenance than she really did. 'Probably worth quite a bit.'

The boy nodded silently, rolling the pen in his palm and inspecting every inch of it. 'And what does that say?' he asked, pointing to the inscription engraved on the lid.

Orinthia's brow furrowed. 'You mean . . . you can't read?'

The boy shook his head. 'Nope. Nor write. Wasn't

one for school, me. Left before I'd even learnt to spell my own name.'

Orinthia heard Séafra gasp, and she glared at him. It wasn't nice to draw attention to a person's short-comings, *especially* when said person had your life in their hands.

'It says, *Happily Ever After* . . .' said Orinthia, pointing to each of the words in turn. 'Like at the end of a fairy tale.'

The boy's eyes widened and he began to move his hand up and down as if to test the pen's weight. He seemed tempted by it and Orinthia pressed him for an answer. 'Well?' she said. 'Do you want it?'

The boy sighed heavily. 'Well, don't get me wrong, it *is* a nice pen. But I'm not really sure that it's worth me keeping quiet about something so important. You know the police are offering a *very* big reward to anyone that hands you over to the authorities . . .'

'Fine. Suit yourself,' snapped Orinthia, snatching back the pen and putting it back into her pocket. She wasn't in the mood for bartering with this horrible boy and, even if he *had* accepted the pen, she'd started to suspect that he probably wouldn't have kept his word anyway. She grabbed Séafra by the arm – they needed to get a head start and find a good hiding place, fast!

'Hang on! Hang on!' called the boy. 'Don't get all uppity.' He thought for a moment, scratching his chin. 'How about, as well as you giving me that pen, you teach me to read and write as well?'

Orinthia wheeled round to face the boy once more. She narrowed her eyes, returning his stare as boldly as she could. 'Really?'

The boy nodded. 'Really. I can't go my whole life not knowing my bowels from my continents, can I?'

'You mean your vowels from your consonants?' said Séafra.

'Yeah, that's the one! It would be quite nice to be able to read a book properly and not just look at the pictures on the cover. So, what do you say? *You* let me have that pen and give me some lessons, and *I* won't tell nobody that you're on board. In fact, I might even sneak you a bit of grub, too.'

Orinthia didn't know what to do. Should they trust this boy? Would he really keep schtum if they did as he asked? She glanced over at Séafra, whom she could tell was wary, but really, they didn't have much choice.

'Well?' said the boy, readjusting his cap. 'We got a deal?'

'OK,' said Orinthia tentatively. 'But we won't have

time to teach you everything about reading and writing before we get to America.'

'That's all right, we can make a start at least.' The boy thought for a moment. 'In fact, I clock off in about an hour. Why don't I come down to you then and we can make a start?'

'OK,' said Orinthia, holding out a hand for the cabin boy to shake. 'I'm Orinthia, by the way. And this is my brother, Séafra.'

'I'm Mog,' the boy replied, returning a hand to seal the deal. It was rough and covered in blisters.

'Nice to meet you, Mog. I'm glad we could come to an arrangement.'

'And you won't tell anyone about us?' asked Séafra, warily. 'You promise?'

Mog nodded, the fierceness in his face that they'd witnessed only a few minutes before completely gone. 'Sailor's promise. It'll actually be nice to have you around. I get so bored of spending all of my time with the rest of the crew. All they want to talk about is grog and girls! Bunch of barnacle brains, the lot of them!'

Just then a miaowing came from beneath the bed and the ginger cat poked her head from under the valance.

'Sally! What on earth are you doing in here?' Mog exclaimed, quickly grabbing the creature by the scruff of the neck and scooping her up on to his chest. 'What have I said about going into the cabins, eh?'

'She's yours?' Orinthia asked, having almost forgotten that the cat was the reason she and Séafra were in the cabin in the first place.

'She's the ship's cat. Captain Binnacle got her to catch vermin, but she ain't got the speed to even chase a dormouse, let alone run after rodents. Unsinkable Sally, the crew call her, on account of . . . well, I'm sure you can guess.

'Anyway, I best get going. Don't want the coxswain on my back again.' He moved to the door before turning and nodding to the box of chocolates on the bedside table with a wry smile. 'Oh, and by the way, the pink ones are the best.'

25

'Well, you two really *have* had an adventure,' said Mog as he sat on an upturned crate in the cargo hold with Orinthia and Séafra later that evening. Unsinkable Sally was curled up on his lap, her tail swept around her body as she purred. 'You're a right pair of daredevils, ain'tcha!'

Orinthia smiled. As they'd agreed, Mog had come to meet them after he'd finished his duties, and they'd been telling him all about their miraculous journey so far. With the *Mollusca* rocking gently through the waves, they'd talked all about their life at home, Grandy Brock and his children, the Mailbox Menagerie at Tupenny Mill, and finally Taber's disappearance. As Orinthia relayed their journey in the *Penny Black*, Mog's jaw had dropped further and further open, and even she had to admit that the words coming out of her mouth seemed almost unbelievable. A few weeks ago they'd been dreading the summer holidays and the boring days at home, and now they were on an international expedition searching for their lost brother.

'I can't believe you actually posted yourselves!' said Mog. 'You're mighty brave, that's for sure. I've been out on some pretty rough seas but I don't think I'd be courageous enough to stick a stamp on my head and send myself to the other side of the world!'

Orinthia smiled proudly, and even Séafra seemed to be enjoying receiving praise from their new-found friend.

'I love the sound of those animal posties, too,' Mog continued, in response to which Unsinkable Sally let out a loud snore. Mog laughed and rubbed her belly. 'Don't worry, I'm not getting any ideas. You're not going to have to do any work, you lazy thing!'

'And what's *your* story, Mog?' asked Séafra. 'You said that you're a cabin boy?'

'That's right,' said Mog. 'I do a bit of everything, really. Moppin' the decks, running food from the galley to the mess, scraping dishes in the scullery. All pretty miserable tasks, but at least it means I have some pennies in my pocket at the end of the month.'

'And how did you end up on board?' asked Orinthia.

Mog bristled awkwardly. 'Well . . . erm . . . after I quit school my parents said that I couldn't just mope around at home, so they sent me off to sea. Keeps me out of trouble . . . supposedly!' He looked to the floor before quickly changing the subject. 'Anyway, shall we make a start on my lesson? I brought my new pen.'

'Yes, of course,' said Orinthia, sitting up straight. She reached for the notebook she'd packed in her duffel bag, ripped out a piece of paper and began to write out some letters. 'So I take it you know your alphabet?' she asked Mog. 'Your A-B-Cs?'

Mog looked to the floor and shook his head. 'Nope. Don't know none of it. Just looks like gobbledegook to me.'

Séafra gasped again. 'What? Even Taber knows his A-B-Cs!'

Mog's face saddened. 'Oh. Does that mean I'm a lost cause?'

'No, of course not!' said Orinthia, glaring at her brother. 'We'll just need to start from the very beginning, that's all. You just let me know if I'm going too fast, OK?'

Mog nodded. 'Oh . . . and do I have to call you "Miss", like we used to in school?'

'No!' Orinthia laughed as she pictured herself as a cantankerous old schoolmistress, striding around the classroom dishing out detentions. '*Definitely* not!'

The next hour passed by in a haze of letters, serifs, ampersands and full stops. Mog wasn't the fastest of learners (and had held the pen upside down for the first ten minutes), but he was enthusiastic and eager to improve.

'So how have I done? Are these letters OK?' he asked, pointing to his notepad as the lesson came to an end.

Orinthia looked down at the cabin boy's work. His sheet was an inky mess, with only a few lopsided 'A's followed by some very squashed-looking 'B's. 'Erm . . . yes . . .' she lied, trying to sound encouraging. 'You've made a . . . bold start.'

Mog could obviously sense that she was lying, and he threw down his pen in frustration. 'I give up!' he said, before crossing his arms with a huff. 'It's too difficult. I can't even remember which letter is meant to come after B.'

'It's the one that looks like a half-moon,' said

Orinthia, taking the pen and writing out the letter 'C' a few times. 'Remember?'

Mog huffed, his face forlorn. 'Maybe I should just stick to scrubbing decks.'

'Don't be silly, you've done really well,' said Orinthia. She gave her brother a gentle nudge. 'Hasn't he, Séafra?'

Séafra coughed. 'Erm . . . yes, of course. Really well.'

'Well, if you say so,' said Mog with a shrug, though Orinthia thought he looked secretly pleased. 'Anyway, we should probably call it a day. I've got to be up at sunrise to polish the captain's shoes.' He pushed back his crate before brushing himself down and straightening his hat. 'Oh, and I almost forgot,' he said, reaching into his bag. He brought out a small loaf of brown bread and a chunk of ham, as well as a bottle of milk thick with cream. 'It's not much, and the bread's as solid as a shark's fin, but it should fill a hole.'

'Oh Mog, thank you,' said Orinthia, taking the food with delight. 'That's so kind of you. It looks delicious.'

'Ha! I wouldn't go that far,' said Mog. 'Not compared to what that posh lot up in first class get for dinner. You should see what they're eating the night after tomorrow – it's the last night of the voyage and they're throwing a special banquet in the dining saloon. Cook's doing potted shrimp, poached salmon, lamb, duckling. And for pudding, a pineapple royale!'

'A pineapple *what*?' asked Séafra.

'*Royale*,' Mog replied. 'Meringue, fresh pineapple, orange sherbet and coconut cream.' He let his tongue loll from his mouth, making a drooling sound.

'Wow, I'd love to see what a banquet looks like,' said Orinthia, picturing the scene. 'The tables, the glassware, the chandeliers, the decorations . . .'

'Me too,' said Séafra. 'But mainly just for the pudding! That pineapple royale sounds amazing. I wish I could try some.'

Mog had gone suspiciously quiet, and Orinthia knew from the glint in his eyes that he was contemplating something. 'Well, there is *one* way to make that possible,' he said mischievously.

Séafra looked confused. 'Really? How?'

Mog looked around before bringing his voice down to a whisper. 'Well, what if I said that I could get hold of a couple of the uniforms that the first-class waiting staff wear?'

'And?' said Orinthia, not catching his drift.

'Well, you and Séafra could put them on and pretend to be a waiter and waitress for the evening. You'd have access to the dining saloon and get to see everything that's going on at the banquet!'

'But what about the other party guests?' asked Séafra. 'What if someone recognizes us from the wanted posters?'

Mog threw down his hands dismissively. 'Séafra, relax! Take it from me – those posh toffs don't so much as look the crew in the eye. Act like we're invisible most of the time.'

'But where will you get the uniforms from?' asked Séafra.

'My sister works in the galley, so I know where they keep the spares.'

'You have a sister?' asked Séafra.

'Oh, yeah. She's my twin,' he said with a scowl. 'Winnie, her name is. Just imagine a more annoying version of me with longer hair and cleaner nails. A right pain in the bum, she is.'

'Like *most* sisters,' said Séafra, immediately attracting a painful punch to the arm from Orinthia. 'Joking!'

'So, what do you think?' asked Mog, eyeballing the siblings expectantly.

Orinthia looked to Séafra. 'What do you think, Séa?'

Séafra grinned. 'If it means I get to try some of that pineapple royale, then definitely yes!'

26

The next day passed with little incident. Mog visited a second time, bringing down another food parcel and the uniforms as promised. For Séafra there was a stiff white jacket with tails, alongside a pair of black trousers, bow tie and gloves. Orinthia received a black dress, complete with black stockings, a frilly white apron and a white lace-edged headband. The three of them had giggled as the uniforms had been tried on, the Shalloo siblings waddling around as if they were penguins in their monochrome attire.

Later, Orinthia had helped Mog with his reading and writing once more – this time concentrating on punctuation. On more than one occasion, Mog had mistaken an apostrophe for a full stop, and had frequently mixed up his commas and question marks, but Orinthia couldn't fault his effort.

'I'll be readin' *War and Peace* in no time!' he'd exclaimed at the end of the lesson.

And then it was the final evening of the voyage – and at last it was time for Orinthia and Séafra to don their disguises and go up on deck.

'Wow, it's so fancy!' whispered Orinthia, as she and Séafra loitered with their platters of vol-au-vents and canapés later that evening. The party was already in full swing and the deck was buzzing with first-class guests.

It was like nothing Orinthia had ever seen before. The deck had been decorated with flowers and balloons, and strings of little paper lanterns twinkled softly against the slowly rising moon. At the bar, groups of moustachioed gents in blazers sat drinking glasses of port, and next to the grand piano, elderly ladies sat listening to the dulcet sounds of classical concertos. Elegant women were milling around in cocktail dresses, quaffing champagne while admiring each other's jewellery. The glasses which they held were so thin and delicate that every time they brushed against one of the ladies' lipsticked mouths, Orinthia feared they might shatter.

'They're the poshest people I've ever seen,' Séafra replied. 'Have you seen the amount of diamonds the women are wearing? And they're so huge! The size of rocks!'

The jewellery was no doubt beautiful, but Orinthia thought that it would be pretty difficult to do anything other than sip champagne wearing such heavy, ostentatious pieces. No exploring, no climbing trees, no splashing around in the sea. Surely these women must get bored of just . . . well . . . looking pretty?

It's really nice to be outside again, though, Orinthia thought, closing her eyes a little as the wind tousled her hair. She took in a lungful of fresh, salty air and immediately felt her shoulders soften.

'And what little morsels are you two serving, *hmmm*?' came a haughty voice from behind. 'Anything exciting?'

Orinthia turned to find an Indian lady wearing an emerald-green sari, arm in arm with a horsey-looking woman draped in a fox-fur stole. They swooped in with their eyes on the children's trays of canapés, without as much as a smile.

'These ones are . . . erm . . . smoked salmon parcels with cream cheese and dill,' Orinthia replied as demurely as she could muster.

'And mine are asparagus tartlets,' said Séafra, pointing to his offering.

Before the guests had arrived, Cook had quickly briefed all of the waiting staff on what was on their individual trays. Luckily for Orinthia and Séafra, with all the pots and pans that were bubbling away on the stoves, she was far too distracted to pay them any proper attention. The siblings had even managed to pop a couple of the canapés in their mouths, just to make sure they knew *exactly* how they tasted. It was only professional!

'*Ewww*,' the lady in the stole exclaimed in disgust. 'Smoked salmon and asparagus – how common. You're not serving any caviar this evening?'

Orinthia gulped. She had no idea what caviar was, let alone whether they were serving it. She looked to Séafra, who was equally perplexed. 'I-I think it's coming later,' she guessed. 'With dessert.'

'With dessert?' quipped the Indian lady. 'How very avant-garde! I've never had fish eggs as a sweet before, but there's a first time for everything, I suppose . . .'

Realizing her mistake, Orinthia felt her cheeks starting to burn as the pair of women wandered off into the crowd, tittering.

Orinthia sagged. Maybe pretending to be a waitress hadn't been such a good idea – she didn't really fit in here, did she? Another mistake and she might give the game away.

She was turning to Séafra to suggest they escape back down to the *Penny Black* when a shadow crossed over her.

Before Orinthia understood what was happening, a burly arm had swept around her neck. She dropped her tray of canapés but nobody appeared to notice – the party was full of loud conversation and a swing band had started up on the dais.

'Gotcha, you little squid!' A familiar voice hissed into her ear. She recognized it from the docks, when they'd been hiding in the *Penny Black*, and later in the engine room. *Drake*. His breath was hot on her neck, stinking of fish, and within the blink of an eye he was dragging her backwards, away from the party.

'Let me go!' hissed Orinthia, kicking and squirming. She could barely move under the man's vice-like hold, but she managed to twist her body just enough to see that a woman had also arrived on the scene. *Duffel*. She had an arm locked around Séafra's waist and a hand over his mouth. Séa was wriggling like an eel, trying to call out from under the gag of her calloused palm, but with little success.

Seeing her brother like that gave Orinthia a fresh spurt of energy. 'LET. US. GO!' she shrieked, her shoes slipping and skidding across the slippery wood as she tried to kick out. 'LET. US. GO!'

Drake clapped his hand over her mouth to silence her, but Orinthia bit down hard on his fingers. He recoiled in pain, and with a loud yelp he stumbled backwards into a group of unsuspecting partygoers, bringing Orinthia down with him.

'*Arghhh!*' screeched a turbaned woman, tipping a glass of red wine over her cream-coloured gown.

'Good grief!' bellowed a monocled gentleman as his prawn vol-au-vent went flying into the sea.

Momentarily free and with chaos ensuing, Orinthia seized her chance. She began to claw her way to safety, digging her fingers into the salt-encrusted deck and pulling herself along on her tummy.

But before she'd even managed to move a few metres, Drake reached out and grabbed hold of her ankle. 'Oh, I don't think so!' he snarled, yanking her back towards him by her legs. 'You're goin' nowhere, missy! NOWHERE!' He looked to his left. 'You got hold of the boy, Duffel?'

'Oh yes!' Duffel replied, tightening her grip on Séafra with vigour. 'The police are gonna give us a fat reward when we hand you over. You're bounty, you are. Wanted criminals. The two of you are gonna spend the rest of your young lives in a borstal!'

By now the rest of the deck was completely silent and everyone was glaring in the Shalloo siblings' direction. The band had stopped playing, and the elderly ladies were sat on the edges of their seats as if they had front-row tickets at the theatre.

'DRAKE, DUFFEL! BRING THEM TO ME!'

A voice hacked through the salty air, and Drake stopped in his tracks. Without loosening his grip for a second, he whirled Orinthia around and she found herself across the deck from a sharp-cheeked man with piercing green eyes. He was dressed in a blue double-breasted jacket which was embellished with a row of shiny gold buttons, and two gold epaulettes accentuated his already broad shoulders. He was taller than anyone else on board, the thick mast of his body making the rest of the crew look like tiny winkles in comparison.

Orinthia felt the blood rushing from her face. There was no doubt about it – this was Captain Binnacle. And they were really in trouble now.

27

'So it's true,' crowed the captain, looking the Shalloo siblings up and down. 'We *do* have a couple of stowaways on board.'

Séafra's captor grinned widely, throwing back her flaxen hair with pride.

'So you thought you'd try and get free passage on board *my* ship, hmm?' asked the captain, meandering towards them. He walked with a swagger, with one hand on his hip.

Orinthia had no idea what to say.

'Well . . . I'm waiting!' snapped Captain Binnacle, stomping down a heavy boot. 'Explain yourselves!'

Orinthia's mouth began to tremble. 'W-we're just trying to get to America,' she said.

Captain Binnacle nodded. 'Well, you've made quite the name for yourselves. The whole world's looking for you, you know. And there's a handsome reward for anyone who finds you. Give me one good reason why I shouldn't hand you over to Inspector Snodgrass, hmmm?'

Orinthia gulped, looking around. She was desperate to lay eyes on a friendly face – someone who might come to their aid. But no one spoke up. The party guests offered nothing but contempt, their mouths twisted in disapproval, their arms crossed with scorn.

'Well?' said the captain, raising an eyebrow.

Orinthia opened her mouth, hoping that something might spill out which would convince the captain to give them safe passage, when a familiar voice stopped her short.

'Pa, no! Please don't hurt them – they've done nothing wrong!'

Orinthia looked across deck to see Mog bursting through one of the hatches. He had obviously been running, and was now doubled over, trying to catch his breath.

Orinthia looked to Séafra in confusion. Had Mog just called Captain Binnacle *Pa*? The severe captain of the *Mollusca* was his . . . father?

'Pa, just let them be,' Mog continued, panting. 'They're not criminals, they're my friends.'

There was a sharp intake of breath from each of the party guests.

'Mog, what on earth are you talking about?' said Captain Binnacle, confused. 'What is the meaning of this?'

Mog edged towards his father, still breathless. 'I mean, you should let them stay on board. They're not causing any harm. And they've been teachin' me to read, Pa.'

Captain Binnacle scoffed, affronted. 'I don't care if they've been teaching you to do one-handed cartwheels, sonny. You've jeopardized the reputation of this vessel, and the safety of its passengers. How long have you known that we had two dangerous criminals on board?'

'Pa, look at them! Don't tell me that you actually believe they're dangerous. They just want to find their little brother and—'

'I don't care!' snapped the captain. 'They shouldn't be on board this ship, and that's the end of it.'

Mog looked over to Orinthia and Séafra, tears glistening in his eyes. 'I'm . . . I'm so sorry. I didn't mean for this to happen. It was Winnie, my sister. She saw me taking the uniforms from the kitchen yesterday and got suspicious. I didn't know it at the time, but she followed me down to the cargo hold and overheard our plan. She knew you'd be here tonight, and organized for Drake and Duffel to be waiting for you—'

'It's your own fault, Mog,' a smug voice cut in. 'You had it coming to you, sneaking around like that.'

Orinthia looked up and almost did a double take. Standing at the top of the hatch that Mog had just appeared from was a girl with long red hair, her arms crossed firmly across her chest. She was the spit of Mog, and it would have been difficult to tell the difference between the two if it weren't for the long plaits which hung down her back.

She crossed the deck towards their father, coming to stand by his side. 'I did the right thing, didn't I, Pa?' she asked, looking up at him with a saccharine self-righteousness. 'I thought it was the proper thing to do.'

'Oh shut up, Winnie!' said Mog angrily. 'You just like being a little snitch!' His cheeks were red and he was trying his hardest to stop himself from crying. 'I hate you! I HATE YOU!'

Captain Binnacle's face darkened. 'Your sister did what any good crew member would have done, Mog.' He put a hand on his daughter's shoulder. 'No one gets away with sneaking aboard a vessel under the command of Captain Nelson Binnacle! Imagine if the American authorities had found these children hiding on board at the dock. I'd never be allowed to set sail again.'

He looked to Duffel and Drake. 'Keep the children tied up until we get to shore. And don't take your eyes off them.'

Orinthia gulped, not knowing what to do as Duffel and Drake started to manoeuvre her and Séafra towards the hatch leading down into the ship. She looked over to Mog, who seemed equally flummoxed, raking his fingers through his auburn mop. Winnie, on the other hand, was obviously enjoying herself, her chin jutting forth with smugness as she oversaw proceedings.

For a moment, all seemed lost.

Orinthia felt her body crumple, resigning herself to the fact that she and Séafra were going to be handed over to the police as soon as they reached shore. The fact that Drake and Duffel were already discussing how they were going to spend their reward money only added to her panic.

'I'm gonna get myself some new tattoos,' Drake said, tightening his grasp on Orinthia. 'Some *really* nasty-lookin' ones. And if there's any left then I'll have myself a few flagons of grog and one of them nice pies at the Whiskered Kipper.'

Duffel considered this before saying, 'Nah, it'll be a nice new pair of boots for me, that's for sure—'

But then it happened.

As if from nowhere a loud *squawk* came from above, and Orinthia craned her neck skywards. A bird was circling high above them, silhouetted against the sky in the evening light. Its wings were flapping so fast that they were little more than a white blur, and it looked as if it were coming straight towards them.

The children looked at each other.

'No!' Orinthia began. 'Is that . . . ?'

'It . . . it can't be,' replied Séafra, obviously sensing her thoughts.

But as the bird dipped, and the siblings caught sight of the yellow bucket-shaped beak, they knew it was their beloved baby pelican. He'd found them!

'Gungho!' squealed Séafra as the bird dived towards the boat. 'Gungho, you're back!'

On seeing the children's captors, the little pelican let out a battle cry of a *squawk*. He swooped down with his webbed feet outstretched, and like a plane coming in to land, he locked his eyes on Duffel. The sailor flinched but Gungho landed with a thump on her head, and immediately began pecking at her eyes and ears, his wings beating aggressively against her face.

'Oi! Get off me, you devil!' shouted Duffel, momentarily releasing her grip on Séafra's arms in order to shield her face. Free from his shackles, and seizing his chance, Séafra quickly bolted across the deck. He collided head first with Captain Binnacle, who went flying into a couple of nearby barrels. Orinthia watched in amazement as her brother then broke into a sprint, barging through the crowd of confused party guests to the quarterdeck before disappearing down a hatch.

The whole ship seemed to gasp, eyes fixed on the captain as he rubbed his head and sat up, his epaulette askew. Unnoticed – except, perhaps, by Orinthia – Mog slipped after Séafra.

'Well don't just stand there, Duffel, you numb-skull!' shouted Captain Binnacle from the floor, pink as a prawn with embarrassment. 'After him! After the boy, now!'

Dumbfounded, and with her face scratched and bloody from Gungho's attack, the sailor quickly righted herself.

'Run, Séa, run!' encouraged Orinthia, shouting towards the hatch in the hope her brother could hear her. Gungho, meanwhile, had swooped back up on to a tall steel mast.

'Ha! And where's he going to run to?' mocked Captain Binnacle, finally pulling himself to his feet. He limped forward, straightening his hat. 'In case you've forgotten, we're in the middle of the Atlantic. There's nowhere to hide. Duffel will find him in no time.'

Orinthia looked out at the vast expanse of blue-black surrounding them, and felt her heart sink. He was right. Despite Gungho's intervention, she and Séafra were stuck.

28

'Where is he?' bellowed the captain after ten minutes had passed. 'Where's the boy?' Duffel had yet to return with Séafra, and he was growing impatient, pacing back and forth.

Orinthia's hands had been pinned behind her back by Drake, but after several minutes of waiting, he too appeared to be tiring – his grip loosening slightly around her wrists. They'd moved to a more secluded area of the deck so the partygoers could resume their celebrations. Every second Séafra remained below deck, Orinthia felt her hope dwindling. But after a few more minutes, a flash of movement caught Orinthia's eye. She looked up to see Gungho taking to the sky. The pelican had been watching over her from the mast, but now he wheeled in the air and swooped with purpose to a spot behind her.

But where was he heading? She was at the railing, and behind her was . . . the sea!

She glanced over her shoulder and looked down, and to her absolute surprise, she saw the *Penny Black* bobbing amongst the waves like a tiny escape raft. Inside it was Séafra, with his duffel bag flung across one shoulder, and her knapsack over the other. He was using a broom to hold the crate against the side of the ship, and was beckoning at her to jump. Gungho had flapped down and landed proudly on his head.

'There's no use looking down there,' crowed Captain Binnacle. 'You *could* try escaping overboard of course, but you'll be sleeping with the fishies before too long! I'm sure the electric eels would be more than happy with a bit of young flesh for their supper.'

'We'll see about that!' Orinthia said determinedly, and summoning every ounce of bravery in her being, she swung her legs over the railings and launched herself over the side of the *Mollusca*. It was terrifying but exhilarating – the cold wind hacking against her skin as she plummeted, the spray showering her with crystals of salt. She landed feet first in the *Penny Black* with a *thump*, sending the tiny vessel rocking back and forth.

'Rinthi, are you OK?' said Séafra, panicked. 'You haven't hurt yourself, have you?'

Orinthia, slightly dazed but fine, shook her head.

'Oh Rinthi, I didn't know what else to do. Mog and I couldn't launch any of the proper lifeboats. They were just too heavy. The *Penny Black* was all we could manage.'

'Séafra, you did brilliantly!' Orinthia cut in. 'But we need to get this thing moving under its own steam, and fast. Did you pick up any oars?'

Séafra nodded at his broom and then at another propped against the side of the crate. Orinthia snatched it up. She didn't know how long the crate was going to hold, but considering the circumstances, it was their only hope of escape. They had to start rowing. Land shouldn't be far, since there had only been a few hours of sailing left on the *Mollusca* anyway!

'HEY!' bellowed a loud, angry voice from the deck above. 'Come back here this instant!'

Orinthia and Séafra looked up to find Captain Binnacle leaning over the side of the *Mollusca*, his jaw nearly touching the deck.

Mog appeared by his side clutching Unsinkable Sally, and as he laid eyes on the Shalloo siblings in their makeshift escape raft, he beamed. 'Row!' he shouted, flapping his arms frantically. 'Follow the setting sun to the west, and don't stop until you reach New York! It's not too far off now. You can get there!'

'No!' shouted Captain Binnacle, smashing his fist on to the railings, his brow darkening. 'Stop what you're doing immediately! Stop, I say!'

'Ha! I don't think so!' shouted Séafra, with a look of steely determination in his eyes that Orinthia had never seen before. He plunged his oar into the inky water, and with a loud groan, he eased the *Penny Black* out into the waters. 'New York here we come!'

'Woohoo!' shouted Mog, as the engines of the *Mollusca* propelled it away from the now-adrift *Penny Black*. 'Just don't stop rowing! I'm going to miss you both!'

'We'll miss you too!' Orinthia shouted, as they drifted further and further away from the steamship. 'And don't give up on your bowels and your continents!'

Through the waves the siblings pushed, throwing their backs and shoulders into every movement as the *Mollusca* receded into the distance. Even if Captain Binnacle ordered the ship after them, by the time it slowed and turned, finding the siblings on the ocean would be like looking for a needle in a haystack.

The cold spray of the waves doused their faces, the saltiness catching at the back of their throats, but at least the sea was relatively calm. Gungho circled above their heads, and for a while they didn't talk at all, concentrating all of their efforts into getting away from Captain Binnacle and his dastardly crew.

It was only after an hour, and when the *Mollusca* was nowhere to be seen, that Orinthia and Séafra lifted their makeshift oars from the water and flopped back into the crate, exhausted.

'Well, the party turned out to be fun!' said Séafra, with a wry smile.

Orinthia snorted. 'Probably the most excitement those posh guests have had in years, stuffy old snobs!'

'I can't believe Mog's father was the captain of the *Mollusca*, though,' Séafra said.

'No wonder he wasn't very talkative when we asked him about his background.' Orinthia lay back, and patted her stomach. 'Anyway, have we got any of that dry bread left in my knapsack? I'm starving!'

'Oh, I think we can do better than a bit of dry bread,' said Séafra cheekily. He reached into the bag's front pocket and pulled out the half-eaten box of chocolates they'd found in the royal suite. 'Ta-daaaa! Whoever's room it is clearly hasn't touched any since we were last there – so I'm sure they won't be missed.'

'Séafra, you absolute hero!' said Orinthia, feeling herself beginning to drool at the mere thought of what was inside. 'Did you really sneak back into the royal suite?'

Séafra nodded proudly. 'Mog and I sneaked in there to hide from Duffel, knowing it would be empty because of the banquet – it was too good an opportunity to waste.'

The pair dug in, and even though their lips and fingers were encrusted with salt, they didn't let that detract from the deliciousness of the chocolatey treats. For the next hour they watched the moon floating through the sky as they feasted on caramels and creams, butterscotch and brittle. Orinthia's particular favourite was an unctuous white chocolate sphere, and she let it melt across her tongue, savouring every bit of its velvety sweetness. Even Gungho joined in with the celebrations, albeit feasting on the shimmering silver mackerel which he'd caught in his beak pouch. It was so good to see the bird once more, and Orinthia couldn't wait for him to be reunited with Taber as soon as they reached New York.

For a while, nothing could dampen the children's spirits. The American coast was in sight, and as long as the sea stayed calm and they didn't veer off in the wrong direction, they'd be there by morning!

But just as Orinthia was considering closing her eyes to take a little nap, something rumbled overhead.

'Rinthi, what was that?' said Séafra, his posture spiking as he turned his gaze skywards. 'It-it wasn't thunder . . . was it?'

Orinthia looked up and gasped. Gungho had shot into the air, his wings flapping furiously. Within the blink of an eye the sky had darkened and all of a sudden it felt claustrophobically close. It was whirling with metallic swirls of purple and grey, angry-looking clouds closing in quickly. A droplet of rain fell on to Orinthia's forehead, and as another rumble of thunder rang through the air, it quickly began to pour.

'Oh no!' whimpered Séafra, shielding himself from the rain and looking to his sister in terror. His hair was already sopping wet, sticking flat against his face. 'What now?'

Orinthia didn't know the answer. The waves were growing by the minute, and bolts of lightning were splitting the sky into pieces. The rain was coming down in shards, and she could already feel ice-cold water swilling around her ankles. There was no way the *Penny Black* was going to last for much longer in these conditions.

But she couldn't let Séafra see how scared she was. She had to stay brave for the both of them. 'Séafra, listen to me!' she shouted over the din. 'We need to hold on to the sides of the crate and keep our heads down. Whatever we do, we can't let go, OK?'

Séafra nodded sheepishly and did what he was told. The two children hunkered down, grasping so hard on to the sides of the *Penny Black* that their knuckles turned white. Orinthia could feel her wet clothes clinging to her like slimy, wet fish skin, her hair plastered across her cheeks.

'Rinthi, I'm scared!' yelped Séafra as they crested an especially large wave and came crashing down with a splash. 'We're going to drown!'

'It's going to be fine!' said Orinthia, frantically trying to scoop some of the rising water out with her hands. But it was coming in faster than she could bail it out, and the *Penny Black* began to tilt. Orinthia persisted, wiping sea spray from her eyes as she tried to steady the vessel. 'The storm won't last long, and then we can—'

The words died in her throat.

A huge maelstrom had crashed into the side of the

crate, smashing it into pieces.

Orinthia screamed as she was thrown head first into the icy depths of the Atlantic, salt water rushing up her nose as she plunged beneath the waves. Blood pounded hard in her ears. It was dark, murky and indescribably cold. She thrashed about in blind panic, not knowing which way was up and which way was down. All around her, bubbles were jetting upwards and distorting her vision. A shadow passed across her, and she felt something brushing against her leg. Was it a fish? An octopus? Worse? Was she going to end up as the kraken's supper?

Hope was beginning to fizzle out. Her sodden clothes felt like an anchor around her, pulling her further and further and further down . . .

Then she saw it – a glimmer of moonlight, reflecting on the surface of the water like a bright-white beacon. She kicked her legs hard, pushing herself up. She *had* to get her head above water. She *had* to get air in her lungs.

With a mighty thrust, Orinthia broke the surface with a gasp, spluttering and coughing as she tried to catch her breath. Immediately she looked around for Séafra through the blue-black waves.

There he was! Clinging on to the broken lid of the

Penny Black!

'Rinthi, over here!' he shouted, pulling himself on top of it. 'Get on! Quick!'

'I'm coming!' Orinthia gasped, spitting out a mouth of salty seawater. But the ocean was ferocious now, its foamy spray almost blinding her. She swam as best she could, but the tug of the current was strong. Very quickly her lungs began to tighten, pain searing through her chest as if she were being crushed in a vice. Seaweed began to tangle around her ankles, shackling her like rope . . .

She had almost given up hope when all of a sudden she felt Séafra's hands on her shoulders, yanking her up on to the makeshift raft. She flopped on to it like a fish, her throat itchy with salt and grit.

'Rinthi, don't let go!' shouted Séafra. 'I can see the shore. We just need to keep afloat for a little while longer!'

He pointed, and through the rain Orinthia looked into the distance. Not too far off, she could see the beam of a lighthouse, and the twinkle of street lamps. A surge of relief flooded her icy body, as Gungho flew on ahead, guiding the way.

They'd done it!

They'd reached New York!

29

Feeling the dry land beneath her feet brought Orinthia to her knees, and she curled her fingers into the sand, full of excitement. 'Séafra! We did it!' she gasped. 'We did it!'

The storm had died down as suddenly as it had started, the sky now clear and the ocean calm. For a while they both lay on the beach, letting the gentle waters lap over them as they caught their breath. Orinthia's body felt so heavy, so sore, and if it weren't for the fact that she was desperate to get to Taber, she probably would have lain there forever.

Gungho, who had flown on ahead, was nestling amongst the seaweed-strewn rocks, trying to dislodge some mussels with his beak.

'Come on, let's lay out our wet clothes,' Orinthia said, pulling herself up and extending a hand to her brother.

Séafra nodded.

'Oh! But there's just one thing I want to do first. Wait here, I won't be long!' Orinthia trudged back to the shoreline and, with all her might, dragged what was left of the *Penny Black* out of the surf.

'Erm, Rinthi, what are you doing?' asked Séafra.

'I want to keep the stamp as a keepsake,' Orinthia replied. 'As a reminder of our first overseas expedition. So we never forget how far we've come.'

She gently peeled the stamp off the wooden lid, and held it out on her palm like a little wet starfish. It was soaking wet and the background had faded a little, but you could still make out the design of the beautiful yellow flower, even in the moonlight. Orinthia thought back to the morning that she'd attached the stamp to the crate and she felt tears welling in her eyes – it felt like a lifetime ago.

The siblings laid out their sopping wet clothes on the rocks and lay down in their smalls on the dry sand at the top of the beach. Luckily it was a warm night and Orinthia wasn't cold at all. Their bags had been washed away during the storm, but Orinthia was delighted that her diver's watch was still on her wrist and working perfectly. Closing her eyes, she curled her hand around the stamp protectively – and the sigh of the ocean soothed her to sleep.

Morning felt amazing – the warmth of the sun's rays softened Orinthia's aching muscles, the fine white sand was smooth beneath her skin. She opened her eyes.

Séafra was sitting nearby, running a finger up and down Gungho's feathered chest as the bird chirruped happily.

'It's nice having him back, isn't it?' said Orinthia.

'*So* nice!' Séafra replied. 'But I *still* don't know how he found his way to us on the *Mollusca*, having been gone all that time.'

'Who knows? I guess all the training we did with Geronimo in the Mailbox Menagerie rubbed off on him,' Orinthia remarked with a shrug. 'Or maybe it was just a pure stroke of luck and—' She stopped halfway through her sentence and leant over to the pelican. 'Hang on a minute, what on earth's that?'

Séafra frowned. 'What's *what?*'

'*That!*' Orinthia pointed to Gungho's right leg – a little piece of rolled-up parchment had been tied on to it with twine.

Séafra's brow wrinkled and he quickly hauled the bird on to his lap. 'It looks like it could be some kind of note,' he said, briskly unpicking the twine.

Orinthia lunged to his side, watching with anticipation as he unfurled the rolled-up paper to reveal a message:

To Rinthi and Séa,
HELP ME!
Come to 25, West 13th Street in Noo York on Saturday at 7 p.m. They haf tied me up. I am fery scared.
TABER x x x

'Oh my goodness!' said Orinthia, seizing the note from her brother and re-reading it again and again. 'It's from Tabs and he's in trouble! Gungho must have found him in New York, and he wrote this message to bring back to us!'

The pelican squawked as if in agreement, his wings flapping furiously.

'It says *they've* tied him up!' said Séafra. 'But who's *they*? And what's West 13th Street?'

Orinthia looked at the note again. 'It must be Grandy's brother Jobe!' she said, feeling sick at the thought of her little brother tied up and frightened. 'He's holding Taber against his will at the animal sanctuary!'

'Really? Surely Taber would have explained to him

248

why he was there?' Séafra replied.

'Well, I guess Grandy and his children didn't think twice about betraying us. Maybe the Brock family aren't as nice as we thought.'

'Unless . . .' said Séafra with a gulp. 'It's the police. They're after us for some reason – everyone seems to think we're hardened criminals, not just runaways. Maybe Taber's been arrested? Maybe being *tied up* means that he's being held at a police station and has been put in handcuffs?'

The thought made Orinthia's stomach lurch and she jumped to her feet. The relief she'd felt at reaching America was quickly diminishing. She did some quick calculations in her head then gasped in horror. 'We need to get to this West 13th Street immediately. Saturday is tomorrow!'

Leaping into action, the siblings pulled on their clothes, and with Gungho in tow made their way up the white wooden steps leading to the headland.

But when they reached the top, they came to a sudden halt. A large wooden sign was looming over them, but instead of welcoming them to New York, it bore the words WELCOME TO CAPE COD.

30

'Erm . . . Rinthi, where exactly is Cape Cod?' asked Séafra, looking up at the sign in horror. 'And why are we here, instead of New York?'

Orinthia gulped. She had absolutely no idea where Cape Cod was. It sounded like an imaginary fairy-tale land where mermaids might live! Was it anywhere near New York? Was it even in America? She thought hard, trying to remember if she'd seen it on the world map in Ophelia Pearcart's diary, but she couldn't.

'I'm sure we can't be too far from New York,' she lied, trying to remain optimistic in front of Séafra. 'We must've been blown off course in the storm. We'll just have to ask someone to point us in the right direction, that's all.' She looked around before her gaze landed on a row of ramshackle huts and wagons swarming with people, not too far in the distance. 'Look!' she said, pointing. 'We can ask someone over there. Come on!'

Without a moment to lose, the children made their way across the seafront promenade. It was a sprawling stretch, complete with a long boardwalk, a bandstand and a quaint red-and-white striped lighthouse. Fishermen were already bringing in the morning's catch, their chatter mixing with the caws of the seagulls and egrets that circled overhead. It would have been a lovely place to visit, thought Orinthia, if you weren't meant to be somewhere else!

The siblings crossed a wide road, and as soon as they reached the row of huts and wagons, Orinthia realized that they had, in fact, stumbled across a food market. All around there was a strong smell of fried fish, and clouds of steam were rising up from bubbling pots. The bellows of the stallholders rang through the air, each one trying to get their sales pitch heard through the din:

'Get your oysters! The best on Cape Cod!' called one.

'Broiled lobster for sale! Freshly caught today!' shouted another.

'Cornmeal pancakes!'

'Boston beans!'

'Saltwater taffy!'

The siblings stood for a moment, taking in the sights with wide-eyed wonder. Orinthia had never heard of most of the delicacies on offer, but the aromas wafting up from the various pots and pans were mouth-watering. If only they had the time – and the money – to sit down and have a good feed. They hadn't eaten a proper meal since being on the *Mollusca*, and her stomach suddenly felt very empty.

'Rinthi, let's ask that woman for directions,' said Séafra. 'She looks kind.' He pointed to a plump woman wearing a floral headscarf, who was standing behind the counter of one of the little wooden huts. The words 'Big Betty's Clam Shack' were emblazoned across its front, and the counter was decorated with strings of tiny shells which tinkled gently in the wind. A samba song blasted out from a little wireless radio, evoking the atmosphere of a party despite there only being a couple of customers.

'OK,' said Orinthia. 'But don't say a word about Taber.'

'Good morning!' bellowed the stallholder, dancing to the music as the children approached. 'I'm Big Betty and welcome to my clam shack.' Her voice was deep yet mellow, as if she were speaking with a tongue covered in syrup. 'And what can I get for you young ankle-biters this morning, hmmm? I've got fried clams, steamed clams, breaded clams, clam spaghetti, clam chowder, buttered clams, clams with corn, clam ice cream . . .'

'Erm, we actually just wanted to ask for some walking directions, if that's all right?' said Orinthia, pulling herself up on to her tiptoes to see over the counter.

'Sure!' said Betty. 'Where you headed to?'

'We need to get to New York,' Séafra replied brusquely. 'It's not too far, is it?'

Betty snorted. 'Ha! Are you kidding me? New York's over two hundred miles from here!'

'What?' said Orinthia, her face dropping. 'I mean . . . is there any other way for us to get there?'

'Well, your best bet is to get the westbound locomotive from Central Station,' said Big Betty. 'That'll take you about three hours. Or there's a bus which leaves a couple times a week, but that'll be much slower. Well . . . not as slow as walking!' She turned to serve another customer, shaking her head in disbelief and chuckling. 'Walking to New York City from Cape Cod! Who ever heard of such a thing?'

Orinthia and Séafra looked at each other glumly.

'What should we do?' whispered Séafra, trying to keep a low profile. 'We can't get the train or the bus – we don't have any American money!'

'I know,' said Orinthia gloomily, running a hand through her hair. 'But don't worry, Séa, we'll think of something. We've come this far, I'm not giving up now.'

Betty turned back round, appearing to sense the glum mood which had settled over the children. 'Say, why don't you take a seat and I'll getcha a couple bowls of my famous clam chowder?' She gestured to the two rickety stools beneath the counter.

'Erm . . . I'm afraid we came out without any money,' said Orinthia, a little embarrassed.

Betty smiled. 'Well, I tell ya what, because I like ya, I'm gonna give you a couple of bowls on the house. How does that sound?'

Orinthia licked her lips. 'Well that's very kind of you,' she said, unable to refuse – after all, the sweets Séafra had taken from the royal suite hadn't exactly been nutritious. 'Thank you so much.'

'Yes, thank you,' added Séafra.

Betty nodded, and pulled up the lid of a large soup kettle which sat atop the counter. Steam rose from it, sending an earthy, faintly fishy aroma wafting up Orinthia's nose. Her tummy began to rumble.

'There you go,' said Betty, ladling out two bowl-fuls. 'What were your names again? I'm not sure I even asked.'

'Erm . . . my name is Dotty,' Orinthia quickly improvised. 'And this is my brother . . . Waldo!'

On hearing his pseudonym Séafra snorted loudly, but luckily Betty was too busy sprinkling parsley on to the chowder to notice. 'Well, bon appétit,' she said, pushing the bowls towards the children. 'I hope you enjoy!'

Orinthia picked up her bowl and supped deeply. She instantly felt her body soften. The chowder was so rich, so creamy but laced with the fresh, salty tang of the sea. She sipped slowly, trying to make the warming loveliness last for as long as she could – who knew when they might eat again? Especially if they had another 200 miles to travel.

Séafra was enjoying the chowder too, but he was gulping his down with gusto, barely stopping for breath. '*Ahhh!*' he said, wiping his mouth with satisfaction as he finished the bowl in record time. 'That was delicious!'

But the joy of Betty's clam chowder was over before it had begun. All of a sudden, the music on the radio was interrupted as a news anchor began to speak.

'*BREAKING NEWS,*' came the voice across the airwaves. '*Orinthia and Séafra Shalloo, the two children wanted by the British authorities, were recently caught on board the RMS Mollusca, a packet ship headed for New York City. The crew were able to detain the children momentarily, but following a struggle, they managed to escape on a makeshift vessel. It is believed that they are being accompanied by some type of bird. American police are now on the lookout for them, and are asking members of the public to be vigilant. Our international correspondent, Siân Smith, is in the English village of Little Penhallow, where she's been speaking to the children's mother . . .*'

Orinthia flinched on hearing the last word. Mum was looking for them too. *At last, we've got her attention*, she thought bitterly.

'*Please, my darlings,*' came her familiar voice. '*Hand yourselves in. I miss you so much and just want you home . . .*'

Big Betty looked at the Shalloo siblings, her eyebrows raised. Orinthia knew the penny had dropped, and without needing to say a word she and Séafra leapt to their feet, pushing back their stools with a screech.

'Hey, hold on a second,' Big Betty said nonchalantly

as she carried on stirring her pots, as if she'd heard nothing. 'You know, there *might* be another way for you two to get to New York.' She nodded to a poster which had been pasted across the side of the next hut along, and winked knowingly. It was decorated with pictures of hot-air balloons and at its centre were the words:

THE NEW ENGLAND AVIATION SOCIETY's 25th ANNUAL HOT-AIR BALLOON RACE

CAPE COD TO NEW YORK CITY

Come and watch this celebration of flight, where the county's finest balloonists will compete to be the first to reach Central Park.

Last year's winner, the renowned aeronaut Faris Huckabee, will be competing once again in the world-famous balloon, the *Zeppherino Blue*.

The race will start at 2.30 p.m. sharp, but come early to enjoy the food and festivities!

THIS SATURDAY!
Cape Cod Fairground
ADMISSION FREE!

'You're saying that we should go by hot-air balloon?' Séafra asked with a gasp.

Big Betty smiled. 'I'm not sayin' nothin'. But it just so happens that Faris Huckabee is a good friend of mine. And their balloon workshop isn't too far from here either. Why don't you head on over there and explain your predicament? Just say that I sent you.'

A smile tugged at the corners of Orinthia's lips. 'Thank you,' she said, realizing how much this woman was risking by helping them. 'Thank you so so much.'

'No problem,' said Big Betty, giving another of her pots a stir. 'Now be off with ya! Good luck, and if I don't see you again, don't forget to tell all your friends back home about Big Betty's Clam Shack! The finest seafood in town!'

31

Orinthia and Séafra gazed up at a set of tall wrought-iron gates with signage arching over their top: HUCKABEE'S HOT-AIR BALLOONS.

Beyond, Orinthia could see a small yard laden with sheets of scrap metal, planks of wood, spindles of rope and all manner of tools, gears and mechanical parts. Orinthia wondered what Mr Huckabee might be like. She imagined him as a suave commander of the skies, dressed in a shearling-lined leather flying jacket, with a moustache waxed into perfectly precise curls. He'd definitely own some impressive flying goggles too. Maybe they'd even get given a pair of their own to wear during the flight?

'OK, let's do this,' she said, pushing open the gate before turning to her brother. 'We know what we're going to say when we're inside, yes?'

'Yup,' Séafra said, confidently. They'd been through their cover story several times on the way.

'Good,' Orinthia nodded. 'And remember, we're not going to take no for an answer. We *have* to get a ride in this balloon!'

As if in agreement, Gungho swooped down and landed on Séafra's shoulder, squawking wildly.

'But maybe you should keep Gungho hidden for a while?' suggested Orinthia. 'Faris might not like animals, and we don't want to give him any reason not to let us fly.'

Séafra nodded, and stroked back the pelican's feathers before hiding him inside his coat. 'Don't worry, we'll get you out soon,' he whispered. 'And as soon as we reach New York, I'm going to treat you to the juiciest hot dog I can find.'

A sudden round of loud hammering from within the workshop snatched the siblings' attention. They scampered towards the front door, which had been left slightly ajar, and listened. There was more hammering, followed by the shouts of a rather cross-sounding woman.

'Damn, you blasted thing!' she yawped. 'Why won't you hold?' Her accent was American, but very different to that of the other people they'd spoken to in Cape Cod. Orinthia thought she sounded a bit like a cowgirl – her words gravelly and drawn out, as if she were dragging them up from the pit of her throat. Maybe it was Faris's wife, Orinthia thought. Or his daughter?

'Hello?' she called out over the din. 'Can we come in? We'd like to talk to Mr Huckabee please . . .'

There was no answer.

'Hello!' she tried once more, giving the door a sharp knock. 'We're looking for Mr Huckabee! Big Betty has sent us.'

Again, there was no reply, so the Shalloo siblings pushed open the door.

They found themselves in a sprawling industrial workshop, with high ceilings reinforced with thick metal dowels. The floor was carpeted with wood shavings, the air almost sweet with the heady aroma of varnish and glue and oil. Metal tools hung from a pegboard on the wall, and gigantic rolls of jewel-coloured silk were propped up in one corner. The late-morning light shone through the upper windows, picking out the dust particles dancing through the air.

And at the centre of the space, a large wicker basket hung from the ceiling. Someone (presumably the woman with the cowgirl voice) was lying beneath it like a mechanic working under a car. Only her bottom half was visible – stout legs in oil-stained overalls, culminating in a pair of hobnail boots. She was hammering away at something, grunting loudly as she worked. 'Gosh-all-potomac!' came her raspy drawl. 'Stay put, you wretched nail!'

The siblings exchanged nervous looks, before Orinthia edged forward tentatively. 'Erm . . . hello. Sorry to interrupt, but we're looking for Faris Huckabee.'

The pair of legs jerked and the hammering came to a sudden stop. 'Who's asking?' came the woman's cross-sounding reply.

'Erm . . . well my name's Dotty,' said Orinthia, remembering the pseudonym she'd thought up at the clam shack. 'And I'm here with my brother Waldo. Big Betty sent us. She said Faris might be able to help us—'

The clang of a hammer missing a nail rang through the air and the woman cursed loudly. 'Odds bodkins! Pass me that screwdriver on the table, will you?' she called out.

'Erm . . . pardon?' Orinthia replied in an uncertain tone.

'My screwdriver! The one with the flat head on the

workbench. Pass it to me.'

Orinthia gestured to her brother to follow the orders, and Séafra fumbled for the screwdriver. He crouched down next to the basket and passed it to the woman, who snatched it from him without even a hint of a thank you.

'Now, what were you saying before?' she snapped, as she continued to work. 'If you're here trying to sell me home-made lemonade or girl-scout cookies, then I'm not interested. The last batch gave me terrible indigestion!'

'No, no, we're not selling anything,' protested Séafra. 'We're looking for Mr Huckabee. Could you tell us where we can find him?'

The hammering stopped abruptly and the woman pushed herself out from under the basket. She was much younger than Orinthia had anticipated, probably barely out of her teens. Her hair was in a full Afro, and a scar ran across her left cheek from her nose to her ear. She pulled up the safety goggles covering her eyes, and blinked the workshop into focus. '*Mr* Huckabee?' she said incredulously. '*I'm* Faris Huckabee, and the last time I checked I wasn't no mister, that's for sure!'

Orinthia gasped. Faris Huckabee . . . was a girl?

'Yeah, yeah, I know what you're thinkin',' said Faris, as if reading her mind. 'How can an unsalted young broad like me be one of the finest balloonists in the country? Well, through hard work and determination, that's how! And through not givin' a toot about what other people think! Especially men!'

She picked up a large file and began to smooth down the edge of a sheet of metal on the workbench beside her.

As she watched her work, Orinthia felt a sense of shame and embarrassment flood through her. Why had she assumed that Faris was a man in the first place?

'So, are you gonna tell me what I can do for you, or not?' asked Faris, blowing away a cloud of tiny metal filings from her tool.

'Yes, of course,' replied Orinthia, quickly shaking herself from her thoughts.

'Well, spit it out then, girly!'

'Well, I know it's a big ask,' Orinthia replied. 'But could we fly with you in the balloon race tomorrow? My brother and I need to get to New York you see, and we thought we could race with you in the *Zeppherino Blue*.'

'Race with me?' Faris swatted the comment away dismissively. '*Pah!* What do you think I am, a taxi service? What do you need to get to New York for anyhow?'

Séafra glanced quickly to his sister before clearing his throat. 'To . . . erm . . . visit our grandfather. He's very ill and we want to see him as soon as possible.'

'And why won't your parents take you?'

'They don't have a motor car. And no money for the train or bus.'

'I see,' said Faris, remaining completely expressionless.

'We thought we could be your crew!' added Orinthia, trying to twist the balloonist's arm. 'Help you navigate maybe? Or . . . or pour you cups of tea?'

'And what makes you think I need a crew?' said Faris. 'I've been flying solo perfectly well since I was a little girl, thank you very much. Don't need no help from nobody.'

The siblings looked at each other blankly and Orinthia began to panic. They had nothing else to offer the aeronaut – no expertise, no money, not even any interesting trinkets to trade.

Faris pulled her goggles back down and picked up a wrench. 'Now, if that's all, I'll be getting back to work. Don't have time for no hogwash and hooey. Let yourselves out . . .' She made for the basket.

'Wait!' Séafra said, reaching out a hand to the woman's shoulder. 'Can I just show you something? I think it might be of interest to you.'

Orinthia's brow furrowed. What was he doing? What did they have that might be of interest to a world-class balloonist? She sincerely hoped he wasn't going to try and woo Faris's favour with the couple of soggy chocolates they had left over from the *Mollusca*!

Faris wheeled around and sighed. 'Go on then, but make it quick.'

Séafra unbuttoned his coat and lifted Gungho out carefully. The bird let out a relieved honk and flew a lap of the workshop before settling on Séafra's shoulder.

'Thunderation!' exclaimed Faris. 'Is that a pelican?'

'Not *just* a pelican,' said Séafra proudly, running a hand down the bird's white tail feathers. 'He's a homing pelican. He's extremely intelligent and I think he could be a real asset on board.'

Faris pondered this for a moment. 'Go on.'

'Well, he can go miles and miles and always navigate his way home. I thought you could let him fly from the balloon during the journey tomorrow, to find out what kind of weather was lying ahead. It could give you a real advantage.'

Orinthia shot her brother a smile. What a brilliant idea!

There was silence for a moment, before Faris's face seemed to soften slightly. 'Well, I have to say he's a fine-lookin' specimen,' she said wistfully. 'May I?' She held out an arm for Gungho to perch on.

'Yes, yes, go ahead,' said Séafra, ushering the pelican towards the balloonist. He flew from his shoulder, landing gently on Faris's arm. 'He's very observant,' Séafra continued. 'And ever so good-tempered. You couldn't want for a better bird.'

The young balloonist studied Gungho intently, and as she stroked his wing he let out a long, contented *caw*. 'And you say he can detect a change in weather?'

'Yes,' said Séafra proudly. 'The air pressure affects how low or high he will fly, you see. So if he swoops nearer to the ground, you know you can expect rain. But if he soars upwards, the weather will be fairer.'

Faris nodded, the closest thing to praise that she'd offered so far. Silence hung in the air as she continued to inspect the bird, and Orinthia crossed her fingers tightly. Was the balloonist going to let them fly? Had Séafra managed to convince her? If this didn't work out, then she didn't know how they'd get themselves to New York. Would they have to come to terms with the fact that they wouldn't get to West 13th Street for 7 p.m. tomorrow? That they wouldn't get to Taber in time?

Faris passed Gungho back to Séafra, and let out a long sigh.

'So?' pressed Séafra, tentatively. 'What do you think? Will you let us come with you? We'll make it worth your while and, and—'

'All right, cool your heels, will ya!' Faris cut in. 'I'll see you at the fairground at 2 p.m. sharp tomorrow.'

Orinthia gasped in disbelief. 'Really? We can fly with you to New York in your balloon?'

'Yes,' said Faris. 'But don't be late! The *Zeppherino* don't wait for nobody.'

Orinthia's heart began to race. 'We won't,' she gushed. 'We promise!'

'And don't be bringin' no toys nor books or nothin' with you neither, you hear me? And if there's any misbehaving you'll be over the side of that basket quicker than you can say *double-barrelled jumping jiminetty*, you understand?'

Séafra let out an involuntary snort and Faris scowled. 'Something funny?'

'No, no, nothing funny . . .' Séafra backtracked,

quickly turning his laughter into a string of pretend coughs. 'Just a frog in my throat, that's all.'

'Well, make sure you get rid of it before tomorrow,' said Faris. 'Don't want no amphibians hopping around in my balloon. Having two children and a bird on board is gonna be enough of a challenge, that's for sure.'

'Yes, Miss Huckabee,' Séafra replied, slightly embarrassed.

'And please, just call me Faris, would ya? Miss Huckabee makes me sound like one of them straight-laced bluenoses that works at the bank. And who'd wanna be one of those?' She reached for her goggles and pulled them back down over her eyes. 'Now, I'm gonna get back to work. Got a lotta things to do before tomorrow. Make sure you get a good night's sleep tonight. Don't want my crew snoozing mid-air.'

The children nodded, and as they left the work-shop, Orinthia beamed. This time tomorrow they'd be cruising through the clouds, on their way to New York!

All they needed now was somewhere to spend the night.

32

Orinthia awoke to the heaviness of Séafra's hands on her shoulders, shaking her from her sleep. 'Rinthi, we need to get up!' he gasped, as she opened her eyes. 'We've overslept. It's nearly midday!'

Orinthia jolted upwards in panic. 'Midday? Oh my goodness, Séa, we're going to be late to meet Faris!'

They shot to their feet and began to pull on their clothes in such a blind hurry that Séafra nearly ended up with a sock on his hand and a leg through one of his jumper's armholes. They'd spent the night in a derelict barn which they'd found behind an old farmhouse not far from Faris's workshop. It was far from luxurious, but it was warm and dry and the hay bales made for surprisingly comfy beds. They'd even found some apples in the surrounding trees which, combined with a handful of gooseberries from the hedgerows, had made for quite a tasty supper. When it was time to sleep, they'd covered themselves with loose straw and bits of lambswool, and listened to the sound of the farm animals braying outside until they'd drifted off.

'OK, we need to go,' Orinthia ordered, beckoning to Gungho, who was perched atop a hay bale next to a barn owl. 'Come on, boy. This isn't the time for socializing.'

The siblings crept out of the barn, and checking that the coast was clear, scampered across the farmyard and back to the main road.

The sky was wide open and hinting at a fine day ahead. Gungho circled above and the pair headed off, following the plentiful signs to the fair. Thankfully, having slept so soundly, the children were full of energy, and they made short work of the journey. It wasn't long before they were standing in line at the entrance to the County Fairground.

'Come on, come on,' said Orinthia impatiently, looking down at her watch as they waited to go through the turnstiles. It was already approaching half past one – they only had thirty minutes left until they had to meet Faris! Was the *Zeppherino Blue* going to leave without them?

Luckily for them, the queue moved quickly, and soon enough the siblings were at the front, being greeted by a cherry-cheeked woman in a floppy straw hat manning the turnstile. 'This way,' she said, trying to usher them through. 'That's it, nice and quick.'

'Erm . . . excuse me,' said Orinthia, trying to get her attention. 'Could you tell us where we can find the hot-air balloon field, please?'

'It's at the far end,' replied the woman, pointing into the distance. 'Take a left at the livestock tent, then another left at the helter-skelter, before taking a sharp right across the tractor field. Keep going straight until you reach the pumpkin patch. Then jink right before cutting across the pig-racing track. The entrance to the hot-air balloon field will be on your left next to the chuck wagon. You can't miss it.'

'Erm . . . thank you,' said Orinthia, pushing her way through the rickety turnstile, and hoping that she'd remember those rather convoluted directions.

'Have a good day!' shouted the woman. 'Who are you both rooting for? Faris Huckabee?'

'You bet!' Séafra replied, following behind his big sister with a knowing chuckle. 'We wouldn't be rooting for anyone else!'

On entering the field, the children were immediately

hit with a kaleidoscopic onslaught of sights and sounds. It was a bit like the village fete that was held on the green in Little Penhallow every summer, but much busier, bigger and certainly much louder. Canvas tents were decorated with bunting and balloons, and paddocks were filled with cattle, flicking away flies with their tails. Up ahead, a ginormous Ferris wheel had already attracted a crowd of wide-eyed children, craning their necks to watch as the passenger cars rose and fell. There were coconut shies, fortune tellers and a multitude of food stalls, with each vendor competing to lure in the passers-by.

'Right,' said Orinthia, hiding in the shadows of some nearby trees as she tried to get her bearings. 'The woman at the door said to first take a left at the live-stock tent . . . now where is it?' She scanned their surroundings until she clocked a man with a wheat stalk in his mouth, leading a herd of goats into a canvas marquee. 'Ah! That must be it over there!'

Not wanting to draw any unwanted attention, she slipped Gungho inside her coat, and arm in arm the siblings pushed off across the field. The afternoon sun was hot now and the ground dry beneath their feet. They passed stallholders spinning sugar into clouds of pink candyfloss, and a woman urging them to guess the weight of a gigantic marrow. As they skirted a carousel, lustrous wooden horses with names like Baby, Dante and Prince flew by, their painted nostrils flaring as they rose and fell on their poles. *It all looks so much fun*, thought Orinthia.

The children pressed on, and as instructed they took another left at the helter-skelter before heading right across the sprawling tractor field. But at the pumpkin patch, Orinthia faltered. They were surrounded by hundreds upon hundreds of the bright-orange gourds, and all of a sudden she felt completely disorientated. Which way had the turnstile woman said to go now? Left, right or straight ahead? She began to panic a little as she looked down at her watch once more. In fifteen minutes they'd be officially late to meet Faris. Orinthia couldn't afford to take them the wrong way . . .

'What's wrong, Rinthi?' asked Séafra, his voice shaky on seeing his sister's obvious panic. 'Are we lost?'

'No, of course not,' lied Orinthia, turning on the spot as she wracked her brains for an answer. 'Just catching my breath for a minute, that's all. It's so hot.'

She thought for a moment, and was just about to take a chance on swinging left when the cries of a passing toddler wearing bright-red dungarees made her ears prick up. 'MOMMY, I DON'T WANNA GO SEE THE HOT-AIR BALLOONS!' he wailed, dragging his feet through the dirt as he reluctantly followed his parents through the mountains of pumpkins. 'I WANNA GO BACK TO THE FERRIS WHEEL!'

His mother stopped and turned sharply. 'That's enough, Donald!' she scolded. 'I told you we'd take another ride after lunch! But if you keep on hollering like that, you'll be going straight back in the car. Now, pick up your feet!'

The little boy scowled, and as the family took off, Orinthia seized her chance, breathing a sigh of relief as she and Séafra followed in their footsteps. Thank goodness little Donald had been screaming so loudly about the balloons. If she was going to become a famous explorer then she'd have to work on her inner compass – a good sense of direction was the backbone of any successful expedition.

But that didn't matter now. Orinthia's thoughts were interrupted by the sound of little Donald suddenly letting out a screech of delight. 'Look, Mommy, colours! Pretty colours.'

Orinthia looked ahead and felt her eyes widen.

There, in a vast field stretching out in front of them, dozens of balloons were hovering above ground, aglow in the afternoon sunshine like beautiful multi-coloured light bulbs. Their designs were magnificent – one was yellow with red stripes like those of a candy cane twisting from top to bottom, and another was blue with bright-pink polka dots. Some were adorned with zigzags, and some with diamonds. Some had even been fashioned into unconventional shapes, and Orinthia beamed at the sight of one resembling a gigantic world globe.

Discarded peanut shells crunched underfoot as they approached the entrance to the field, causing the man standing guard at the gate to look up. A cowboy hat was perched atop his mop of white hair, and a smoking pipe hung limply from one side of his mouth. Orinthia smiled politely and, remembering her manners, said, 'Good morning, sir, we'd like to come in please.'

The man inhaled from his pipe, the bowl of tobacco glowing red before he let out a feathery ring of smoke. 'Tickets?'

'Well . . . we're actually here to meet Faris Huck-abee,' said Orinthia proudly. 'We're flying with her today.'

The man guffawed, nearly choking on the smoke he'd just exhaled. 'Yeah, yeah, of course you are, and I'm Abraham Lincoln. Beat it, kids! No ticket, no entry!'

'It's true,' said Séafra. 'We're Faris's crew for the day. She's allowing us to race with her to New York.'

The man shook his head incredulously. 'Listen kids, nice try and all, but Faris Huckabee is a solo flyer. She never has any crew, especially not ones your size.' He shot the siblings a self-important scowl. 'Now get outta here! Go and get yourselves some cotton candy or somethin'.'

Orinthia felt her fists curl, and was just about to retort when she saw Faris trudging towards them across the field. She was wearing a shearling-lined jacket in chestnut-brown leather, with a matching aviation hat which buckled beneath her chin. She looked so strong, so powerful, exactly the type of woman Orinthia wanted to grow up to be. Blood rushed through Orinthia's veins at a pace, and for some reason she felt her heart flutter.

'Don't worry, Hank,' Faris called out to the man on the gate. 'They're with me, let 'em through.'

Hank's brow furrowed in confusion and he took his pipe from his mouth. 'Really? Not like you to have

277

a crew, Faris. Goin' soft in your old age?'

'Somethin' like that,' said Faris begrudgingly.

'In which case I apologize,' said Hank to the children. He emptied his bowl of tobacco and put his pipe into his top pocket. 'This your first flight in a balloon?'

The siblings nodded.

'Well it's a damn shame that you're takin' it with this cranky curmudgeon! She's the grumpiest balloonist in all of New England!' He gave Faris a playful punch on her shoulder, laughing at his own joke. 'Nah, just kiddin'. You'll have a whale of a time I'm sure.' He unbolted the gate and ushered the children through. 'Hope you have a good flight!'

'You and me both,' muttered Faris as she turned on her heel, and headed back across the grass. 'Come on, Dotty, come on Waldo, this way.'

33

'Here she is,' said Faris as they reached the far end of the field. 'The *Zeppherino Blue!*'

Orinthia looked up and felt her heart quickening. Tethered by two lines of rope, a gargantuan balloon hovered over them, as wide and as tall as an oak tree. Its silk envelope was the colour of midnight – a blue so deep that it was almost other-worldly. It was embellished with golden stars and moons, each one stitched with gilt thread and shimmering brightly. The passenger basket was constructed from varnished wickerwork, dressed with swaths of flowing fabric and trimmed with tassels.

'Wow!' Séafra enthused, as they edged closer. 'Are we really flying in this?'

'Well, of course we are,' said Faris. 'What did you think we were flying in, a garbage pail?'

'It's so beautiful,' said Orinthia, almost lost for words. Not only were they finally on their way to Taber, but they were going to reach him by travelling in the most impressive hot-air balloon in the world. 'I've never seen anything like it.'

'Well, you won't have,' said Faris, hoisting herself into the basket. 'One of a kind, this is. Built especially for me by my great-great-grandfather, Papa Huckabee.'

'So you come from a family of balloonists?' asked Séafra, still mesmerized by the sight in front of him.

Faris nodded. 'Yup. My daddy was a balloonist, his daddy was a balloonist, and his daddy's daddy was a balloonist. I was even born in the basket of a balloon!'

The siblings looked at each other in disbelief. 'You mean, one that was on the ground?' asked Orinthia.

'Nope,' said Faris, 'one that was a thousand feet up in the air!'

'No way!' said Séafra. 'You're pulling our legs.'

'It's true! My parents were takin' a flight over the state of Texas one evenin', when my old momma went into labour. It started just as they was passin' over El Paso, and I was born by the time we'd touched down in Dallas.' Her eyes twinkled and she smirked mischievously. 'Made front page of the gazette before I was even a day old.'

Orinthia laughed. She wasn't sure if Faris was telling the truth, but it was a good story nonetheless.

'Anyway, we can't stand around beating our gums all day,' said Faris. 'The race is gonna start soon and I wanna show you what's what. You got the bird with you, yes?'

Orinthia nodded. 'But I'll keep him in my coat until we're up in the air, I think. I don't want him to get spooked.'

'Good idea,' said Faris. 'Now, hop in!' She nodded towards the small rungs on the side of the basket and gestured for the Shalloo siblings to ascend.

As she and her brother climbed up the wickerwork, exhilaration prickled across Orinthia's skin. She was going to do something that not even Ophelia Pearcart had done – race through the skies at 2,000 feet!

Once they'd clambered into the basket she gazed up at the dome of colourful blue silk. As the sun shone through the panels she felt as if she were inside a giant paper lantern. This was something that might transport you through a dream, not across mountains and fields and lakes. It made her head spin.

'Now, you're gonna need these,' said Faris, reaching into a wooden trunk. She pulled out two hats, two sets of brown leather gloves, and two pairs of flying goggles, and handed them to the siblings. 'They might be a bit big, but they'll have to do. I've never had rugrats in the basket with me before.'

The garments were indeed too big, and Orinthia couldn't help but chuckle as Séafra pulled on his gigantic goggles. 'You look like a human insect!' she said. 'Like a weird, curly-haired fly!'

'Pah! You should see *yourself*,' said Séafra in retort. 'You look like a googly-eyed fish!'

'All right, all right,' said Faris. 'That's enough of that. You both look as ridiculous as each other! Now make yourselves nice and comfy. The race begins in ten minutes. I'm gonna do my final checks.'

Faris got to work, and Orinthia took her seat and looked out across the field. All around, the other balloonists seemed to be doing their last-minute preparations too – adjusting nozzles, checking baskets, tightening goggles. Family and friends had begun to gather around the other baskets to wave off the competitors, their words of enthusiasm filling the air.

'What a load of fuss and ballyhoo!' tutted Faris as she caught another balloonist sharing a farewell smooch with the woman standing on the other side of his basket. 'It's an air balloon race, not a mission to the moon!' A sudden hiss of white noise came from the stage, and Orinthia looked up.

'Ladies and gentlemen, boys and girls,' bellowed a bespectacled man who'd come to stand at the microphone. He was wearing a smart suit complete with bow tie and was addressing the crowd as if he were talking to an arena. 'My name is Jackson Riviera, and as the governor of this fine peninsula, it is my great honour to welcome you all to Cape Cod's twenty-fifth annual hot-air balloon race! And what a fine New England day it is. Are you all having a swell time?'

There was a huge cheer from the crowd and Orinthia felt excitement fizzing through her.

'Now, it's nearly two thirty,' continued Governor Riviera, 'so I'll try and keep this short . . .'

'Thank goodness for that,' Faris muttered grumpily under her breath. 'I was nearly asleep by the time you'd finished gassin' last year.'

' . . . so I'd just like to wish all racers the very best of luck. Fly safely, and I'll look forward to awarding the prize to the lucky winner on their return. Everybody, I would love you to join me in counting down to the beginning of the race.'

The crowd erupted once more, and as the mayor began to count, they chorused in unison:

'Ten . . . nine . . . eight . . . seven . . .'

Faris adjusted her goggles.

'Six . . . five . . . four . . .'

Orinthia looked at Séafra, biting down a smile.

'Three . . . two . . . one!'

The sound of a horn pierced the air, and a huge cheer erupted from the crowd of spectators. With a sharp nod from Faris, the crew on the ground untied the ropes, and as gravity released its clutches, the *Zeppherino Blue* rose from the ground.

They had lift-off!

34

As the balloon lifted up, Orinthia peered overboard in awe. They were gaining height rapidly, the village below quickly losing clarity until all the people and houses and cars were no more than multicoloured specks. She had expected the ascent to be jerky, but it wasn't at all. In fact, it was so smooth and so gentle that if she'd closed her eyes she probably wouldn't have even known they were moving. She wriggled her toes in delight. There was now nothing but a wicker basket between her boots and the distant ground beneath – she was practically walking on air!

'*Waldo*, isn't this incredible,' she said, looking over to her brother, who was also taking in the view and just as mesmerized. The wind was sweeping through his hair, and the smile on his face was perhaps the most joyous she'd ever seen.

'It's amazing, *Dotty!*' he said, his fists clenched with excitement. 'I-I feel so free. I feel' – he looked up at Gungho, who was now circling around the basket – 'like a bird!'

The balloon continued to rise at an incredible pace, and when they were high enough Faris switched off the burner and let the vessel cruise. Orinthia had expected it to be noisy so high up, to feel the strength of the wind fighting against them, but it was quiet, serene – one of the most peaceful places she had ever found herself.

'Where are we now, Faris?' she asked, peering over the side of the basket and taking in the incredible view. They'd left the coast behind and were now flying over vast stretches of green.

'That's the Taconic Range,' said Faris, pointing to the north-west. 'Part of the Appalachian Mountains. That big peak right there is Equinox Mountain. One of the highest summits in Vermont.'

'Wow,' said Orinthia, feeling her feet itch as she imagined trekking to the top of it, on the hunt for black bears or bobcats! It would *definitely* have to be added to her list of places to explore in the future. It would be an incredible starting point for an expedition.

'So, your grandpa,' asked Faris. 'What's wrong with him?'

'Excuse me?' Orinthia replied, momentarily forgetting the lie she'd told Faris the day before.

'Your grandfather,' Faris pressed. 'You said he's sick or somethin'?'

'*Oh!*' Orinthia exclaimed, suddenly realizing what the balloonist was talking about. 'Yes, he's in hospital with . . . erm . . . pneumonia.'

'Doesn't sound good,' said Faris. 'I hope he gets better soon.'

'Me too,' Orinthia replied, before quickly slinking down against the side of the basket, hoping to avoid any more questions. She hated having to lie, especially to someone like Faris whom she admired so much, but she had to stick with their story until they reached New York. She definitely didn't think it would be wise to come clean so many thousands of feet above ground!

The next hour or so passed by in a hazy dream. Séafra let Gungho fly free as they passed over Rhode Island, in the hope that he would bring back news of any inclement weather up ahead. Occasionally another air balloon would pass by above or below, but they would never stay in the lead for long. As soon as she clocked that they were being overtaken, Faris adjusted the nozzle of the burner to take them in a different direction. It was like watching a conjurer at work, a magician of the skies!

They sailed west rapidly, and as they began to get closer to New York, Orinthia sat back, enjoying the warm sun on her face as she thought about how far she and Séafra had come. She pulled the postage stamp she'd taken off the *Penny Black* from her pocket and ran a finger over it. This little square of paper had enabled them to travel halfway across the world. It had given them passage not only to new places, but to new people, new friendships. Noah, Mog, Big Betty, Faris – she'd *never* forget the friendly faces that had shown them such kindness along the way.

'And what's that you've got there, hmm?' asked Faris, peering over her shoulder. 'Looks interestin'.'

Orinthia jumped and quickly stashed the stamp back into her pocket. 'Oh, it's . . . it's nothing,' she said, feeling her cheeks redden. 'Just a silly stamp.'

'Oh,' said Faris. 'Is that so? Because for a moment there I swear I just saw you looking at an example of the very rare and very sought-after "Inverted Narcissus".'

Orinthia frowned with uncertainty. 'The inverted *what*?'

'Inverted Narcissus. Named because the flower on the front was printed the wrong way round on one of the print runs, making it one of the most collectible stamps in the world.' She nodded to Orinthia's pocket. 'Look, pass it here and I'll show you.'

Orinthia flinched, and as if sensing her hesitation, Faris smiled. 'Don't worry, I'm not gonna pinch it.'

Tentatively, Orinthia passed the stamp to Faris. Surely she'd made a mistake? Surely this wasn't the philatelic rarity Faris thought it was? Orinthia looked to Séafra, who seemed equally dumbfounded at the revelation.

Faris reached for a magnifying glass before pulling up her goggles. She inspected the stamp thoroughly, her right eye appearing gargantuan under the circle of domed glass.

'As I thought,' she said after a while. 'An Inverted Narcissus!' She put down the magnifying glass and pointed to the flower on the front of the stamp. 'You see the way the stem and head are leaning? Well, they should be bending left, not right. Most of the print run was correct, but a few were printed like this.'

'How do you know so much about stamps?' Séafra asked.

'Well, I've dabbled in a bit of philately over the

years. Used to pick up a stamp from every country I visited in my balloon, but the designs ain't so interesting these days. And I never had an Inverted Narcissus in my collection, that's for sure. What a treat to see one!'

'So . . . let me get this straight. People want the stamp because of the *mistake* on it?' asked Orinthia. 'That seems odd.'

'People like things that are rare,' Faris replied. 'Rare coins, rare animals, rare books. And this is as rare as they come. Someone'd pay you big bucks for this. BIG bucks!'

Orinthia gasped. All of a sudden everything began to make sense. If this stamp was worth a lot of money, then that's why the wanted posters had described her and Séafra as criminals! Mrs Pauncefoot obviously knew its value, and wanted it back, so she'd got the police involved. If only Inspector Snodgrass knew that Mrs Pauncefoot was a criminal herself, then he definitely wouldn't have been so eager to help her.

Faris coughed. 'So where exactly did a young chickabiddy like you get an expensive thing like that from anyway, hmmm? Quite a spendy thing to be carryin' around.'

'I found it,' said Orinthia, her gaze darting to the

floor. She was trying not to reveal her guilt, but she feared it was there, emblazoned in her eyes for Faris to see. 'In a . . . erm . . . junk shop.'

Faris nodded, giving her a knowing look. 'Yeah, yeah, of course you did.' She pulled her goggles back over her eyes and turned back to the barometer. 'No more questions asked. But I'd keep that stamp safe, if I were you. Don't let it out of your sight, OK?'

Orinthia nodded, and just then Gungho swooped back into the basket. He was screeching, flapping his wings furiously.

'What is it, boy?' asked Séafra, reaching out to calm him. But the bird wouldn't stay still. He knocked Séafra's hand out of the way with his beak, continuing to shriek and beating his wings harder and faster by the second.

'What's wrong with him?' asked Faris. 'Is there a storm brewing or something? I hope it ain't a twister!'

Gungho pecked repeatedly at Séafra's shoulder, nudging him towards the edge of the basket. He squinted, trying to tell if the bird was warning them of something. But soon enough a smile broke across his face. 'Look!' he cried, pointing ahead. 'Gungho was trying to tell us that we're nearly in New York!'

Orinthia and Faris leapt to their feet, and through

the nebulous mass of clouds, the city skyline was coming into view.

'Great snakes, he's right!' said Faris. 'We've been yapping so much that I completely lost track of time!' She raised an eyebrow playfully. '*That's* why I usually choose to fly alone!'

'Oh my goodness, the view is incredible!' said Orinthia, taking in the enormous buildings. She recognized the Chrysler, the Empire State, the skyscrapers of Wall Street and Times Square. And there, rising up from the harbour, wielding her golden torch and robed in verdigris, was the Statue of Liberty.

'There she is,' said Faris with a smile. 'The famous lady herself! *Liberty Enlightening the World.*'

'Woah! She's huge!' said Orinthia. 'Even bigger than I thought she'd be.'

'Weighs over two hundred tonnes. And see that crown on her head? It has seven rays – each one representin' one of the seven seas and the seven continents.'

Orinthia hugged herself as an overwhelming joy surged through her. 'Séafra, we did it!' she gasped, reaching for his hand and gripping it tightly. 'We made it! We made it!'

'Hang on a minute! *Séafra?*' Faris blurted out in

confusion. She turned to Orinthia and scowled. 'What are you talkin' about? You told me his name was Waldo! What's goin' on here?'

Orinthia's stomach lurched as she realized the error she'd just made. She felt sweat blooming on her forehead as Faris's gaze bored into her, demanding an answer.

'Erm . . . Séafra is . . . erm . . . his middle name,' Orinthia said, trying to backtrack. 'I call him by it sometimes, that's all—'

'Don't lie to me, girly,' said Faris, her voice rising. 'You can't kid a kidder!' She was fuming now, her cheeks turning from white to pink to red with rage. 'Now quit with the cacklin', and tell me what on God's earth is goin' on!'

35

'**W**ell? I'm waiting! Are you two gonna tell me what's goin' on here or not?' Faris's nostrils were flaring, her eyes protruding.

Orinthia knew she couldn't keep up the lie any longer. It had gone too far. 'Our names aren't Dotty and Waldo,' she whimpered, dropping her chin to her chest in shame. 'I'm Orinthia and this is my brother, Séafra.'

There was a moment's silence before Faris's hand shot to her mouth and she gasped out loud. 'Holy catfish! You're them whippersnappers they've been talking about on the radio!'

'Faris, we're so sorry,' said Orinthia, guilt burning her cheeks. 'We didn't want to lie to you, we just didn't know what to do. Our little brother is in New York all by himself and we're trying to find him.' The whole story came tumbling out, then. 'We thought that if we could fly with you then we'd be able to get to him quicker,' Orinthia finished.

Faris pulled up her goggles, blinking as she took in the children. 'Why on earth didn't I put two and two together?' she said, shaking her head in disbelief. 'What a dummy!'

'I think they're looking for us because of the Narcissus,' said Orinthia. 'We stole it, but we had no idea it was valuable, I promise! All we wanted was to find our little brother.'

Faris nodded, as if everything was suddenly making sense.

Séafra's eyes filled with tears. 'So are you going to hand us over to the police when we land? We'd understand if you did.'

Orinthia nodded glumly in agreement.

'Hand you over to the Blue Force?' said Faris, as if she'd just been sworn at. '*Pah!* Anyone that's been through what you have to get to their little brother ain't gonna be shopped in by me. I thought *I* was brave, but you two, you're somethin' else. And besides, I ain't no dime-droppin' rat. I'd *never* go to the cops!'

Orinthia was taken aback by the balloonist's

unexpected tirade. She felt shocked and grateful in equal measure. 'Faris, I don't know what to say,' she stuttered. 'We really can't thank you enough . . . for everything—'

'Oh bosh!' said Faris, pulling down her goggles. 'And besides, there ain't no time for thank yous. We've still got a race to win!'

She adjusted her leather gloves before calibrating the nozzle on the burner. 'Now hold on tight, we're goin' down! Central Park is just over there. Unfortunately that fog is going to make for a tricky landing . . .'

The balloon lost height quickly, making its way towards earth as smoothly as it had ascended. As they disappeared through the patch of fog everything went hazy and the siblings huddled together as they prepared to land. When they came out the other side of the mist, the ground was only a few hundred metres below them.

There was a huge gust of wind and as the balloon approached the ground, the basket began to swing from side to side. 'OK, brace for impact!' Faris ordered, concentrating hard as the park rushed towards them. 'Hold on tight! We're coming into land. Things might get a little—'

DUMPFFFF!

The balloon hit the ground with an almighty thump, and the whole world tipped sideways. Central Park flashed past as Orinthia fell from the *Zeppherino*'s basket, and when she looked up she found herself splayed across the grass, her clothes twisted around her like bed sheets after a nightmare.

'Séafra!' she called out, her thoughts immediately turning to her brother. 'Are you OK?' Her vision was swarming with blotches of yellow and black and for a moment she couldn't spot him.

'Rinthi! I'm just here!' came a reply from behind her. 'But I think I might have broken Faris!'

Orinthia turned to find Séafra splayed across the grass a bit further across the field, with a squashed-looking Faris sticking out from underneath him. She had her leather hat clutched tightly in her hand, but was only wearing one shoe.

'OH NO! Faris, are you OK?' called Orinthia, running towards her and kneeling at her side. 'Should we call for an ambulance?'

'No, no. I'm fine,' she croaked, pulling up her cracked goggles and rubbing her eyes. 'Just help me up. But then the two of you need to scarper before the crowds and the press start arrivin'. You don't want any nosy old camera lenses pokin' around in your affairs.'

Orinthia nodded and extended a hand. 'Thank you for everything, Faris,' she said, pulling the balloonist to her feet before throwing her arms around her neck. She smelt of gasoline and sawdust and adventure and kindness. 'We'll write soon, and when all this is over we'll come back to Cape Cod for another ride! We won't forget you, Faris!'

Faris smiled warmly. 'And I won't forget you two, neither,' she said. 'I never thought that flying with two rugrats could be so . . . well . . . wonderful.' Orinthia saw a tear glistening in the corner of her eye and she quickly looked away. 'Now go! Get out of here! Follow the signs for Times Square, then when you hit that, don't stop running south till you find your little brother.'

36

Standing in the middle of Times Square was like being trapped inside a giant kaleidoscope. Everywhere Orinthia looked there was light and colour and life. It couldn't have been more different to Little Penhallow, and there was so much to take in that she wondered if there was enough space in her brain to store every new sight, every new sound.

She gazed upwards. A huge news ticker loomed overhead, flanked by a neon sign shaped like a big apple and an advertisement for 'JOHNNY'S ALL-AMERICAN FRANKFURTERS' which blinked from red to white to blue. Even the roads seemed glamorous somehow – with overhanging yellow traffic lights and steam rising up through the manholes, as if a conjurer was about to appear from their depths. Orinthia wished she could join the queue of people to see a show, or grab one of the delicious-smelling hot dogs from the cart on the corner. She suddenly remembered how Grandy's children had made her promise to bring some back and felt her eyes sting. She still couldn't believe their betrayal.

'So, where should we go now?' asked Séafra, tugging Orinthia from her musings. Gungho was stood at his feet, watching the cars whizz by, but luckily the New Yorkers were giving the pelican barely a second glance. *The people who live in this bonkers city must be used to strange sights*, Orinthia thought.

She looked at her wristwatch. It was nearly six o'clock. 'I think we should take a taxicab!' she said, heading to the kerbside and sticking a thumb into the road, the way she'd seen people do in old films. 'Look – that's 46th Street, so there are still loads to go! We don't know how long it'll take us and Taber's message said to be with him on West 13th by seven p.m. We can't be late, his life might be at risk!'

'But Rinthi, we don't have any money,' said Séafra. 'How are we going to pay for a taxi? We can't jump in and expect a free ride.'

Orinthia paused for a moment, watching the traffic rush by. Her brother was right – they had nothing to offer as payment, nothing at all. But they couldn't give up now. They'd come too far to let something as trivial as a taxi fare get in their way. 'We'll think of something,' she said, sticking out her hand even further. 'We always do! Now pick up Gungho and hide him in your coat again!'

Within moments, a boxy yellow taxicab, chequered with black and white squares, had pulled up alongside them. The driver, a portly man with thick black eyebrows, wound down his window. 'You two gettin' in?' he called out over the hubbub of the city.

'Yes!' Orinthia shouted back, skipping over and reaching for one of the rear door handles. She jumped in and shuffled across the vinyl-clad back seats, tapping the empty space beside her as Séafra followed suit.

'So, where you headed?' asked the driver, adjusting his front mirror. There was a string of orange rosary beads dangling from it, and statues of the Virgin Mary and Jesus on the cross adorned his dashboard. A photo ID card bearing the name 'Salvador Lopez' was displayed on the glovebox.

'25, West 13th Street, please,' said Orinthia urgently. 'But we're in a bit of a rush, so do you think you could try to avoid the traffic?'

The taxi driver snorted loudly. 'Avoid the traffic? *Ha!* We're in New York City, honey! You'll be lucky!' Still laughing, he checked his mirrors before pulling out into the road with a screech.

The city sped by in a blur of colours and bright lights, and the Shalloo siblings sat with their faces pressed to the taxicab's windows. On one street corner a group of men were unloading pickle barrels from a truck, while on another, a woman in a sparkly leotard tap-danced for money while singing a doo-wop. They saw the star-spangled American flag flying over the entrance of a fancy hotel, and a delicatessen with a sign in the shape of a giant salami. All around, skyscrapers jutted upwards like the gleaming walls of a fortress.

Like Salvador, the driver, had warned, the traffic was terrible, and the cab had crawled at glacial pace from block to block. But eventually they arrived at West 13th – a quiet, dimly lit street perpendicular to the main road.

'Here we go,' said Salvador, pulling up alongside the kerb. 'Number twenty-five is just up there.' He pointed to a dilapidated grey-brick building up ahead, the words 'MANHATTAN MANURE PROCESSING CO.' emblazoned across its front in faded letters. 'That place hasn't been open in years though. You sure you've got the right address, kiddo?'

'Erm . . . yes,' lied Orinthia, despite the confusion she felt on seeing the run-down old building. Manhattan Manure Processing Co? Why on earth had Taber told them to come here? Especially as it seemed to be completely deserted. *Well, at least it's not the police station*, she thought.

'So, that'll be three dollars fifty please,' said Salvador, looking to the numerical meter next to his steering wheel. 'And that *doesn't* include a tip.'

'Erm . . . well . . . about that,' began Orinthia, having completely forgotten to figure out how they were going to pay the driver. 'We *might* have to owe you the money another time, if that's OK? You see I've forgo—'

'Don't tell me, you've forgotten your purse?' interrupted Salvador, shaking his head. 'Or you've run out of pocket money, or you come from a poor family?' He tutted. 'I've heard it all before, honey, and it ain't gonna wash with me.' He reached for his car radio and pressed the button. 'Let's see what the cops have to say about this, hmmm?'

'No, wait!' said Orinthia, leaning forward as he put the device to his mouth. An idea had come to her which she was reluctant to use, but she knew she didn't have much choice. 'We might not have any money, but' – she reached into her pocket and pulled out the Inverted Narcissus – 'we do have this.'

She heard Séafra gasp loudly beside her, and she knew he was probably glaring at her with disapproval. But this was their only hope. The stamp might be worth a bit of money, but finding Taber was priceless. Parting with the Narcissus was their only choice.

'Are you kidding me?' said the driver indignantly. 'A stamp ain't worth three dollars fifty! It ain't even worth a nickel!'

'This one is,' protested Orinthia. 'And possibly a lot, lot more. It's extremely rare and a real collector's item. It's called the Inverted Narcissus.'

The driver took the stamp and inspected it closely. 'The Inverted Narcissus, hmmm? Sounds like somethin' you've just made up to me.'

'Trust us, it isn't,' Séafra corroborated, much to Orinthia's relief. He leant forward and pointed to the design. 'Look, the head of the flower points left when it should be pointing right. There's only a few of these in the world.'

'*Please* accept it,' Orinthia pleaded. 'It's all we have.'

Salvador sighed heavily, rolling his eyes. 'Well, at least it's not a candy bar I guess. Been offered enough snickerdoodles instead of payment in my time.'

'So you'll take it?' pressed Séafra.

'All right. But next time, if you want a taxi ride, come prepared, OK? Not everyone in this city's as friendly as me, that's for sure.' He put the stamp into his top pocket before unlocking the doors.

'Thank you,' enthused Orinthia, already halfway out of the cab. 'Thank you so much! And have a good evening!'

She leapt out on to the pavement, and with Séafra close behind, they pelted towards the deserted building. It had turned chilly now, but the thought of being reunited with Taber warmed Orinthia more than any hat or scarf ever could. She and Séafra had travelled so far, overcome so many obstacles, and now the prospect of seeing their baby brother was within their grasp! She just hoped he was OK.

At the gates, Orinthia slid to a halt. The place was still – the front door boarded up and every light switched off. She stood looking up at the building, panting as she scanned its facade for any doorways or openings they could clamber through. *Bingo! There's one!* A window on the second floor, not too high above ground, had been left ajar. Orinthia was just figuring out the best way to reach it when she heard Séafra calling her name.

'Rinthi! Rinthi! Come here, quick! You need to see this!'

She whirled around to find her brother at a standstill, staring across the street. 'What is it, Séa?' she called back. 'We haven't got time to hang about! I've already found a way in.'

'Over there!' Séafra replied. 'Look!' He pointed to the opposite corner, where an old woman, bundled up in a big woollen coat and fingerless mittens, was selling hot pretzels from a cart. She had a grubby-looking pigeon perched on one shoulder, and all around her other birds were pecking ferociously at fallen crumbs. There were sparrows, finches, blue tits and . . .

. . . a pelican!

'NO!' Orinthia gasped, feeling her heart skip a beat. She looked to Séafra, almost speechless. 'It can't be! Is that Geronimo?'

'Yes!' Séafra replied. 'Taber was right all along! She *did* make it to New York!' Without a moment to lose, and barely stopping to check for oncoming traffic, the siblings dashed across the road.

They tore over to the pretzel cart, and without even

an 'excuse me', Orinthia slammed a hand on to the counter. 'That bird,' she blurted out breathlessly, pointing at Geronimo. 'Where did it come from?'

The old woman looked up. Her eyes were crinkled and her cheeks were weathered and dry. 'What, the pelican, you mean?'

'Yes,' said Orinthia impatiently.

'It turned up a couple of weeks ago, and has been coming back ever since. I always feed the birds my leftovers at the end of the day, you see. It's pigeons mostly, so it was nice to see something a little more exotic.' She ripped off a big piece of bagel and threw it into Geronimo's open beak. 'Even if this one's appetite is bigger than the others'.'

Not knowing whether to laugh or cry, Orinthia dropped to her knees and wrapped her arms around Geronimo's neck. 'It's so good to see you, girl,' she whispered, hoping that the pelican would understand. 'We've missed you so much.'

'Hold on a minute,' said the pretzel woman, coming to stand beside them. 'You mean this bird belongs to you?'

'Yes,' Séafra replied. 'We thought we'd lost her. Look, we even have one of her young ones with us!' He reached into his coat and lifted out Gungho who, on seeing his mother, began to *cheep* and *rasp* excitedly.

'Well isn't that lovely,' said the woman, watching as the two pelicans were reunited. Séafra gave Geronimo a cuddle too. 'But it's very strange,' she said to Séafra. 'You're the second boy to have hugged that pelican today.'

'WHAT?' said Orinthia, leaping to her feet immediately. 'Who was the other boy? Describe him!'

The pretzel woman thought for a second. 'Well, he was so high,' she replied, holding a hand to her shoulder. 'With black hair . . . and a dimple in his chin. He was here just an hour or so ago, actually. The woman he was with bought a cup of coffee from me and then they both went into the old manure processing building over there. Struck me as odd, since it's been closed for so long. Didn't see them come out either . . .'

Woman? Taber was with a *woman?* A chill rushed over Orinthia and she felt each of her hairs stand on end. Séafra was looking equally concerned.

'This woman, what did she look like?' he asked.

'Hmm, let me see . . . well, she was quite old, and quite small, with curly grey hair . . .'

Orinthia and Séafra looked at each other with sheer horror, and in unison gasped, 'Mrs Pauncefoot!'

The pretzel woman flinched. 'Are you two all right?' she asked. 'You seem a little nervy.'

'We're fine!' said Orinthia, shuffling from foot to foot as adrenalin fired through her body. 'But we need to go and do something. Will you keep an eye on the pelicans for a little while longer?'

'Well . . . erm . . . yes . . . I guess so,' said the woman, clearly befuddled. 'But don't be too long, OK? I'll be packing up shop soon.'

'We won't!' Séafra called back, and within the blink of an eye, the Shalloo siblings had scaled the gates of the Manhattan Manure Processing Co. and were scrambling through the half-open window.

37

The siblings took the main stairwell of the building at a sprint, their boots clanging against the metal steps as they made their ascent. Apart from a few glowing exit signs and the orange light of the slowly setting sun coming in through the gaps in the boarded-up windows, it was dark.

'Taber!' whispered Orinthia and Séafra, scampering from one floor to another, and searching every room and chemical store and production area that they came across. 'Taber, are you here?' But much to Orinthia's growing dismay, there was no sign of their little brother.

'OK, where now?' she gasped, looking around frantically as they reached the top floor of the building. It had led them to a sprawling landing, with more rooms and corridors stretching in all directions. There was so much ground to cover, so many places to search, it was like a labyrinth. 'Which way shall we go, Séa? Do you think we should split up?'

'I don't know Rinthi, is that wise?' said Séafra in panic. 'What if *we* lose each other, we'll—'

'HELP! HELP!'

Séafra stopped mid-sentence, as a guttural scream from behind a set of double doors cut across him. The Shalloos turned towards it. There was a sign above the doors which read MANURE MANAGEMENT ROOM, and a plaque bearing the words PROTECTIVE CLOTHING TO BE WORN AT ALL TIMES.

'HELP ME!' came another high-pitched cry from within. 'HELP ME SOMEONE! PLEASE!'

The siblings' eyes met.

They knew that voice.

It belonged to Taber!

They tore across the landing and burst through the double doors, stumbling into what was perhaps the smelliest room that Orinthia had ever had the displeasure of finding herself in. The stench of old animal poo was overwhelming – and it was all Orinthia could do not to turn straight back.

'Urghhh, that's disgusting!' Séafra groaned, just as repulsed. He quickly covered his face with his sleeve, spluttering as if he were going to vomit. 'It's like we're in a giant toilet!'

'We pretty much are!' said Orinthia. 'They can't have cleaned out this place since it closed down!' She held her nose as she took in their surroundings. The place was vast – with thick metal joists girding the high ceilings, and gigantic pipes protruding from walls. All around, fabricated steel platforms loomed over them like the rising tiers of an amphitheatre. There were barrels and tanks and cisterns and butts, no doubt filled with slops!

'Rinthi!' came a sudden scream from above. 'Séafra! Help me! I'm up here!'

The siblings looked up. There, looking down at them from one of the metal platforms, and teetering precariously close to the edge, was Taber. He was a little dishevelled – his face grubby and his hair even more wild than usual. His wrists were tied together, and there was a look of sheer terror on his face. It didn't take Orinthia long to work out why – directly beneath him was a huge metal vat, the words HORSE DUNG stamped across it in big black letters.

'Taber, don't move a muscle!' she screamed, running towards him. Every instinct in her body told her to turn around and get help, but she couldn't leave her little brother alone for a minute longer. One slip, one wrong move, and he'd plunge head first into the vat of ancient poo below. He'd never be able to get out!

'Don't worry Tabs!' she shouted, looking around frantically before her gaze landed on the spiral stairwell that led up to his platform. 'Everything's going to be OK. Just stay where you are. We're going to come and get you.'

'Is that so?' came a voice from behind. The words were cold and threatening, and despite their brevity, Orinthia knew exactly who had spoken them.

She and Séafra whipped around.

Mrs Pauncefoot was standing in the doorway they'd just come through, dressed in her usual ensemble of cardigan, blouse and knee-length skirt. But even though she still looked like the meek and loveable postmistress they'd come to know in Little Penhallow, Orinthia knew that her true identity couldn't be more at odds with that kindly public persona.

'Well, hello there, children,' snarled the old woman. 'How nice to see you.'

'Get away from us!' shrieked Orinthia, grabbing Séafra's arm and edging backwards. 'Don't come any closer.'

'Well, that's not very friendly,' Mrs Pauncefoot replied, letting out an exaggerated gasp of offence. 'You children were always so polite when you visited the post office. Don't I even get a hello?'

Orinthia felt her temperature rise, and with single-minded focus she shouted, 'NO YOU DO NOT! We know you're not the person you claim to be. We know about your black-market stamp business, we know what you did to Grandy Brock, and we know why you're here now! You're trying to get back the Inverted Narcissus!'

Mrs Pauncefoot flashed a mocking smile. 'Well, aren't you clever. And you're not wrong. That stamp is worth a lot of money. A lot of money indeed!'

'Well, you're not going to get it,' shouted Séafra. 'Now get away from us, or we'll call the police. Everyone's looking for us, so they'll be here in a flash.'

Mrs Pauncefoot flashed a mocking smile. 'Oh, you're not wrong about that. In fact, I think I can hear an officer coming now . . .'

The sound of approaching footsteps made Mrs Pauncefoot turn, and she put a hand to her ear dramatically. 'Is that you, Jeremy?' she called out across the landing. 'I have some children here that have been asking for you. They want to report me to a police officer!'

To Orinthia's surprise Inspector Snodgrass came pacing across the landing in his shiny black boots. He had a truncheon in his hand, and his police hat cast a dark shadow over his face.

It wasn't relief that Orinthia felt on seeing him, however – it was fear.

Something wasn't right.

The look on Inspector Snodgrass's face wasn't that of a police officer coming to their aid, it was the look of someone dangerous. And why was Mrs Pauncefoot so calm? She had a six-year-old tied up in a closed warehouse; why wasn't she trying to run from the law?

'They turned up!' grinned Inspector Snodgrass, coming to stand at Mrs Pauncefoot's side. He ran a hand over his thick moustache. 'The Narcissus is ours again at last!'

What? Orinthia looked to Séafra, not quite believing what she'd just heard. Inspector Snodgrass and Mrs Pauncefoot knew each other? They'd been working together to retrieve the Narcissus?

'He's in on this?' she shouted to Mrs Pauncefoot, eyeing Snodgrass in disgust. 'He put a warrant out for our arrest, just to get your stamp back?'

The postmistress smiled. 'Yes. It's rather handy having a brother in the police force.'

'Hang on a minute,' Séafra blurted out. '*Brother*? He's . . . he's your brother?'

Realization hit Orinthia as she thought back to the old photograph she'd spotted in the post office, the night she and Kipling had broken in. The teenage boy standing next to the young Mrs Pauncefoot wasn't Mr Pauncefoot – it was Inspector Snodgrass!

'Hilda's my big sister,' the detective inspector said, looking to Mrs Pauncefoot with a smirk. 'Can't you see the family resemblance? I thought we'd both inherited our parents' good looks.'

Orinthia snarled. 'I just see ugliness,' she spat. 'Ugliness and greed and lies!'

'It was him who made me write those things on the message they wanted Gungho to deliver to you,' yelped Taber, beginning to cry. 'He said they would put Gungho in the oven if I didn't do it.'

Inspector Snodgrass shrugged with nonchalance. 'It's amazing how persuasive the words "pelican casserole" can be!'

'It's OK, Tabs,' Séafra shouted up. 'Gungho is absolutely fine. She brought us your note and now she's outside with Geronimo and the other birds—'

'*Sshhhh!*' Mrs Pauncefoot snapped. 'I don't want to hear another word.'

She slunk across the floor to where Orinthia and Séafra were standing and ran her tongue over her teeth. 'Now, give me my stamp. I'm sure you can understand why I've been so eager to get it back, and why, if you don't hand it over to me, things are not going to end well for your little brother.' She looked up at Taber with disquieting glee and it was obvious enough what she was thinking.

'So, where is it?' said Inspector Snodgrass, cracking his knuckles as he approached. He began to circle around the siblings, as if he were interrogating suspects in the interview room of Little Penhallow Police Station.

'We don't have it!' Orinthia blurted out.

'Oh, I think you do,' said Inspector Snodgrass. 'We know what's been going on. You see, I *saw* you and your little friend Kipling stealing the Narcissus from the post office! You thought you were so clever, breaking in while wearing those ridiculous disguises, but you didn't fool me. And besides, I'd recognize one of Amos's brats from a mile off.'

'Smell them from a mile off, more like,' added Mrs Pauncefoot, twisting one of her grey curls around her finger. 'Those horrible little urchins have been running amok in Little Penhallow ever since Amos adopted them. It was better when they were locked up at Guttersnipes.'

'They did come in handy when we needed help with our investigation, though,' said Inspector Snodgrass. 'I confronted Kipling and his siblings about why you'd stolen the stamp, you see. They didn't want to divulge anything to begin with but' – he smiled cruelly, flashing a mouth of yellowing teeth – 'they didn't have much choice, really. I made it very clear that if they didn't come clean, I'd inform my superior that their precious Grandy Brock had stolen it. After all, who would people believe, hmm? Me, a pillar of the local community? Or him, a known felon who'd already been fired from the Royal Mail for stealing?'

Despite the severity of the situation, Orinthia's shoulders softened momentarily – so their friends *hadn't* betrayed them after all. Inspector Snodgrass had threatened Grandy Brock's freedom, so they'd had no choice but to reveal her and Séafra's secret. She'd have done exactly the same to protect her loved ones. How she wished she hadn't doubted them without hearing the full story first.

'Now,' Inspector Snodgrass repeated, 'where's the Narcissus?'

'I told you, we don't have it,' shouted Orinthia. 'I

promise you, we don't!'

Mrs Pauncefoot sighed heavily, sauntering over to the vat of manure. 'You're playing a rather dangerous game here. And it's going to get rather "pooey" for your little brother if you keep on lying. Just one little push and—'

'No, don't do that!' Séafra blurted out, leaping forwards. 'My sister's telling the truth! We *did* have the stamp, you're right, but we don't any more!' He looked to Orinthia. 'We . . . we gave it to someone.'

Mrs Pauncefoot's face dropped. 'What do you mean, *gave* it to someone?' She gritted her teeth, and Orinthia could see the anger flashing in her eyes.

'We gave it to a taxi driver here in New York,' Séafra replied. 'We didn't have any money to pay for our ride, so we offered it to him as payment. *He* has it now.'

Mrs Pauncefoot let out a nervous laugh. 'You . . . you can't be serious? You gave one of the world's rarest stamps to . . . a taxi driver?' The colour had started to drain from her face as if she'd just been told the most frightful of stories, and she fell to her knees, banging the floor with her fists like a tantrumming toddler. 'Nooooooooooo! My stamp! My precious, precious stamp! How could you have given it away?

It's worth a fortune!'

'We don't care how much it's worth!' shouted Orinthia, knowing all too well from the long hours that Mum worked that wealth definitely didn't necessarily bring you happiness. 'You probably acquired it using dishonest money in the first place. Money you made from your awful black-market stamp business.'

Mrs Pauncefoot looked up, her nostrils flaring like those of an old dragon, her eyes fixed on Orinthia. 'You're going to pay for this!' she screeched. 'Jeremy, tie them up and take them to join their brother!' She pointed to the platform where Taber was being held and stamped her foot. 'Then I want you to go and find out the names and addresses of every New York taxi driver who was working tonight. I'm not letting these children out of my sight until the Narcissus is back in our hands.'

Inspector Snodgrass nodded, and grabbed Séafra by the scruff of the neck before snapping a pair of handcuffs around his wrists.

'Hey, get off him!' shouted Orinthia, trying to pull her brother free. She kicked and jabbed at the crooked policeman, screaming and hollering, but it was no use. Inspector Snodgrass yanked her hands behind her back, twisting so hard that it felt as if her arms might come out of their sockets. He reached into his pocket, and just as he'd done to Séafra, handcuffed her too.

Soon enough they were being pushed in the direction of the stairwell leading to the overhanging platforms. Orinthia's heart was thundering as they reached the top, in part because they were now closer to Taber than they had been in weeks, and in part because she was terrified that they might not get the happy ending they'd hoped for.

'Right,' said Mrs Pauncefoot, rubbing her hands together as she brought up the rear. 'I'll take it from here, Jeremy. You go and do as I asked. I want that taxi driver found, and the stamp back in my hand before morning!'

'No problem, sis,' he replied, pulling his police badge from his pocket and flashing it cruelly for the children to see. 'It shouldn't be too difficult. It's amazing how quickly people begin to talk when they see this.' He turned on his heel, laughing, before stomping back down the staircase.

'Well, there we are,' said Mrs Pauncefoot, clapping her hands together. 'I guess all we do now is wait until he gets back. I just hope for your sake he doesn't return empty-handed.'

'But he won't hurt the taxi driver, will he?' asked Orinthia, suddenly overcome with guilt at having put Salvador in danger. 'He was a nice man, he doesn't deserve this.'

'My brother will do what he feels is necessary, I'd imagine. As I'm sure you've realized by now, he'd do anything for his big sister. Now, be quiet. I have it on good authority that the contents of that vat aren't conducive to a pleasant swim. If I hear another word from any of you, you know what'll happen.'

But it wasn't another *word* that Mrs Pauncefoot heard next.

It was a whistle.

Taber had managed to twist his bound wrists up enough to put his thumb and forefinger to his lips, and just as he'd done when training Geronimo at Tupenny Mill, he let out a sharp, shrill *tweeeeeeeeet*.

'Oh, for goodness' sake, child, stop mucking around!' shrieked Mrs Pauncefoot. 'Stop it immediately!'

But from the steely look of determination on his face, Orinthia sensed that Taber wasn't mucking around at all. He put his fingers to his lips once more and let out another whistle, this one louder and even more ear-piercing than the last.

Then something amazing happened.

There were some almighty *honks*, and through an open window, in flew Geronimo and Gungho. The beat of their wings was strong as they soared, their yellow beaks piercing the air like the noses of two feathered aircraft. Behind them, swooping through the manure management room in a huge V formation, came the other birds they'd seen at the pretzel cart – the sparrows, the finches, the blue tits and even a pigeon or two. Their avian cacophony was deafening, and if her hands hadn't been in cuffs Orinthia would have covered her ears!

'Wh-what's going on?' shouted Mrs Pauncefoot, swatting her hands above her head as if the birds were wasps. 'Get those creatures out of here!'

Her face was changing by the minute – her smug smile being replaced with confusion, then bewilderment, and finally terror as the birds headed straight for her. Orinthia was amazed at Taber's quick thinking. He'd obviously hatched the plan when Séafra had told him that Geronimo and the other birds were congregating outside! It was genius!

'OK, get down!' Taber screeched to his siblings. 'They're going to attack! They're going to attack!'

Orinthia and Séafra obeyed their little brother without question, falling to their knees immediately. Mrs Pauncefoot tried to duck too, putting up a hand to protect herself as the birds approached – but the winged heroes were relentless, and they swooped down, pecking at the grey-haired old woman like scavengers at a carcass.

'Arghhh! They're eating me!' cried Mrs Pauncefoot, striking out wildly. 'Get them off me!' She threw out a leg, trying to kick the birds away, but as she did so, she lost her footing.

The children watched wide-eyed as she began to wobble, flapping her arms wildly to try and regain her balance, but failing miserably.

She didn't even have time to scream before she fell backwards . . .

Her feet left the platform . . .

Her legs shot into the air . . .

And as she hit the foul-smelling contents of the vat there was a huge splash, causing globules of the sticky brown gloop to shoot up like the most unpleasant of fountains.

The siblings looked over the edge of the platform and gasped. Mrs Pauncefoot was splashing around in the revolting bath, waving her arms violently to keep herself from going under. She looked like a monster who had just arisen from a muddy swamp!

'Help me, please!' she spluttered, trying to wipe the oozing excrement from her eyes and face. 'It's pulling me down! This stuff's like quicksand!' Her coiffured tresses had flopped to one side now, as if she'd slicked her hair down with the gluiest of chestnut-coloured pomades.

'Come on, you two!' Séafra shouted to his siblings, shuffling from foot to foot impatiently, and attempting to wriggle free from his handcuffs. 'Don't just stand there gawping at her. Let's get out of here!'

He made to move, but Orinthia stopped him.

'Séafra, wait!' she said, peering back into the vat. 'I didn't think I'd ever say this, but I don't think we should leave Mrs Pauncefoot to drown in there. We might be runaways, but we're not heartless. I don't want that on my conscience for the rest of my life.'

She thought for a moment before saying, 'I tell you what, I'll stay here and make sure she doesn't go under. You take Taber to the pretzel cart and ask the old lady to call 911. She needs to tell the authorities where we are, who we are, and mention the words Operation Narcissus.'

'But Rinthi, I don't want to go without you,' said

Taber, his face crumpling. 'I don't want to leave you with the horrible lady. She might hurt you.'

'I'll be fine, Tabs,' said Orinthia. 'I promise.' She nodded to Mrs Pauncefoot, who was now doggy-paddling helplessly like a small child learning to swim. 'She's not going anywhere!'

38

That night, Orinthia slept better than she had done in weeks.

It had been a long evening – within minutes of being called, patrol cars from the New York Police Department had arrived at the Manhattan Manure Processing Co., their blue lights flashing and sirens screeching. On finding Mrs Pauncefoot splashing around inside the vat of manure, the chief commissioner had been quick in ordering his officers to come to her aid, but not, Orinthia had noticed, before stopping to cough back a rather unprofessional fit of laughter.

Orinthia and her brothers had giggled too, as they'd witnessed Mrs Pauncefoot being hauled out of the vat by two burly policemen, looking (and smelling) like a dishevelled sewer rat. She and Inspector Snodgrass had then been arrested, and taken into custody for questioning. It later transpired that a worker at the United States Postal Service who was an old friend of Mrs Pauncefoot's had agreed to intercept Taber's crate at the sorting office before it got delivered to the Brock Family Animal Sanctuary. Mrs Pauncefoot and Inspector Snodgrass had then taken Taber captive in a motel on the outskirts of town, knowing that they could use him as a bargaining tool to retrieve the Inverted Narcissus from his older siblings. Orinthia couldn't believe the lengths they had gone to just to get the stamp back, but then again, she knew that greed made people do awful things.

The most important thing was that she and her brothers were back together again, and it had been arranged that Grandy Brock's brother, Jobe, was to look after them until Mum arrived from England to take them home. Jobe was a rosy-cheeked man with a bald head and a laugh that rang out like a bell. The way he spoke was similar to Grandy Brock, albeit with a slight American twang which he'd obviously picked up over the years. The Shalloo siblings had warmed to him immediately, especially as he'd treated them to hot dogs and cream soda, before taking them back to the Big Apple Plaza – the grand hotel they'd all be spending the night in.

It was the size of a palace, with a large revolving door leading to a colossal lobby, and a grand staircase spiralling up to the floors above. Jobe had explained that it was one of the oldest hotels in the city, and Orinthia had been delighted to learn that even Ophelia Pearcart had stayed there once, on her way to an expedition at Lake Erie.

Once they'd checked into their room the children had relaxed for a while, watching all the goings-on of the city from the comfort of their private balcony. The housekeeper had run them all hot baths with oodles of strawberry-scented bubbles, and the hotel manager had even arranged for fresh cotton pyjamas and dressing gowns to be brought up. It felt amazing to be snuggling down into a big comfy bed, rather than curling up on the hard floor of the *Penny Black*, and it wasn't long before Orinthia was fast asleep, with her two brothers curled up at her side.

The next morning, Jobe took the Shalloo siblings downstairs to the dining room for breakfast. They were greeted by a waiter wearing an emerald waistcoat and matching bow tie, who handed them each a menu before escorting them towards a secluded table in the window.

The room was already buzzing with the hotel's other guests – families, businessmen and -women, couples and tourists. Orinthia grinned. It felt so nice to be able to walk freely amongst other people, without fearing that someone might recognize them and call the police.

'Well, what y'all fancy then?' asked Jobe, nodding to the buffet table as they sat down. 'Eggs? Cereal? Griddle cakes?'

Orinthia hadn't expected such a delicious selection of foods to choose from. She looked over at what was on offer, her mouth watering while Jobe talked them through all of the unfamiliar delicacies they could try. There were hash browns with sausage, bagels smothered with cream cheese, French toast, blueberry muffins and a towering pyramid of sticky cinnamon rolls. Eggs were served *sunny side up* (which meant that the bright-orange yolks were still deliciously runny), and there were bowlfuls of a thick, grainy porridge called 'grits' which were to be sprinkled liberally with brown sugar.

In the end, all three children opted for stacks of fluffy pancakes, dripping with maple syrup and topped with crispy bacon. Glasses of milk and a jug of freshly squeezed orange juice were also brought to the table, with a huge pot of black coffee for Jobe.

'Mmmm, this is so incredible,' said Orinthia, spearing up a salty-sweet forkful, and stuffing it into her mouth. 'Americans certainly make good food!'

'We sure do!' replied Jobe. 'Well, speaking as an *honorary* American of course! Breakfast is our favourite meal of the day. Well . . . apart from lunch that is . . . and dinner . . . and maybe supper!' The children laughed. 'What about you, boys, you like your breakfasts?'

Taber (who *had* initially been slightly disappointed that there were no hot dogs on offer at this time of the morning) supped deeply from his glass of juice, before letting out a satisfied *ahhhhhh*. 'I *love* it. American food is the yummiest!'

Séafra nodded in agreement. 'Apart from the peanut butter and jam thing. That's just weird.'

'You mean peanut butter and *jelly*,' corrected Jobe with a wry smile, before ruffling Séafra's hair. 'Anyway, are you looking forward to seeing your mom this morning? She should be here any time.'

The three siblings looked at each other and shrugged.

'I guess so,' said Orinthia. 'Although, I think we're going to be in a lot of trouble. I can't imagine that it'll be the happiest of reunions.'

'Poppycock!' said Jobe. 'Your mom is going to be so relieved to see you that shoutin' and yellin' is gonna be the last thing on her mind.'

'I doubt that,' said Séafra. 'She'll just be annoyed that she's had to take time off work.'

Jobe sighed. 'Well, maybe I'm wrong, but something tells me that maybe, just maybe, work won't be the most important thing on her mind from now on.'

The siblings didn't have to wait long to find out if Jobe's hunch was right. Ten minutes later, the hotel manager strode into the dining room, with Mum following behind him.

For a moment, Orinthia barely recognized her. She was carrying her briefcase as usual, but the polished, glamorous woman that had sped off to London in her vintage car only a week or so before had been replaced with a pale, sunken-eyed zombie. She had no make-up on whatsoever, hadn't even combed her hair, and looked as if she hadn't slept for days.

'Oh my goodness,' she gasped, her hand shooting to her mouth. 'Children!'

She burst into tears, and seemingly uncaring that half of the dining room was staring at her, she ran towards them. 'Oh my babies!' she gasped, dropping to her knees and throwing her arms around her three children. 'I've been so worried. So, so worried.'

Orinthia allowed herself to melt into the moment. Her mother hadn't given her a proper cuddle in ages, and the embrace felt like the safest, loveliest place in the world.

When she finally let her children go, tears were tumbling down Mum's cheeks. 'Oh my loves,' she wept. 'I'm so, so sorry. I've let you down terribly. I've been an awful, awful parent. That ghastly Inspector Snodgrass managed to convince me that you were criminals. He made me believe that it was best for me to stay in Little Penhallow, rather than coming to look for you here in America. Oh, what a fool I've been.'

'It's OK, Mum,' Orinthia replied, suddenly feeling enormous guilt for all of the times she'd complained about her mother. 'You're here now. We're *all* here.'

Mum nodded wistfully. 'But from now on, things are going to change. There's going to be no more working late, no more business trips, no more weekends in the office. In fact' – she got up and began to upturn the contents of her briefcase – 'there's going to be no more work at all. I QUIT!'

Everyone else in the breakfast room was staring at them now. Cutlery had been put down, cups of coffee were going cold, and even the queue for the hot buffet was at a standstill.

Orinthia's face dropped as she watched her mum's things clatter to the floor – her pen, her diary, even her precious accounts folder! 'Mum, are you sure you know what you're doing?' she asked. 'You don't have to quit your job *completely*. We just want to spend a bit more time with you, that's all.'

She looked to her brothers, who were nodding in agreement.

'Oh, I don't need to work!' said Mum, who was now grinding her handbag into the floor with her foot. 'I've got plenty of money in the bank. More money than I'd ever know what to do with, if truth be told!'

'But what about Grandad's legacy?' asked Séafra, looking agitated. 'You can't just get rid of the used-car business.'

'I won't get rid of it,' Mum reassured. 'But Uncle Max can take care of the day-to-day running from now on. I've done more than my fair share over the years, and it's time for that lazy oaf to pay his dues.'

'And when Uncle Max retires, I think I know

someone who might want to take care of things,' said Orinthia with a wink, before nodding in Séafra's direction. 'Isn't that right, Séa?'

'Really, Séafra?' Mum replied in shock. 'You're interested in selling cars? My, my! After the way I've been running things recently, I thought you'd want to stay well clear.'

'Well, I think it would be nice to keep Wheely Good Motors in the family,' Séafra replied bashfully. 'I think Grandad would have wanted that. And after this adventure, I never want to stray too far from home again!'

Mum let out a long, satisfied breath, as if the weight of the world had just been removed from her shoulders. 'That's wonderful news. And from now on, I'm going to be the most attentive, loving, committed mummy I can be! I've got a *lot* of making up to do.'

She pulled her children in close once more, and from across the breakfast table, Jobe caught Orinthia's eye. He winked, and with a twinkle in his smile, mouthed, 'I told you so!'

39

'Children! Lunch is ready! Come on down!'

The sound of Mum calling up from the kitchen rang through the house like a song, accompanied by the smell of baking and the satisfying clatter of a table being laid.

The Shalloo siblings, halfway through a rather competitive game of snakes and ladders in Séafra's room, immediately jumped to their feet and were through the door in a flash. Geronimo and Gungho, who had been roosting on the top bunk all morning, launched into the air, before gliding down the stairs behind their young owners.

'First one to the kitchen doesn't have to help with the washing-up!' Orinthia shouted, deftly overtaking her brothers as they made their way across the landing. 'And the last one there smells like Mrs Pauncefoot!'

'What? You can't just make up rules like that!' replied Séafra. 'That's not fair!' He reached for his little brother's hand and quickly picked up speed. 'Come on, Tabs, let's get her!'

'Yeah!' agreed Taber, fizzing with determination. 'Let's get her! Let's get her!'

Orinthia laughed, and with her brothers hot on her tail, she made her way down through the house, her nose being led by the delicious smells that were wafting up from the kitchen. Since they'd returned from New York the previous week, Mum had kept herself busy by scouring her collection of newly acquired recipe books, and was quickly becoming quite the home cook. Pots and pans that had previously never seen the light of day were now being used to roast meats, simmer soups, fry eggs and boil potatoes, and the family were sitting at the table to eat together every evening.

And it wasn't just the Shalloo family whose lives had changed. Having tracked down Salvador Lopez, the Royal Mail had decided to sell the Inverted Narcissus and use the money to transform Tupenny Mill into a proper home for Grandy Brock and his children. The stamp had attracted interest from philatelists from all around the world, but it had eventually been sold at auction to the famous German stamp collector, Leopold Stempel, who'd offered a more than fair price for it, despite its slightly worn condition. Of course, Salvador had been handsomely compensated as well, and had decided to leave the hustle and bustle of New York behind him in favour of a quieter life living on a cattle farm in the mountains of West Virginia.

Taking three steps at a time, Orinthia bounded down the stairs. 'I'm gonna win! I'm gonna win!' she taunted, poking her tongue out at her brothers as they tried to catch up with her. 'I hope you've got your washing-up gloves ready—!'

But as she reached the bottom, she stopped suddenly.

'SURPRISE!' shouted Mum and Mrs Gastaldini from the kitchen doorway. There was a loud *bang* as party poppers were fired, showering the Shalloo children in candy-coloured confetti. There were balloons everywhere too – tied to door handles, floating up to the ceiling, hanging from shelves. And above the fireplace, a string of bunting had been hung, each of the flags embroidered with either the letter O, S or T.

'W-w-what's going on?' Orinthia asked, almost speechless as she took everything in.

'Well, we're having a party, of course!' said Mrs Gastaldini, her hands shooting into the air. '*Una grande festa*, to celebrate us all being back together.' She was wearing a shimmering knee-length skirt and matching blouse, embellished with a string of beautiful pink pearls. She was certainly dressed for a celebration.

Mum smiled. 'I know I can't turn back time, my darlings, but today I'm going to try and make up for all of the celebrations I've missed out on over the years because of work. For all of the Easters, all of the Halloweens, all of the Bonfire Nights. Does that sound like a good idea?'

The three siblings looked at each other before letting out a huge 'YEEEEEES!' They leapt from the stairs, throwing their arms around their mum and jumping up and down with excitement.

'And we have *another* surprise for you too!' said Mrs Gastaldini, turning in to the kitchen. She beckoned to whoever was inside, before whispering, 'OK, you can come out now. They're here.'

There were a few giggles from within, before Grandy Brock jumped out from behind the door with his children in tow, each one smiling from ear to ear.

'WELCOME HOME!' they screeched, shooting

even more party poppers into the air.

'Wow! You all look so nice,' gasped Orinthia, who had never seen the brood looking so smart. Their faces had been washed, their nails had been scrubbed, and they were all dressed up in brand-new party outfits (albeit paired with their trademark wellington boots!).

They'd also brought with them at least half of the animals from the Mailbox Menagerie, who'd been adorned with paper streamers! Peggy had Millicent the grass snake hanging around her neck like a scaly necklace; Kipling was wrangling one of the porcupines; Bramwell had a litter of baby chinchillas that couldn't have been more than a few days old; and Suki had Betsy, the pygmy hippopotamus, on a lead. Even Milky, who was toddling now, had a silver-coloured chihuahua nestled in the front pocket of his dungarees!

'Scrub up well, don't they?' said Grandy Brock with a wry smile.

'As do you!' said Orinthia, looking him up and down. He was sporting a new three-piece suit complete with pocket watch, and a jaunty grey fedora with a feather in its brim. His hair had been brushed (a little) and Mr Malagasy was perched on his shoulder. 'Very dapper indeed!'

'Well, thank you,' replied Grandy, blushing slightly. 'It's been a while since I've had an occasion to get dressed up, and it's an honour to be here to celebrate with you.'

Orinthia was just about to reply when yet another voice cut across her from inside the kitchen. 'All right, all right, enough of the smushy stuff! What *we* really want to hear about is the rest of your adventure!'

Orinthia blinked and to her complete surprise Mog appeared from behind the door with Noah in tow! 'Mog . . . Noah . . .' she gasped. 'It's so good to see you! But what are you doing here? How did you know where we lived?'

'Your lovely ma sent us party invites,' Mog replied cheekily. 'And thanks to you, Rinthi, I could even read mine *myself*!' His nose wrinkled. 'I had to ask me dad what RSVP meant, though. One language at a time!'

Mum put a hand on Mog's shoulder and beamed. 'I'd heard so much about you two from Orinthia and Séafra that I knew you had to be here. And here you are!'

'I wasn't gonna miss out on a party, that's for sure!' said Noah with a chuckle. 'But anyway, tell us all about what happened in America. Is it really true that you used the *Penny Black* as a boat to escape across the Atlantic? What was it like in Cape Cod?'

Noah's questions came thick and fast, and soon enough the Brock children had begun to quiz the Shalloo siblings too:

'How was the ride in the hot-air balloon?' asked Suki.

'Did you really push Mrs Pauncefoot into a vat of manure?' added Kipling.

'How fast did the mail train go?'

'Did you remember to bring back hot dogs?'

If it weren't for Grandy Brock cutting in, Orinthia thought that the questions might have gone on all night. 'All right, all right, that's enough chatting for now,' he said, playfully ushering his children away. 'I'm sure Orinthia, Séafra and Taber will tell you all about their adventure in due course.'

Just then, the dinging of an egg timer sounded from the kitchen, making Mum jump. '*Ooh!* I better see to that!' she said, darting into the kitchen and gesturing for everyone to follow. 'Come on in, everyone. And take a seat.' Flinging a tea towel over her shoulder, she made for the oven, while the children rushed in and scrambled to get a seat at the long wooden table.

It was laden with the most mouth-watering spread of food Orinthia had ever seen, and with Taber sat on her lap she took in the various plates and bowls and platters. Her mouth began to drool. There were cheese-and-pickle sandwiches, pork pies, crisps, chicken drumsticks and scotch eggs. A three-tiered cake stand was laden with scones and butterfly cakes, and at the centre of the table, a bowl of trifle was heaving with strawberries and whipped cream. A party hat had been left at each place, and soon enough the sound of pinging elastic was ringing through the air as the children pulled them on.

'And the pièce de résistance . . .' said Mum, bringing over a huge copper pot from the stove. 'Clam chowder!'

There was a chorus of *ooooohs* and *ahhhhs* as the partygoers took in the magnificent sight, noses twitching as the delicious savoury smell wafted towards them.

'That's what we ate at Big Betty's Clam Shack on Cape Cod!' squealed Séafra excitedly.

'And it was Big Betty herself that sent me the recipe,' Mum said, placing her culinary masterpiece down at the head of the table. 'You haven't stopped going on about how delicious it was, so I wrote to her asking how to make it!'

'And I provided the clams!' said Noah proudly. 'Came straight off the boat from the south coast this morning.' He brought his voice down to a whisper and winked. 'Don't tell my boss, though – they were meant to be going to the kitchen at the Ritz!'

Orinthia smiled. 'Well, the Ritz will just have to make do with the jellied eels today!'

As the kitchen filled with laughter, Mum raised a glass. 'Cheers everybody! I'm so glad that you could be here today to celebrate with me and my three wonderful children. Now, everyone tuck in! Fill up your plates. I don't want any leftovers!'

'Ha! There won't be any leftovers,' said Grandy Brock with a grin. 'Not if my children have anything to do with it, that's for sure! I've known hogs who eat less!'

There was an eager commotion as the children dove in, fingers reaching excitedly for the delicious treats on offer. Bowls and terrines were passed around the table like a game of pass the parcel, with sandwiches being exchanged for pies, and cakes being swapped for iced buns. Mrs Gastaldini served the chowder, taking the guests' bowls and returning them filled with creamy broth to eager hands.

Even the animals of the menagerie had been

catered for. Geronimo and Gungho had wasted no time in swooping across the kitchen to get to a bucket of fresh sardines, and Betsy had almost knocked over the plant stand as she swift-footed it to a trough of cabbages. There were bone-shaped biscuits for the dogs, fresh cream for the felines, crickets for the reptiles, and even a dish of deliciously ripe peaches for Mr Malagasy, which had been served to him under a silver cloche.

'Mrs Shalloo, this is amazing,' enthused Bramwell, biting into a scotch egg. 'I had to admit I was a bit scared about eating your food to begin with. Orinthia always said that you were a terrible cook!'

Mum chuckled. 'Well, it wasn't that I was a terrible cook, so much as not a cook at all! Up until recently the most adventurous thing I made for my children was jam sandwiches.'

'And you didn't even make them, very often,' quipped Séafra.

Everone laughed, but Orinthia could tell that the admission had actually rather upset their mother. Tears were forming in her eyes, so Orinthia quickly took her hand and squeezed it tight. 'Don't be sad, Mum,' she whispered with a smile. 'You're more than making up for it now. I promise.'

Mum sniffed back her tears and smiled. 'Thank you, darling. What would I do without you, eh?'

A doe-eyed Mrs Gastaldini, who had been attending to Grandy Brock's every need since he'd arrived, refilled the old man's glass with ale. 'And what about you, Amos? There's been a fair few changes in your life too, I hear. How's the new *casa*?'

'The house?' Grandy Brock exclaimed. 'Oh wonderful. Just wonderful! Although it's going to take me a while to get the hang of that vacuum cleaner thingamajig that the Royal Mail insisted on buying me.'

Mrs Gastaldini batted her eyelashes. 'Well, maybe I could come and help you with it, then perhaps cook you supper one evening? Do you like *carbonara*?'

'Oh . . . well . . . yes,' spluttered Grandy Brock, much to the amusement of his brood. 'That sounds wonderful.'

'And the Royal Mail have given you your old job back as well, I hear, Amos,' said Mum.

'Not *just* his old job,' Suki answered, putting an arm around her adoptive father proudly. 'He's been promoted! The postmaster general loved the idea of the Mailbox Menagerie so much, that he's made Grandy Brock Head of Innovations. He's going to be training up a new fleet of animails for the Royal Mail to test run! And we're going to help him.'

'Well I never,' Mum replied. 'That's wonderful. Congratulations, Amos.'

Grandy Brock's cheeks reddened. 'Well, it's all down to the children really. They're the real workforce behind the Mailbox Menagerie. Yours included, of course.'

'That's very nice of you to say so,' said Mum proudly. 'And I couldn't agree more. In fact, I have a little treat for all of you youngsters.' She nodded to the sideboard where a huge mound of what looked like boxes was hidden beneath a large cloth. 'Geronimo, Gungho, could you do the honours?' she asked. And with that, the pelicans swooped across the room, pulling away the cloth with their beaks to reveal a mound of beautifully wrapped presents beneath.

The children gasped in amazement.

'Woooow!' said a wide-eyed Peggy. 'It's like Christmas.'

Séafra rubbed his hands together with glee. 'Come on, let's see what we've got!'

A stampede of excited children darted over to the table and Orinthia watched as they dove in, tugging excitedly at multicoloured ribbons and ripping back shiny wrapping paper with gusto.

'Wow! Look what I've got,' said Séafra, holding up a huge book entitled *The Encyclopaedia of Motor Cars*. 'I love it!' He waved the tome around with glee, although everyone else was far too busy examining their own gifts to take much notice.

Taber was wrestling with silver paper and sticky tape, his little body vibrating with delight. 'It's a fire engine!' he shouted as he whipped out his present. He immediately dropped to his knees and, accompanied by an ear-piercing *nee-naw, nee-naw, nee-naw*, began to navigate the shiny red vehicle across the floorboards. 'Don't worry, Geronimo!' he called out, charging over to where the pelican was now roosting contentedly on top of the fridge. 'Fireman Shalloo is here to rescue you!'

The present-opening continued with relish. Mog and Noah both got bags of jelly beans from Mr Barnabas's shop, handfuls of which were swiftly scooped up and gobbled down. Kipling was over the moon with the tap-dancing shoes he received, and Suki was delighted with her new hockey stick. Peggy got a whoopee cushion, and Bramwell couldn't believe his luck when he opened up a box containing a new fountain pen engraved with his name.

'I can start writing a story all about your adventures now,' he enthused to the Shalloo siblings. 'How you posted yourselves in a wooden crate, the journey on the packet ship, the hot-air balloon ride, New York City, the expensive stamp!' He looked into the distance as if imagining inking his words on to a page of his notebook. 'I'm going to call it . . . *The Adventures of the Parcel Tape Trio!*'

Orinthia laughed. To anyone on the outside, the tale would have sounded like a complete work of fiction! But it was real. She and her brothers had done it. They'd posted themselves to the other side of the world.

'Come on, Rinthi, why don't you open your present now?' said Taber, passing his big sister a parcel wrapped in gold paper and adorned with a blue bow. 'Yours is a *really* big one!'

Orinthia took the gift and began to carefully unpick the ribbon. She couldn't remember the last time she'd had a proper present, and her hands started to tremble with anticipation. What had Mum bought her?

'Come on, Rinthi, just rip it open!' said Kipling, coming to stand beside her. 'You're being so slow!'

'All right, all right!' chuckled Orinthia. The blue

ribbon unfurled between her fingers and she began to tear at the shiny paper. As her gift came into view, her eyes began to widen. 'No!' she gasped, glancing over to her mother. 'It's not, is it . . . ?'

She quickly pulled away the remainder of the wrapping to reveal a beautiful world globe standing on a polished wooden stand. 'Oh my goodness, it's beautiful!' she exclaimed, running a finger along the brass meridian which ran from pole to pole. 'It's a proper globe! I've always wanted one of these!'

'So, you like it?' asked Mum, with a smile.

'Like it?' Orinthia replied. 'I *love* it!' She spun the globe around, watching with glee as the countries she'd one day explore whizzed past. Russia, Morocco, France, Germany, Peru, the USA . . .

But a sudden shout from Séafra drew her from her daydreams.

'Rinthi, come look at this!' he gasped, pointing frantically through the kitchen window to the garden. 'It's Faris! It's Faris!'

Pushing back her chair with a screech, Orinthia ran to the back door and flung it open. With everyone else in tow she ran on to the lawn, just in time to see the *Zeppherino Blue* descending through the sky and coming to hover above the greenhouse. Faris, dressed in her usual flying leathers, and with a brand new pair of goggles, gave the awaiting throng a big wave.

'Faris!' Orinthia squealed, jumping up and down as she waved back to the aeronaut. 'I can't believe it! What are you doing in England?'

Faris peered over the side of the basket. 'I'm taking part in the London Air Balloon Regatta tomorrow, and thought I'd drop by,' she shouted down. 'You fancy a little ride?'

Orinthia felt her heart racing at the thought of being in the skies once more, and she spun round to her mother. 'Can I, Mum? *Pleeease?*'

Orinthia's mother put a hand on her daughter's shoulder. 'Of course you can. The world is yours, my darling girl. But be careful up there, OK? And make sure you're back in a couple of hours.'

Orinthia's skin prickled with excitement as Faris lowered down a rope ladder. 'Don't worry, Mum,' she said, planting a kiss on her mother's cheek before running off towards the hot-air balloon. 'From now on, wherever I go, the best journey will always be coming home.'

ACKNOWLEDGEMENTS

This book was written during the global pandemic. When all of our worlds suddenly became much smaller, writing an epic adventure set across land, sea and sky seemed like the perfect antidote. With all of the restrictions we were facing, penning this story let me travel the world without leaving my desk, and was very much a tonic. But I couldn't have written it without the love, support and wisdom of so many people.

First, thanks go to my nearest and dearest. Mum and Graeme, Dad and Mary, Jacko – thank you for saying all the right words at all the right times. You are all lifelines. *Caru chi i gyd.*

Next, to my moon-shooting lockdown household – Manda, Beth and Chlöe – thanks for the games, giggles and gossip. And not forgetting Mr Glen, who baked each week despite the flour and egg shortages! Grandma and Mamgu – even in your nineties you continue to inspire, touch and amaze me always. And to the rest of the Rivers, Smiths, Marstons, Foxford-Marstons, Lawrences and Argentas – you make for a huge and wonderful family.

Many thanks to my editor extraordinaire, Kesia Lupo, for helping me to tell this story and for all of your support and care. And to everyone else at Chicken House and beyond who've worked so hard on this book – Barry, Rachel H, Jazz, Laura M, Laura S, Rachel L, Sarah, Esther, Elinor, Helen, Sara and Fraser – your passion for bringing authors' stories to life is humbling and heart-warming.

This book's gorgeous illustrations are by the incredible Caroline Bonne-Müller. I cried when I first saw the drawings of Orinthia, Séafra, Taber et al., and my eyes still turn glossy when I look at them now.

Next, big love to my agent, Kate Shaw, for being a shoulder to cry on, a motivational emailer, a voice of reason, a cheerleader, a dog-walking companion, and a really special person.

A big shout-out to all my dear friends, especially The Pyramid of Truth, Merched Moist, The Cackles Alumni, The Greenacre Walk Gang, Clan CIC and Huevos de Oro. You bring so much merriment, creativity and adventure into my life. I'm giving a special cuddle to Gabi for always providing me with enough work to keep a roof over my head while I write – I love having you as my boss. Another big hug goes to Julia at Ottie and the Bea bookshop for so much kindness and compassion during a tough time.

To all of the wonderful mini people who regularly leap, toddle and crawl through my world – Noah and Thea, Romilly and Indigo, Otis, Hazel and Gwilym, Rocco, Heidi, Luca and Zeno, Alice, Minerva, Gwen Bach – you are all delicious. And to my lovely drama students – I'm so lucky to hang out in imaginary places with you all each week.

And finally, to three plucky Irish siblings whom I briefly met a few years ago. Your names are Orinthia, Séafra and Taber, and even though our paths haven't crossed since, your mischievous faces, loud laughs and twinkly eyes couldn't help but find their way into this story.

DEMELZA & THE SPECTRE DETECTORS

Demelza loves science – she loves it so much that she stays up late to work on her inventions. But she soon discovers she's also inherited a distinctly unscientific skill: Spectre Detecting

Like her grandmother, she can summon the ghosts of the dead. When Grandma Maeve is kidnapped, Demelza and her pasty-faced best friend, Percy, must leap into action to solve the deadly mystery . . .

Talking skulls, family feuds, red herrings and a spirited (in every sense) heroine underpin this funny, fizzing debut . . .
DAILY MAIL

Paperback, ISBN 978-1-912626-03-8, £6.99 • ebook, ISBN 978-1-912626-82-3, £6.99

HOW TO SAVE THE WORLD WITH A CHICKEN AND AN EGG by EMMA SHEVAH

This story isn't just about birds. It's about secrets, the seaside, how seagulls can trick worms into thinking it's raining. It's about mucus, fudge and dogs needing a wide variety of sniffs. But if you want the simple version, it's about what happened here last summer. How a girl called Ivy and a boy called Nathaniel solved a mystery and saved the world's animals: one at a time.

A truly excellent eco-adventure.
M. G. LEONARD

Paperback, ISBN 978-1-910655-47-4, £6.99 • ebook, ISBN 978-1-913322-44-1, £6.99

BEETLE BOY by M. G. LEONARD

Darkus can't believe his eyes when a huge insect drops out of the trouser leg of his horrible new neighbour. It's a giant beetle – and it seems to want to communicate.

But how can a boy be friends with a beetle? And what does a beetle have to do with the disappearance of his dad and the arrival of Lucretia Cutter, with her taste for creepy jewellery?

A darkly funny Dahl-esque adventure.
KATHERINE WOODFINE

A wonderful book, full to the brim with very cool beetles!
THE GUARDIAN

Paperback, ISBN 978-1-910002-70-4, £6.99 • ebook, ISBN 978-1-910002-98-8, £6.99